# Operation: Mistletoe

By Greg Jackson

ISBN: 978-0-6151-6745-9

Cover Design:  Greg Jackson

Thanks to Basil the Nutcracker for taking the time out of his busy day to pose for the front photo.  I appreciate it greatly. Someday I will find your arm.

**Acknowledgements:**

I would like to thank my entire family for their understanding and willingness to listen to me babble for hours on end about everything under the sun, mom and dad, thanks. Thanks to my brother Scott for helping me through this process and my sister Allison for the helpful tips late at night.  Thanks to Jason Williams for critiquing the first copy. Much thanks to Tim "Xavier" Doyle for all the web help.  Thanks to Cecilia for being such a great person, I'm lucky to know you.  Much thanks to Dunkin Donuts and the crew in all of them that I frequent.  You're all incredibly nice.  And everyone else who I know or have known, thank you all for playing the parts that helped me be the person I am today, I am eternally grateful for the good as well as the bad.  It all helps.  And thanks to Patty, someone who pointed some things out and got me on track. And Alex, who is just too cool for words.

The following novel is a work of satirical fiction. The satirizing of Christmas and all of the traditions involved with it was done out of complete respect to them, as I have grown up with them and love them.

**All of the characters in this book are completely fictional. Any similarity to any person, living or dead is purely coincidental. These events never happened.**

For:
Amy,
Thank You.

# Prologue

The courtroom was dead silent. The jury was in deliberation for what seemed like twelve long days. Father Time, who had been serving as Judge for five years now, stared directly at Kris Kringle's defense attorney, Jack Frost, with beads of sweat running down his face. It wasn't normal in December to have sweat running down your face, especially being a Judge in the central courthouse of the North Pole.

Jack Frost stared back with icy intensity, not letting his gaze on Father Time falter for a second. He knew just by looking at Father Time that Time had changed his mind. He was going to let Kringle go free! All of the work and time invested in making all the arrangements: paying the jury, telling Time that his precious Baby New Year would go missing if his Father didn't prosecute Kris Kringle to the fullest extent of the law. Hell, Jack even tipped off the Herald and had his building permits on the way before the trial even came through.

Jack decided the best way to go about this would be to call for an emergency sidebar. This wasn't normally done during deliberation but what the hell? Paying off jurors isn't exactly a common practice either.

"Kris, I will be right back. I am going to see what the holdup is." Jack told Kringle. "I have a good feeling about this. I think you can turn around and give your wife a big 'thumbs up'."

"Jack, this is my life and the lives of millions who believe in me. Can you guarantee that all of these charges are going to be dropped?"

"It's a little late to drop the charges, Kris. We're already done with the trial. The best I can guarantee is an acquittal. And with the multiple counts of gross negligence that the Pole Prosecution brought to the table...that may be a long shot."

The cherry-red cheeks that occupied Kris' face grew a little paler every minute that he sat at his defense table. The tummy that used to roll like a bowl full of jelly was losing the war with gravity and drooped down to the floor.

Jack approached the bench.

"What can I do for you, Mr. Frost?" Father Time asked.

"Is there anything we can do to speed this up?" Jack responded. "I have a hair appointment at three."

"Jack, your hair is always a mess and someone's life and freedom hangs in the balance. Have some compassion or at the very least act like you do." Father Time rolled his eyes.

Jack put his hands through his icy-blue-spiked hair. "With all the money I gave you, you are the last person in the world that needs to be talking about compassion. What I did makes what Capone did seem like child's play."

"It's not up to me anymore. I swayed the proceedings towards a guilty verdict, just like you asked. My work is done here. It's up to the jury now, I'm afraid. Now, if you'll please sit down and wait, we're all nervous here for one reason or another."

Jack smiled with his pointed teeth and returned to the defense table. As his back was turned, the elf jurors came back and sat in the booth. He looked at Kris for a brief moment. "Kris, I don't know how this looks. The jury selection was done based on American courtroom practices, so we have one woman, one African American and the rest of them are white males from the Union. It's not exactly what I call balanced."

The twelve jurors filed in and sat in the jury box.

"Will the jury please rise?" Father Time said, accompanied by three hits of his ice gavel. By the sound of it, the ice cracked under his nerves.

The jury stood up, not that you would notice the elves standing. Either way three feet tall was three feet tall.

"Foreman of the jury, have you reached a verdict?" Father Time cleared his throat and took a drink of water.

"We have your Honor. On the three counts of labor violations, we find the defendant guilty on all counts." Gasps hopped from person to person in the back of the court. "On the count of misuse of Pole equipment resulting in the serious injury of Head Elf Pal Pickman, we find the defendant guilty as charged." More gasps. "On the count of labor violations against the monetary code sixty-six placed into law in the year nineteen-ninety eight, we find the defendant guilty as charged."

At the defense table, Kris broke down into tears. He was going away for a long, long time. He sat there and waited for his sentence, feeling the need to jump up and defend himself. "Your honor, can I say something?"

Father Time wiped the tear from his eye. "Yes, you may."

"Can I fire my lawyer?" Kris said, making Jack almost want to jump up and strangle him.

"Why the hell would you want that? The jury is handing out the verdict! Don't you think it's a little late you fat piece of shit?" Jack yelled.

"Thousands of years of tradition and I have it all stripped away from me for absolutely no reason. Maybe it's because I never got you that bike, Jack Frost, but it wasn't me who had you placed on that naughty list. You, as I remember, had a little problem nipping people's noses. My wife and I looked after you as best we could."

"The facts are the facts, Kringle. You broke the law. Hell, you broke a bunch of them!" Jack almost turned red.

"I broke the laws that were specifically designed to ruin the Holiday traditions." Kringle added. "Father Time, we used to play golf together. You know me. You know the things I do here and the good they bring to people. I don't know what's going on here, but..."

Father Time looked at him and cut him off. "We had a trial in a court, Mr. Kringle among a jury of your peers. The evidence was documented and supported and you were found guilty of all of the charges brought against you by said peers. I have a newborn son to worry about, Kris, so it is what it is, I cannot change the verdict. I haven't even seen him in his new top hat yet because of this trial. But what, only for curiosity's sake, did you want to fire your lawyer for?"

"I think a personal grudge with me prevented him from doing the best job he could have done." Kringle was standing straight up, chin in the air.

"And how would you rectify this?" Father Time asked.

"You know I am not capable of these things, Your Honor, but since the jury was modeled after American Law practices, I am adopting a similar practice and changing my plea to guilty by reason of insanity. I am putting our past behind us as it is painfully obvious there are other ways to get your respect. Possibly thousands of reasons."

"On what grounds?" Jack was ready to go through the roof. "Insanity is not the same as ignorance!"

"I have at least eight different names and no one knows which one is real, including myself. I don't know which one committed these horrible acts of negligence, but it wasn't Kris Kringle. The only thing Kris Kringle is guilty of is beating you in eighteen holes three years running."

Father Time took his time figuring out the clever new twist in his head. On one hand, Baby New Year should be fine as Kringle was still going away. Jack wouldn't do anything to him as long as he still got something he wanted. On the other hand he would never be guilty of anything and probably get out soon. He liked Christmas the way it was, but the Christmas that Frost has envisioned would let Father Time retire early and watch his son grow up, with a lot of money, of course. "I will recommend that Kris Kringle be remanded to the Amazing Grace Mental Institution beginning immediately. There, he will receive daily mental examinations and medication, if needed, to take control his alleged multiple personality disorder. In my professional opinion, people in this state are not suited for prison, for fear of the other prisoners. With that in mind, I am not about to send a man to prison that may be held accountable for things not delivered throughout the course of someone's life time. In the Institution, he will be cared for and examined and we will determine a follow up date in one year to see if he can be rehabilitated." He slammed his gavel down again, breaking shards off, flying in all directions, one of them bouncing off of the court reporter's head.

The guards came over and took Kringle by the elbows, bringing him back to the back room for processing. As Kris turned around, he saw Mrs. Kringle, crying and blowing him a kiss. She was nervously petting the amulet that hung from the chain around her neck. Kris nodded and smiled at her as he walked away into the waiting darkness.

"This doesn't change a thing, Time." Jack said, straightening his suit as he stood up. "It doesn't change a thing at all."

"I will be here when you need me, Jack. It's one thing to get what you want and another to have some compassion about it. Someday you'll realize how truly great he is." He whispered loud enough for Jack to hear it loud and clear. "It's a shame that I didn't have the backbone to stop you."

"We did it together, Time. We're both guilty. And your backbone doesn't begin to compare with my wallet." Jack smiled at him as he turned to leave. He walked outside to talk to the angels of The Pole Herald, who were skulking around outside with their cameras and tape recorders. Jack had to start spinning the story now if he was going to take over this place. It was no easy task but all of the necessary pieces were in place. Within five years the world would be his for the taking. And no one would know the difference.

# One

My name is Will Foster. First, I want to let all my readers know that I never intended to write this. I never intended to have people give a shit enough about me to read about it. Hell, I never even thought I would ever be in a position to be able to write something as bizarre as this. What you will be reading is from a journal I kept of some extraordinary experiences with some extraordinary people.

You will see that I am not what you'd call a typically nice person. Sure, once you get past my layers and layers of put-on crap, I generally last about six weeks and people tire of me. It's not that I am physically bad, I just never stop thinking. And with the thinking comes negativity and then I turn into someone I hate turning into: the insecure, neurotic man who insists that things will get better until I destroy them again.

Sure, I have my hang-ups just like everyone; it would be petty of me to say that I didn't. For instance, I hate driving in front of a sixteen year-old who blew all his fast food money on a stereo that shakes my rear-view mirror when he's behind me. I would love to just shoot those fucking stereos. Whose right is it to make me listen to that if I don't want to? And then the car sounds like a lawn mower when he tries to beat me off the line, showing that twenty grand in a five hundred dollar lemon actually paid off and he can get plenty of poon tang with his crooked hat and shorts that are long enough to be pants. I have no problem with the style, if it is used as a style and not some sort of fashion rite-of-passage to sleep with naïve gang-banger girls that have some sort of affection for guys who like trying to sound like Eminem.

I hate that people use walkie-talkie phones and hold the damn thing only an inch from where it would be anyway if they used it the right way. Is it really that hard to go the extra inch and spare me the misery of listening to find out if Earl picked up his hemorrhoid medicine while I am in line waiting to pay for the DVD that I intend to watch on Friday night? That's what I do since I don't have a crooked hat or wear circus pants. I drive my standard SUV home, think about how much I am NOT the bad boy chicks go for and settle down to watch *Ferris Bueller's Day Off*.

I can't stand when people cut me off when there's clearly no one behind me for miles, only to drive really slow. I can't stand going to the movies and seeing commercials that I just saw on TV right after the preview for the movie I am trying to see. I hate that MTV dropped the M in their programming and at three in the morning when I actually see a video, it's all boom-boom music played by the stereo guy mentioned above with the mentioned gang-banger chicks dressed in short shorts shaking their booty by an old Cadillac. Does she realize he's singing about her woman parts and the easiest way to violate them? Does she realize she's singing about the easiest way to get into her woman parts? I think it's just damn strange that women fought for so long to be equal but in the music world it's cool to be a slut-for-hire. I like all kinds of music, it's all okay, but where's the actual video? I can jump around and sing in a group of jumping people with champagne. Shit, tell a damn story. I don't need to see you sing the damn song already. And can someone please tell Hollywood that we can take a break from computer generated movies?

Yeah, that's me, boring, crotchety old Will Foster. I am the funny guy who eventually began to have distaste for anyone near my personal bubble. I am the guy who has been building walls for a long time silently among the strange people in the world, creating my nest-egg of seclusion. Just give me *The Breakfast Club* or *Top Gun* and everything's okay. I can pop those in when all of my two hundred channels take the same commercial break simultaneously.

Well, I guess things have changed in my life. Some things for the good, some things for the bad, but I guess that completes the person as much as I can be complete. This is more of a working journal, actually. It is December Twenty, Two Thousand and Five and this is the beginning of my journey. As you will soon find out this journey is nothing near typical. More importantly, it is a journal work that helped me discover what's behind my walls, and why, as one of those crazy people doing what they do I was led down the path to discovery in the first place. You'll meet the few people who changed the way my mind works and how it started breaking my walls like sledgehammers to the Berlin Wall.

I don't think I will ever be able to repay those people, and the funny thing is, they have no idea what they have accomplished. I have never thought of myself as a romantic, but if the shoe fits, you know?

It's only a matter of time until I start bitching for my senior discount and my early bird special. It's a right-of-passage that I can't wait long enough for to arrive.

# Two

This journal is being scribbled in a notebook while on a prop plane flying to Anchorage, Alaska. My Uncle Frank lives up there and he thought I should come up for the Christmas season, saying that he needs help with his business. It seems that one of his pilots came down ill and can't help him deliver his parcels so I have to help in distribution to free up another pilot. Yeah, exactly. This is my idea of a great vacation.

Out the window there is nothing to be seen but the wide space of white ice jutting up from the ground, creating beautiful vistas of glaciered mountains. If you spend any time in my mind, you'd discover soon enough that the beauty of those iced stalagmites (or stalactites, I have no idea...I failed science on that question, so I don't care as a matter of principal) turn into many little pinchers of death that are just waiting for the opportunity to rip me apart as the plane glides into them because there was ice on the propeller and we pulled the Ritchie Valenz-Big Bopper-Buddy Holly disappearing act over Alaska. For now it is all about the beauty. Later it's all pain, misery and death, as is normally in life. Brief happiness followed by an enduring pain. Screw it. I think I came out okay. Admittedly a little demented but okay nevertheless.

Anyway, I don't talk much to my family. I haven't talked to Uncle Frank in years, but for whatever reason he called me out of the blue to fly up here. Next to me, snoring in what seems to be bison country by the sound if it was Alyssa Witt. She worked side by side with me on the eight hour days and was and still is the most fascinating creature on the planet, so what was I to do but hire her to be my publicist/agent when my first book took off? You'll learn this about me in this book...I really am not that nice of a person, like I said before. I have a lot of bitterness and an addictive personality, and if it wasn't for Alyssa just talking to me every day, I would have become the most self-mutilating, narcissistic prick that I was gearing up to be. I couldn't risk not talking to her again so I made the obviously selfish move and hired her. Like I said before, it's all about me.

Yeah, I can't tease fate. She absolutely hates me. Fate is a stupid bitch whose only goal is to make me the laughing stock of everyone in the free world. At least now I don't have to go in public. Yeah, Alyssa has a good thing with the guy she's with and I respect that. She only insisted on going because on the way back, we are heading to Seattle where she's catching a flight home to Florida to be with her family. Since I was flipping the bill for the trip, she was more than happy to come. I love the little opportunist. It winds up that we both were from New Jersey and migrated to Florida at the same age. We never knew each other until we started working together years ago.

"We're almost there." The pilot name Gus yelled back to us, loud enough to let a deaf person know on the ground, not realizing we were right behind him.

Alyssa stirred in her seat until she was completely awake. "Are we almost there?"

"Yeah, he just said that." I said in my patented smart-ass tone.

"Simmer down, dork. I just woke up." She was squinting at consciousness, trying to catch some scenery out the window which was a lot brighter than she expected. "Will, how come you don't get together with your family over the Holidays?"

"We've been over this." Truth be told, we never discussed it, but I hated talking about it, so I tried to lie about her forgetting. It never worked with her, she knew my every facial muscle and which ones I used to lie with. In the back of my head I was convinced that she was working with the FBI to take me down.

"Come on! We can finish each other's thoughts and you think I'm dumb enough to forget you telling me that?" She asked, getting into full awake mode.

"It was worth a try. I've known for a long time that I can't get much by you."

"You know, all this time that I've known you and I still don't understand you."

"What's to understand? I'm really not worth the time, Alyssa."

"But you always send out mixed signals. You always compliment me like no one else can do, yet you don't really open up and tell me anything deeper. It's all just the wiseass crap that cracks me up."

"Like what? And further, what's the point?" I asked.

"What are you really thinking about?"

"What makes you think you're ready to know what I am thinking?"

"Shut your mouth! I know that something is on the tip of your tongue and you won't spit it out."

"Man, I hate all this sexual tension between us." I said.

"You're a jackass. *Sexual* tension? Man, you're twisted." She rolled her eyes but looked like she was pondering the thought.

"Listen, you have a life to go back to. You have your fiancé waiting for you back in Florida, and whether you like to admit it or not, it's driving him crazy that you're on a cramped little plane that smells like goat shit, sitting next to me, who's full of goat shit."

The pilot looked back, looking like he was ready to take us into a nosedive for destroying the integrity of his flying vessel. I gave him a look and smiled. If he wants his plane to smell nice, quit carrying the goats with intestinal issues.

"Sorry Gus." I said, kind of apologetically. "But come on, you can't smell that? What the hell do you carry in here, corpses?"

"We carry small animals that need attention to the vets in the area. Problem is, half these people live in BFE and the animals would die if they took them through the snow. We don't do it all the time, only if we don't have other charters available that have the capacity to carry them. Oh, and Mr. Smartass, that smell that you claim is in the plane is on the bottom of your shoe. It seems that Mr. Know-it-all stepped in some moose shit before the flight."

"Nice. Fucking mooses. Meeses." I said, not even bothering to look to see if he was telling the truth. Bottom line was, I was smelling shit and would be until we landed. Nothing I could do about it now. And what the hell is the plural of moose?

"I know I have a life, Will. I like my life. It's just that when you stepped into it, things got a little weird." Alyssa said.

"Yeah, story of *my* life. Live in my head for a while, I dare you." I shot back just as quickly as I looked at the bottom of my shoe.

"Not bad, weird, just *weird* weird."

"*Grease 2.*" I said, not breaking my stare into the bottom of my shoe. It seems that Gus was right. How'd he see that?

"Okay, I don't understand you at all, but you do know me pretty well. No one else even knows there was a sequel to *Grease* and if they do, they'll never admit to seeing it."

"Come on, Michelle Pfeiffer in black stretch pants straddling a ladder? Who wouldn't want to be her cool rider?" I smiled like an idiot. "Oh, when we land we're staying with Ruthie for about an hour until Uncle Frank comes to get us. His cabin is about a hundred miles north of here."

"Oh great, more flying. That's fantastic. I can take another nap."

"Not when you meet Ruthie's grandkids, you won't. Johnny and Bianca will run you out and probably hurt you." I said.

"Great. Why in the hell did I sign on to work with you? You're a damn nuisance. All the people you know are weird too."

"Oh, that's the forty thousand dollar question that *you'll* never answer. Guess that makes us even then? You know. Don't ask don't tell? And by the way, I only know about two people."

"Yeah, I guess you're more pathetic than I would ever give you credit for."

Alyssa looked at me with a face that would give Frosty the Snowman goose bumps. It wasn't a bad face, but the look that would make you hire her just to see her every day. Part smirk, part coy and part defensive…it was all sexy as hell.

Gus turned his head back again and screamed at us, making me jump nearly out of my seat. "We'll be landing in about thirty seconds. If we make it, enjoy Alaska. Oh, and tell Uncle Frank he owes me twenty bucks from the poker game the other night, that cheatin' bastard."

"Got it." I said, silently concocting a scheme to eliminate the asshole that claimed poker a sport and invaded television with it. I will never play the game just on principal. I'll leave that to the cigar smoking secret societies that used to play it in their basements to get away from their wives for a night.

In the matter of about three seconds, our stomachs dropped as it seemed that Gus was attempting to try out for the Blue Angels as he dropped the plane suddenly into the cold, frosty land below.

"Going for the complete vertical landing?" I said, holding my ass cheeks shut as best as I could to avoid any embarrassment.

"Smartass liberal writing son-of-a-bitch." Gus smiled and actually laughed as he navigated our death drop with what seemed to be drunken precision. At least I know that Alaska officially has its resident fucking psycho. If he was any indication as to what to expect from this trip, I was well into a hallucination without the assistance of any acid.

Alyssa looked out the window and was terrified and mesmerized by the scenery coming towards the window at a faster pace that she was accustomed to. Her face went pale as our stomachs dropped. Within another second, her clenched right fist hit me in the shoulder.

# Three

Gus landed the plane much smoother than he led us to believe he would. Alyssa and I didn't even know we were down in Ruthie's back yard, I was expecting maybe the angels greeting me at the Gates of Heaven. We could have been in Heaven and I would have never known. It was all white out here, no matter where you looked.

"We're here." Gus bellowed into the back of the plane, still not realizing that we were not fifty feet away, but right in back of him, not to mention that his plane was off and it was extremely silent in the cabin. I noticed a faint smell of jerky when he talked, making me want to exit the plane immediately, thinking that he ate the moose that was in here before.

"Get out." Gus said. "I have a pickup and a deadline to make."

"Well, thanks for the hospitality, Gus. You're a great man." I said as I tried simultaneously to make sure that I had my duffle bag and that I didn't soil myself on this leg of our Alaskan adventure.

"There's always room for a wiseass." Gus said, unbuckling his belt and getting ready to jump out of his door. "Ma'am, I feel sorry for you having to be stuck with this schmuck over the Holidays."

"No, we're just friends. I can handle him, unless you want to take him." Alyssa adjusted her duffle and started climbing over me to get out. Gus shook his head at her sudden proposition.

"She works for me, Gus. We're not friends." I don't know why I had to clarify that to the snow version of Norman Bates, but I did.

"Oh, that's nice. All this time and you still have that wall up, huh?" Alyssa was getting pissed. I have only seen her like that once before, after some off-handed comment that I made. From that day on, I promised myself I would never again want the look of death from her, so I make it a habit to push the envelope and leave it alone. Judging by her comment, the envelope was almost opened.

"Ruthie should be waiting for us." I said, being crunched by Alyssa's off-centered weight. "I think I lost the feeling in my right leg. Can you hurry up a little bit?"

"Yeah, buy me breakfast one more time and then complain about my weight! That's real nice, Will."

"There's no way in hell that I am ever going to win this, so I will just apologize right now. Plus I pay you so I buy all your breakfasts." I said. "Again, don't read into that."

"Accepted. Now can we get moving before I pee all over you?"

"You are so romantic." I smiled the cheesiest smile anyone can think of. Thank God Alyssa had her duffle bag in the hand with the big ring on it. I'd rather take the chances with the duffel bag.

After a moment or so we ambled out into the snow. To the right of us was Andrew's Lake and by the looks of it, it was either more calm than ever or iced over, I couldn't tell from here. I looked back and Alyssa's mouth was wide open while she was staring at the lake, obviously impressed with the openness of the scenery.

"Far cry from Florida, huh?" I said, amused at her childlike response.

"Far cry from anything I have seen. Even in Jersey there was nothing like this. Why don't you come up here all the time?"

"I've been thinking about it. You may want to close your mouth before it freezes that way. Ruthie's is about five minutes up the trail."

Five minutes later we arrived at the small airport which doubled as Ruthie's house. It was an old log cabin on the outside, untouched from back in the day, when it was crafted by the hands of the local Eskimos. The inside, however, was redone to accommodate central heating and all the amenities that modern tourism would ask for. From what I understand Ruthie also used this place to hold people when they come to port while on various Alaskan cruises, which necessitated the need for a gift shop over in the corner. The original walls were actually still in the main building, redone underneath to make sure that whatever climate that was in the building stayed in the building. As we opened the front door, the smell of fresh coffee and garlic bagels filled the air.

"This is nice, Will." Alyssa looked around like a child who finally understood the grand scale of their favorite toy store. "I could probably stay here forever."

"It's an airplane hangar, Alyssa. It was partially built by Ruthie's father and grandfather and some of the other local Eskimos."

"Still, it's so cozy, you know? I mean, look at the bench seats! They had to have been made in the fifties. And the ashtrays look like the ones that they have in all those old movies where the well dressed guys would sit and read the paper."

Alyssa took out her digital camera and started snapping pictures, making her way to the coffee machine on the "employee" side of the counter. The flash was going off the whole way. As she was taking pictures of the vaulted ceiling, she backed into the counter, making something rattle. I couldn't see what but it was loud.

"I wouldn't go near there!" I yelled quietly, almost in a joking way but passed it off as seriously as I could. "Trust me. Ruthie is going to kick your ass."

"Oooh, I'm so scared." Alyssa said, being as coy as ever. What is it with women that they can be the biggest teases and not even know they're doing it?

"You should be!" Ruthie yelled towards Alyssa, who jumped enough to make her digital camera jump out of her hands, dangling by the protective string on her wrist.

Ruthie came down the steps which connected to the balcony that she was watching us from. She must have been napping when we came in, judging by the mood she seemed to be in. Ruthie was a small Eskimo woman, leathered skin and hair that seemed to whiten the more you looked at it. She couldn't have been more than five feet tall, but her stare was scary as hell. I guess that staring at two grandchildren and the local moose community for so long would make someone lose the touch for simplicities of human etiquette. She'd have gone completely insane if it wasn't for Gus and Uncle Frank coming to see talk to her a couple of times a week. I would probably pay to see her stare Gus down. That sick psychopathic freak would never know what hit him.

"Will, it's you! So nice of you to finally come back to see me! When was the last time you were here? Was it puberty?" Ruthie cracked the leather into a smile.

"Right around there, yeah." I said, wondering how long it would take me to pee my pants. I love Ruthie to death, but she stares a hole into you if you even ask for something mundane like the sugar.

Without a word or a crack in the leather smile, she smacked me in the face which was still frozen from the cold. "It's been too long! You know that I'm getting older and you take this long to see me!"

"I've been kind of busy doing tours for my books. I'm a writer now, you know."

"Ah, big time writer can't afford time to come see the simple folk. It's one thing to not talk to your family, but you always talk to Ruthie, got it?" Her eyes were burning into me. She missed her calling as an interrogator because I had the sudden urge to tell her everything I knew about everything, which wasn't all that much.

"I got it, Ruthie." I rolled my eyes as she turned to Alyssa. I could feel the redness seeping into my cheek from Ruthie slapping my frozen skin.

"Who's the new little strumpet, Will?" Ruthie flipped the facial leather in Alyssa's direction. You can almost hear the sizzle of the heat transfer to her. I kind of feel bad but it's too fun not to watch. Watching Ruthie talk is like watching a horrible accident on the side of the road. You know you'll be holding up traffic and you shouldn't look, but morbid curiosity takes over and you can't resist. It was like a hyena sizing up its prey.

"Alyssa Witt." I blurted out. It never hurts to throw out a lifejacket. "She's my personal assistant."

"She's a hottie, Will. Isn't that how they say that nowadays?"

"She is attractive, Ruthie, but she works with me. She is getting married someday to the fiancé she's had forever now." I looked Alyssa up and down like I needed reassurance that she was hot.

"It's nice to meet you, Ruthie." Alyssa extended her hand, the digital camera swinging from her wrist. "I heard so much about you."

"I'm sure you have. I trust that it was all good?" Ruthie didn't break the stare.

"Oh, absolutely. I can't wait to meet your grandchildren. I heard they'd give me a run for my money. I mean, I think you've given me more of a run than anyone so far. Keep it up, lady. I can take as much as I can dish out." Alyssa's smile was fantastic. She rolled with the punches and stuck to the guns I always knew she had but were never drawn. This situation had the capability of getting ugly real quick.

"Well, then. I like you. Your fast on your feet and can stand up to me. It's nice to see Will with someone who has a mind and a mouth with enough balls to back it up."

"We're not together, Ruthie. I *work* with him." Alyssa said. She was kind of staring at me out of the corner of her eye like I gave Ruthie some false story before we arrived. Yeah, like I would do that.

"And you just happen to be in the same remote place on Earth during the most romantic holiday in the world? I think we could all use a little coffee while we figure out why that is."

Alyssa looked at me and all I could think to do was laugh and shrug. We have chemistry, there's no doubting it. It's not my fault if others can sniff it out. All Alyssa has to do is admit it and the issue would be over. But stubbornness always prevails.

"The kids are outside." Ruthie said. "Alyssa, you can go play with them after you drink your coffee. Will and I have some business to discuss. And since you're not together, you won't mind me excusing you in a few minutes so I can have a heart to heart with this one." An Eskimo finger was pointed in my direction.

"No, I don't mind." Alyssa replied. "I love the scenery and he's getting on my nerves anyway. I guess I have to remember how to make snowballs, huh?"

"Nice." I looked at her and rolled my eyes. We get along like a happily married couple and it's driving me crazy. She takes my money. We argue all the time and never have sex. It definitely sounds like a marriage to me.

Ruthie started for the coffee pot and tray of bagels. They were recently toasted so she must have run upstairs for the sole purpose of terrifying us when we came in. She probably heard our feet crushing snow about fifty yards back and heard Gus yelling at me from a mile away. I was convinced as a child that she too was a Secret Service agent and she was backing up that suspicion to this day. "Normally I wouldn't give anyone bagels, except for the management, but since it's empty today, how do you like them?"

"A lot of cream cheese." I said.

"Is it your goal to make me fat?" Alyssa asked as she back handed me in the shoulder again. "I put on these jeans this morning and had to squat for ten minutes to fit into them."

"Just eat, for God's sake. It is the most important meal of the day. Oh, and you look great in those jeans so shut up." I smiled at her just knowing she wouldn't do anything about it, especially in front of her new friend Ruthie.

# Four

It took us about half an hour to devour two bagels a piece and almost a full pot of Alaskan blend coffee. I consider myself a coffee connoisseur and this was close to being the best I have ever tasted.

Alyssa looked at Ruthie who was seated at the counter. She seemed to be fumbling at her napkin and muttering to herself. I don't know if it was the caffeine or nerves, but something spooked her and Alyssa caught on to it. She doesn't miss much. That's why her agreeing to come up here was so baffling to me.

"Thank you for the coffee and bagels, Ruthie." Alyssa patted her on the hand. "I think I'm going to go find the kids outside. You know, let you guys catch up until Uncle Frank gets here."

"Thanks, Alyssa. We won't be long." I said as I gave her a wink and a smile, silently shuddering as I felt suddenly like a used car salesman trying to get a number from a hot chick with bad credit. "Watch out for Bianca. She's got a wicked sidearm with a snowball. Johnny is the stealthy one, he'll ambush you while she runs interference."

"Thanks for the tip. Come get me when you're ready, Will." Alyssa turned, grabbed her coat and walked to the front doors, exiting out to the white yard that seemed to go on for miles through the trees. Within thirty seconds Ruthie and I heard Alyssa yell about something hitting her in the eye. Bianca was very quick and very good.

"I think Bianca's in trouble, Ruthie. Alyssa's a sidewinder herself." I said like the proud fake husband I was.

Ruthie just continued to stare at the napkin she was fumbling with the entire time we were sitting there.

"Will," she said with a nervous twitch in her voice, "I have to give you something. It's needed now and it's real important."

"What is it, Ruthie?"

Ruthie reached into her front apron pocket and pulled out what seemed to be a ring box. Instead of the black lining around it, this was clear acetate. I tried to look right inside, but with the bluish reflections creating a diamond effect, it was almost impossible to see anything.

"Ruthie, I'm a little young for you, don't you think?" I asked.

"I am not proposing, jackass. I need you to hold onto this for me. For once take something seriously."

"What is it?" My curiosity was officially peaked. Whatever was in that box turned the stone Ruthie into a frenetic box of nerves.

"It's a ring. It's a one-of-a-kind, so it cannot be lost. When the time is right, you will know when to use it."

"Is this where you call me Frodo?" I said.

"I said be serious for one minute! This is very important! There will be…people coming to look for this and it cannot fall into their hands." She gave the box to me. I really didn't want to open it. "It is known as the Christmas Crystal. The contents of the ring were smuggled here, and the contents of that box can save what's been slowly destroyed piece by piece for the past few years."

"I have no idea what the hell you are talking about and why did you hesitate when you said the word people?"

"You will find out, Will. Trust me. You are about to find out who you really are and what you are all about."

"Listen, I don't know if I want this thing. I only came up here to help Uncle Frank with his parcels."

"You are helping Uncle Frank. If this was in his possession he would be an easy target because everyone knows him. You, on the other hand, are a wild card. Not many people know that you exist, thanks in part to your own desire to remain hidden from the world. That's why Uncle Frank has chosen you."

"You mean that he hand-picked me to be part of some cat and mouse bullshit? Alyssa's here and I don't want her involved in anything crazy. She has a family she needs to go home to. And besides, I know myself pretty well already. Trust me on this. I don't want to be the target of some crazy game that Uncle Frank likes to play with his drinking buddies. You know, bet on how long it takes me to make it back to the cabin naked in the middle of winter?"

"There is a reason she's here, Will. There is a reason that you're here and I can assure you it is not for a game concocted by your Uncle and his idiot friends. Be honest with me, didn't you feel a little sense that something was off on the way up here? Like there was a purpose for you and your life?"

"Come to think of it, I wasn't really anxious or anything. Yeah, it did feel like there was something I should be doing, like scraping moose shit off of my shoes."

Ruthie looked at me, her eyes not burning a hole into me this time but melting into a plea for help. She wouldn't give me the satisfaction of commenting on every joke I made about what she was saying. She just slapped me again, this time in the back of the head.

As I rubbed my head I took the ring and put it in my pocket without opening it. My mind raced with every crazy thought of the most bizarre bullshit that you can think of. What was I getting into here? This is only supposed to be a journal for Will the Writer! Easy things like, "Yeah, I smoked a lot of weed but concentrated on writing and found my purpose in life." Not the "I got a mythical Christmas ring from some crazy Eskimo lady in Anchorage, waiting for a charter plane to take me into Hell itself, with a neurotic sidekick whose family doesn't like the idea of her being here with me in the first place." I guess it wouldn't be my life unless Fate intervened and sent me something really twisted to kick me in the crotch.

As I was pondering all of those things, Alyssa came stumbling in the door, holding her left eye.

"What the hell happened to you?" I asked, laughing.

"It's not funny. They were making ice balls and Bianca hit me in the eye. It was crazy! Johnny said he wants Santa to bring him a bike or a snowmobile and while I was listening to his request, Bianca nailed me! It's like you're raising little snow ninjas! It's creepy that they're so tactical."

Ruthie managed a little laugh. "I told them not to make ice balls. They kept hitting the moose with them, making them all crazy."

"They definitely earned the naughty list today. No offense, but that stung! It's like I'm in the *Village of the Damned*!" Alyssa refused to remove her hand from her eye.

"Well, if there was a list anymore, that could be arranged." Ruthie shook her head slowly, looking towards the floor.

"What's that mean? Am I unconscious or something?" Alyssa looked completely baffled.

"It's nothing dear. Will can fill you in later." Ruthie heard something overhead that sounded like it had propellers. "I think that's Uncle Frank. You two best get ready. He's on a tight schedule. Enjoy his *one-bedroom* cabin, you two."

"Okay, Ruthie. That's enough." I said. Some ribbing is fine, I was used to it but I didn't want to have Alyssa's button pushed. Alyssa pushed so many buttons in her life that she's earned the remote control for it, but when hers were pushed I liked to duck for cover. The voice raises three octaves and you can be seven feet tall and within a minute you'd be groveling from your three foot frame. She was good. She was *real* good.

"Thanks for everything, Ruthie." I said. "It was good seeing you again. And seeing Alyssa ambushed? Priceless."

Alyssa back handed me in the shoulder again with the hand not covering her bruised eye.

"Good luck, Will." Ruthie stared at the floor like Jim Phelps after doling out his crazy-ass missions.

"What's going on here?" Alyssa had no idea what just fell into my lap as she stared at Ruthie and me with her one good eye.

# Five

Sixty stories up in the lavish owner's suite of the now-famous Pole Tower Casino, Jack Frost was sitting at his desk, staring out his huge floor-to-ceiling window at the Vegas-style landscape which is the New North Pole. It has become Jack Frost's North Pole and he has no qualms about letting everyone know it. And just to make sure that Jack stays on top of everything going on in his city, all of the walls in his circular suite have been replaced with windows from floor to ceiling and stretch around the entire circumference of the building. Only the inner portion resembled a private residence, closed off to the perimeter. And, as he would have it, he is literally placed on the northernmost point on the globe, so wherever he looks out from anywhere in his suite he is looking south.

Jack smiled to himself, knowing that sitting on the northernmost point of the Earth made him closer to being a god than anyone could ever claim to be.

He sighed loudly knowing that there was still more to do to build his empire. He breathed smoke from the near freezing temperature of the tower itself. He sat here and rested on the laurels of everything that he's created: the gambling Mecca of the world, the nicest casino-hotel the world has ever known, and a stronghold on all of the illegal activity that happens up here and worldwide.

He had eight casinos in the city that were spread out with four on each side of the main strip that went down the center of the town. Each casino had a hotel attached to it and averaged about thirty floors and about three thousand rooms. His casino was the ninth casino on the strip with sixty floors that peaked up into the night sky. There were also about fifty high-end restaurants in the city all with a price tag of no less than a hundred dollars a plate. They ranged from Italian to French to Indian; no matter what you wanted you could get it. Within months the world's most prolific chefs came here to cook, bringing in more tourists than ever.

Outside the actual city in the streets behind all of the action, was the backbone of the Pole operations. They were the real people that made things work up here. There were convenience stores, clothing boutiques and strip clubs all over the place. The hookers were in full swing and advertised on the strip while the not-so-desirable slithered their ways down various candy-striped poles in the shittiest dive bars you can imagine.

Jack stared down at The Yuletide Bar, which was his pride and joy up here. As the biggest manufacturer of Humbug in the world, the bar fronted as a normal hangout for the usual deviants and had the labs in the basement. Jack has made a good portion of his money suppressing the happy urges of the population so they can get down to the more serious business of giving Jack all of their money. All of the people that can make it past the addiction made it to the strip to gamble with the big boys. The others who let the drug consume them can now only dream of being on the strip and not in the gutter. Either way, Jack won.

He caught himself in the reflection, his pale blue face nestled under a head full of straight white hair, which was spiked up like he was some sort of character from a Japanese animated film. He smiled to himself, wondering why he never filed these teeth down. He was born with them and his parents left him because of them, but when they grew into bigger points they were the cause of the only horrible mention of him over the Christmas Holidays. Oddly enough, Jack Frost never nipped anyone's nose. He just figured out a way to get their money…over and over again until they were completely broke. Now he was known for his teeth and would never alter their appearance.

"Mr. Frost, you're package has arrived. Mort and Stan have him here." Sugarplum said suddenly through the intercom. Sugarplum had an actual name once when Jack hired her, but based on her perfect fake-looking breasts and a body that could make the tower melt (not to mention she was a tall *human* female), Jack just started calling her Sugarplum because he caught himself all of the time imagining the visions of her fine breasts dancing in his head.

"Great! Bring him in!" Jack jumped up and smoothed out his icy blue suit. Mort and Stan soon arrived in Jack's room. They were two disgruntled elves that happened to be the meanest sons-a-bitches on the Pole. Mort was the smart elf. On the other hand, Stan was near mentally crippled but could beat a human to death when asked to do so.

In between the elves stood the bulky frame of Frosty. His snowy wrists were shackled in front of his buffoonish body.

"Frosty! It's nice to see you, dear boy. How are things?" Jack smiled as he approached Frosty and got almost face-to-face with him.

"Could be better, Mr. Frost." Frosty kept the befuddled look on his face as he tried to suppress his Jimmy Durante accent.

"No shit it could be better, you fat yellow-piss-attracting shit head." Jack stopped for a second and stared Frosty square in his coal eyes. "I sent you to pick up the rent from The Yuletide. And what exactly happened to the rent, Mr. Snow Shit? What kind of excuse do you have for me tonight?"

"Eddie Drummer took it." Frosty looked straight ahead through his two eyes made out of coal.

"Drop the Jimmy Durante bullshit act, Frosty! You only talk like that because of the film they made about you and now you get all cocky. And by the way, that little Drummer boy couldn't harm a damn fly. He's an orphan, for fuck's sake! That little bastard runs around up in the Pole without sense enough to buy any clothes? He's like a little Tarzan baby running around banging that damn drum. He's fucking harmless and a tad bit crazy and you tag him for stealing my money?! Jesus Christ, Frosty! You can come up with something better than that. All of that damn magic in that old black hat and you're still a fucking idiot. Can't you tell it to make you smarter?"

"He's harmless until he whacks you with the drumstick!" It almost looked like the two eyes made out of coal were getting bigger in surprise. His accent faded away as he yelled at Frost, sounding more and more like he was from Fargo than anywhere else. "Please, I needed the money. I'm really strapped here."

"Oh, grow some snow balls, huh? You're a thief and you know that I don't tolerate thieves. Icon or not I don't like you."

"But you let them live freely as long as they pay you. So, aren't you the biggest thief of all?" Frosty pleaded.

"It's called honor among thieves. You wouldn't know what honor is you pile of white shit. But it is precious of you to point that out. That hat must have told you." Jack smiled through his pointed teeth.

"Alright, alright." Frosty said as he looked around for a moment. Mort and Stan would not be releasing their grip anytime soon, that much was clear. "I took the money to buy some new magic hats for the wife and kids. And it seems that someone stole them to sell them back to that crazy magician so they can eat. Problem is, I go home and my wife is totally cold to me and the kids just sit there. I had to do something to get my family back. You have to understand, Mr. Frost."

"And you couldn't just ask me? I am a reasonable man, Frosty. I could have helped you. But now you've betrayed my trust and I can't have that. Not in this point in my career. I think a punishment is due."

"You gonna lock me up like Claus?" Frosty asked.

"Nope, I have something better for you." Jack disappeared for a second, coming back with a huge tarp that he started laying down in front of Frosty. "Stand on this."

Frosty didn't budge until Stan pushed him onto it, losing part of his hand into the thick, snowy part of Frosty's lower back.

"Frosty, my dear snowman, I am going to melt you right here." Jack pinned up the edges of the tarp in a makeshift way to make sure all of the water was collected in the center. He walked to his desk and hit the intercom. "Sugarplum, turn the heat to eighty degrees."

"Yes sir." Sugarplum responded. "Let me know when to resume normal temp."

"Mr. Frost, please! Take my hat! Take my eyes! Just please don't melt me!" It was almost as if the coal was shedding a black tear.

"If I melt you, you physically have to be rebuilt. The hat restores you immediately. I'll go with melting, followed by an eternity in a mason jar on my desk." Jack smiled at the soon-to-be puddle. "I can wear the hat to some of my events. It is pretty stylish."

"Mr. Frost, no, you can't..." Frosty started talking as he was slowly sinking into the floor. His knees fell into the floor, followed closely by his hips and stomach. One by one his arms melted into the wet pile below him, the shackles clanging to the floor. Frosty was staring at Jack with repentance in his black eyes when suddenly his button nose popped off, bouncing and splashing in the puddle. Within five minutes Frosty's eyes fell to the floor. Jack looked as Frosty's corncob pipe fizzled out, being last thing to drop into Frosty himself.

"Well, that about does it." Jack went over and picked p the magic hat. "Oh, there must be some magic in this old black hat I found!" He started laughing maniacally. "Mort, Stan...bravo! Bravissimo! Well done. Tell Sugarplum on the way out to crank down the air in five minutes. I'm sweating to death. And while you're at it, get that Drummer kid. I want to give him some kind of a job."

"What about The Yuletide?" Mort asked from somewhere in his tiny Armani suit.

"Let it go for now." Jack replied. "They're good for it. It seems that the remaining parts of the Christmas Crystal are in circulation. They seem to be coming from the Alaskan side. Maybe they're coming from that Frank Foster guy. You know him, the pilot? See what you can find out from the guys on the State side."

"You got it, sir." Mort grunted and turned to leave, Stan one step behind him.

Jack stood again facing the window. He smiled to himself as he stood in the pool that used to be Frosty. As he watched the lights buzzing around below him he started moving his feet like a child standing in a rain puddle, skipping in and out of the water and laughing through every minute.

Outside in the streets of the world-famous North Pole the lights were brighter than ever. The sin in the streets was in full gear and dear old Jack Frost was set to have the best year of his life. He could almost smell the body-sprayed sweat of the strippers and the used stench of the hookers through the glass. If he concentrated, he could almost smell the Humbug being cooked over the egg-nog smell that he was pumping into the streets. Tonight was definitely a good night.

"Next step," Jack told his razor-tooth reflection, "the world will be mine as it should be."

# Six

U ncle Frank's cabin was tucked nicely into the edge of the woods, hidden by everything from up above as well as anyone passing by water on a Sunday cruise through the lake. Not that there were that many people in the area, his nearest neighbor was about ten miles away.

The cabin itself smelled old and rustic. It had a faint odor of old cigars and smoked cedar, probably from late night poker games with Uncle Frank and his pilot buddies next to a crackling fire or something. Oddly enough, the wood still smelled new even though the cabin itself was built by the Eskimo people around one hundred years ago.

Uncle Frank walked us in and led us to the living room which was populated by wooden furniture with soft cushions and one lamp. It looked like an old hotel. They weren't the most recent accommodations but with Uncle Frank being out of the house for such long periods of time I don't blame him for not having much. Alyssa, on the other hand, thought the cabin was great. As she walked through the living room, she noticed the antique fireplace and bearskin rug splayed out in front of it, snapping more pictures that she can come back to later.

"Wow, I love the fireplace." She said, in total amazement that we somehow went back on evolution about a hundred years.

"Don't worry about the bearskin rug." Uncle Frank turned around, suddenly enthusiastic that someone was taking a liking to his life. "It's fake. I leave the hunting to the people who know how to do it and have a reason to. Plus, all those environmentalists would somehow get stranded here and have nothing better to do than chastise me. It's just my luck, so fake is the way to go. It's still soft and looks real."

"Either way, I think it's cool. This whole place is cool." Alyssa's head was on a constant swivel as she looked around to look at the wooded haven.

"So which one of you two gets to sleep in the bed tonight?" Uncle Frank winked at me the way two guys do when they know there is an imminent "score" in their future.

"She can take the bed. I'll sleep anywhere." I said. I know Uncle Frank enough to know that he would pounce on my sentence as soon as it escaped my mouth; the words will be floating around just waiting to land somewhere near Uncle Frank.

"No shit." He said, not missing a beat.

"Will can take the bed. I'm just a tag-a-long." Alyssa was still swiveling all over the room like a hungry realtor.

Uncle Frank just laughed. "Well, whoever it is, or both of you, I have new sheets on there. Make sure you change the sheets before you leave. Now, I didn't plan on this, but I can't stay. I have some important things to take care of. There's a turkey in the oven, feel free to enjoy dinner, courtesy of me."

"Oh, you're not staying?" Alyssa finally focused on something other than the wooden walls around her. She stared Uncle Frank right in the face, with a look that said "I really don't want to be alone with him for a week" and "I really want to get stories from Will's past" all at once. Yeah, she was a walking conflict.

"No, unfortunately I can't stay." Uncle Frank said. "But fortunately, Alyssa, you will actually learn more about Will than you ever thought you would. And I think you'll learn a hell of a lot about yourself in the process. I am not talking about intimately, mind you, but on a personal level. I can't explain it all right now, but it will come to you." Uncle Frank stared directly at me, not knowing if I was up to the challenge. What challenge, I had no idea.

"Does this have to do with what Ruthie gave me?" I pulled the ring box out of my pocket.

"It has everything to do with that." Uncle Frank stated, looking at the floor. "And Will, you are the wild card. No one knows that you exist, no less have that ring."

"Wild card in what?!" I yelled, frustrated with mysteries in general. Being part of one that was beyond my control just pissed me off. More than that, I hated all of the poker terminology.

"You'll see." Uncle Frank said, staring again straight in my eyes. "In the mean time, since they will eventually trace you through our family tree, I would recommend that Alyssa become the wild card. I think you should give the ring to her."

"Listen, I am not sure what the hell you brought us up here for, but I think we've been duped into something. Maybe it's coming up with poker losses before you lose your plane, who the hell knows? But I don't plan on bringing Alyssa into any of whatever this is." I really didn't. Out of all the people I have ever really known, I respect her the most and would hate to have her dragged into anything that would put her in danger.

"I can decide that for myself." She piped up. "Will, listen, I didn't have to get on that plane, okay? I'll do whatever it takes, as your editor and agent. I have a feeling that I have to do this. I don't know what it is or what I am a wild card for, but I just know I'm needed. And if you don't make it, who else is going to pay me for a cake job with frequent flyer miles?"

"Do you have any idea how crazy this sounds?" I was in full confusion gear right now and I was becoming crazier by the minute. Alyssa was acting all loony and Uncle Frank seemed to be talking in distracted riddles since we got here. "Uncle Frank, what the hell is going on here? I want to know what kind of weird little game is going on inside of your head. And why the hell would you drag me up here, all the way from Florida, to have me participate in it? And, while we're on the subject, why did I accidentally bring Alyssa into this? Shit, I would have just introduced her to the family. Then again, it's this type of crap that made me not want to talk to anyone in my family again in the first place. Are you willing to risk it?"

"Listen, Will." Uncle Frank seemed to get a stern tone from out of nowhere. It was kind of spooky when it crept up on you. "I asked you up here because of your relationship with the whole family. Or lack thereof, should I say. That ring that is in the box has the power to change things Will, but you are going to have to find out a little something about yourself in the process. If you're not ready to do that and you want to be Mr. Elusive Writer all your life, that's fine, but the world is not going to care about you if it knows you had the power to help it and didn't."

"But I have no idea what the hell this is all about!" I couldn't take it anymore. I was in a crazy house and everyone was sane but me. Maybe Uncle Frank was running weed in his plane. Who knows, maybe they're all stoned. God knows I wished I was right now. Everything would make more sense. Even if it didn't, the refrigerator would be good amusement for five stupid hours. "Would someone please explain to me exactly what I am supposed to be doing with this ring? Am I supposed to be calling you Gandalf the White?"

"Just keep it safe, Will." Uncle Frank walked up to me and stared at me, his eyes were cold like they were buried in the snow outside for about an hour. "Like I said, people are going to be looking for this, and if they find it the wheels that are in motion already will be unstoppable."

"What exactly are we supposed to do? This sounds fun!" Alyssa popped in, making a human triangle, my corner being the only lunatic one. I was the only one who wanted a literal meaning in all of this and they both enjoyed the riddles.

"Will, put the ring on her finger. Like I said, she's not in our bloodline so they wouldn't be looking for her." Uncle Frank said.

"You know what?" I asked, wanting to do something as mundane as pissing my name in the snow right now. But I would settle for Uncle Frank just flying away from here. "I am going to put it on her finger just so we can have some peace and quiet."

I pulled out the ring and got down on one knee. Anyone that knows me knows that I have a flair for the dramatic comedy. I'm a kind of a vaudeville act that's gone completely mad. I have had thoughts of this moment for a while now but knowing that I am in the land of snowballs, moose shit and utter nonsense I can guess that none of those thoughts have a chance in hell, just like the proverbial snowball's chances.

It was more of a fantasy, marrying the perfect woman. But as I learned a long time ago I am not 'perfect' for anyone. I am horrible with relationships and respect Alyssa more than any mere mortal to ruin her with the likes of me. Plus she's already getting married and I respect that, so for now this is going to be vaudeville. Comedy is much easier than real feelings. Hell, if they think you're joking you can take it as far as you want and all parties can walk away at any time without risk of showing anything that should remain hidden. It doesn't change the fact that I really wanted to kiss her right now, even as neurotic as she was acting. She was like a wildly sexual, cute but deranged Looney Tune.

I quickly shrugged off the feeling and slipped the pale blue ring on her finger. I hadn't noticed it before but there was no engagement ring on her finger! Can it be? No! Stop! It's in her bag. She took it off at Ruthie's while she was throwing snowballs. I'll just keep telling myself that I am better off alone. Man, I am neurotic, and I am doing it with the biggest damn grin on my face. This girl is going to be the death of me.

"Oh my God, this ring is really nice." Alyssa held her hand out, staring at the ring like she was trying to figure out how to break it to her family that she was marrying me. It was weird, the signals were weird and I just wanted to go stay in the outhouse.

It really was a nice piece of jewelry. It was just a standard band, made of polished titanium that had a blue tint to it. It barely even looked the least bit titanium anymore.

"Okay." Uncle Frank said, clasping his hands together. "That was the most beautiful engagement that will never be. Alyssa, keep that on until the job is done, okay? You will know the details tonight, but I am forbidden to tell you anything right now."

"Then who is going to tell us?" Alyssa said, still staring at the ring like she was on a commercial. I was waiting for the toothy spin turn, where her hair would whip around in slow motion, shining like gold in the windy sunlight.

"You will know tonight." Uncle Frank said. "Like I said, it sounds a little weird but I cannot say anything. If a person speaks it, it will make it not happen. Just remember these numbers. Will, Alyssa, you listening?"

I nodded along with Alyssa. We both rolled our eyes in our heads.

"Nine. One. Two." Uncle Frank stated like he was waiting for Jim Phelps to give them their impossible mission.

"Nine One Two. Got it." Alyssa stared at the ring again. "What does it mean?"

"Trust the Nine, obey the Twelve." Uncle Frank said. "Trust me on this."

"I am not even going to ask. I just want to lie down." I said, wanting desperately to take a nap.

"Me too." Alyssa said. She was notorious for wanting to sleep all the time. Make that item one hundred that we have in common. Stop, Will! You're better off alone!

"Anyway, there's dinner in the oven and some beer. Oh, I think there's a small bottle of wine and some soda. I don't have a lot of junk food, but we can stock up tomorrow if we can, okay?" Uncle Frank nodded and walked towards the front door.

"Yeah, I could use a drink." Alyssa averted her eyes towards the kitchen cabinets.

"I thought you get 'friendly' with alcohol. That might not be a good idea." I said, secretly wanting to give her the bottle and let her get as friendly as she wants, but I had to stick to my moral guns. Stupid fucking morals. I hate it when morals get in the way of seeing the sexiest woman alive butt naked.

"I can handle myself." She said defiantly.

"I can handle you too, but that would be crossing the line." I shot right back, not taking time to lose the opportunity.

"Damn, you too might as well be married for real. You fight like an old couple." Uncle Frank said, turning around. "Okay, I'm leaving. I will be back tomorrow if I don't see you first. If you light a fire, make sure it's out before you go to sleep. The bearskin is a fake and will go up like crazy. Good luck, guys. And be careful, huh?"

I was never so happy to see Uncle Frank leave. Whatever he was on hopefully was safe to fly on, but at least now I'll be able to rest and let Alyssa cut loose a little. My drinking days are over, but she needed to relax and take a few drinks.

# Seven

Jack Frost was sitting in his office looking over memos and financial statements which had started taking a dip recently. As he looked them over he shrugged and moaned, knowing that his distribution companies based on the Pole should be doing better numbers at this time of year. Since Frost Industries took over nearly worldwide distribution on all products ranging from feather dusters to laptops and bondage outfits and sex toys, he needed to find out why sales were down. Even his blue hair seemed to be turning whiter with every moment he stared at the invoices.

"Sugarplum," Jack said into the little box in the desk, "can you come in here please? And bring something to write with."

"Sure, Mr. Frost." She didn't mean to, but every time she called on that little box, Jack could have sworn she was a phone sex operator. For a minute he pondered putting her on the phones, but even that was stretching his business a little too thin. The door flipped open behind him as Sugarplum's breasts seemed to enter the room. Jack insisted she entered the room at least ten seconds after they did, maybe it was just his perverted imagination.

"Sugarplum, our retail numbers are down. Any ideas on how to get them back up?"

"We can try what I suggested last time you couldn't get something up." Sugarplum hated feeding into him like that but did it only to stay on his good side.

"That's not what I'm talking about. All of the retail chains around the globe are down. Their sales suck. I mean, come on. I had a tap on the new PlayMaster Box 920 two years ago. It's the most anticipated gaming system anywhere. Where else can you shoot someone and they actually feel it? Even that was a near disaster."

"Well, the marketing was weird, Mr. Frost. In my opinion, I don't think it was the best thing to do to sell it the day after Thanksgiving and only send out a fraction of the consoles made. You know how many people were trampled to get their hands on the first ones? And then they got recalled anyway because they exploded."

"Thank you, Sugarplum. I think I prefer you as a gal with a great rack who takes my calls. I didn't hire you for the brain I had no idea you owned."

"Watch out Mr. Frost. A beautiful body and a dangerous mind is a lethal combination. And need I remind you that it was you that asked me in here for my opinion." She smirked at him and pulled down her shirt a little to show some cleavage. She rolled her eyes as she averted him once more.

"Okay, since I know you can think, I really need help here. Do you have any ideas on how to boost sales?"

"Yes. We need more people buying. More people physically going through the lines. How do you make that happen?"

Jack pondered this for a long moment, gliding his snake-like tongue over his pointed teeth. "We get them out faster. It will give them more time to realize they need something else when they get home and they'll come back."

"And how do you suggest that we boost productivity in all of the chains around the globe? That's a tall order this time of year."

"We'll start with the big chains in America. What I want you to do is this: send out an emergency memo to all store owners around the globe. I want you to let them know that from this moment on, anyone uttering the words Merry Christmas in line, to any customer, will be fired on the spot. Happy Holidays, all of it, gone."

"Won't that offend people? I mean, isn't Christmas named after Jesus Christ? I think people would be offended."

"There's no more room for feeling during Christmas. There is a boatload of money to be made, and the archaic notion of Christmas is now gone. Christ has been gone from the holiday for a long time now. Do you think anyone in the world cares about anything other than getting to the mall before everyone else, just so they can spoil their kids that much more? People themselves keep upping the bar that we have to live up to. It's simple supply and demand. It's not our fault that there's no Christ in Christmas, blame the consumers."

"Okay, I get it. Just try to sell that to Mr. Kringle next time you visit the institution, okay?"

Jack looked at Sugarplum like he was about to kill her. "Just send the memo and keep your damn opinions to yourself. You weren't complaining when you got your last bonus, remember? Don't be a hypocrite. Let the consumers and Christmas advocates do that for you. Tell them all shipments will be suspended for all items made if sales don't go up ten percent by tomorrow."

Without a word Sugarplum followed her breasts out of the office. Jack just sat back and waited for the collective sigh across the world to begin. This was his bread and butter. He created mass hysteria with the best of them, but what he had up his sleeve for the remaining part of his plan would cement him as the next big world leader to contend with. The thought made him smile so hard that he cut a hole in his lip with his teeth causing some blue blood to trickle down his chin.

He checked his watch. His visitors should be arriving soon to put next year's plan in motion. It was crunch time; he has three-hundred and sixty-eight days to take over the world.

# Eight

It was about eight o'clock pm. The air outside was pitch black, the only light outside was from the snow glowing in the moonlight as it passed through the naked limbs of the huge trees that protected the cabin. Alyssa was completely wiped out from the trip and from Bianca's ice assault. Pretty soon after we heated the turkey she had a glass of wine and passed out on the fake bear in front of the fireplace. So much for her being "friendly", I thought. The only friendly things that happened were a few well-timed belches by her, followed by her naming the bear rug 'Troy'.

As far as I was concerned I was happy enough just sitting here, curled up in the seat embedded in the bay window staring at the snow outside. It wasn't doing anything in particular, but snow never had to. I just sat there and got lost, thinking about being a kid again. I thought of being up in New Jersey, waiting for the fire station siren to tell me and the rest of the neighborhood that there was a snow day. That was followed by my friends Pete and Kenny running over as fast as they could in the snow as it swallowed their legs up to the knee with each step. We'd run to Goffle Brook Park and sled all day long, not wanting to come home until one of us actually landed in the brook or our hands were frost bitten. Hell, we'd actually wipe wax paper on the bottom and surf all the way down. Man that was fun.

These thoughts come and go frequently. They were mostly gone while I was in Florida, as the actual temperature from hell didn't make you necessarily think of snow days and it was significantly more difficult to surf on sand. It was nice to sit here and think of things like that, because God knows I really never talk about my life to anyone.

I looked over to the fireplace and looked at the sleeping Alyssa who was passed out on Troy. She looked so peaceful that I couldn't bring myself to wake her. And me being the selfish bastard I am I decided to at least be nice on her behalf.

Out the bay window the snow days faded into a snowdrift as the wind carried the adult thoughts into my head. Not like the main things adults think about, where I would sneak over and slip myself inside of her and she would be swept away with hot, sweaty romantic passion that 'Troy' would be in paradise while it lasted for hours. Okay, that thought may have sneaked in there, but the general thought on my mind right now was that I would give about anything to be lying next to her right now, feeling her breathe into me as we were wrapped around each other as we slept. I know, guys shouldn't think these things but she just looked like the perfect person to snuggle up with when life sucks. The smell of her hair was just amazing and sleeping next to that would be something I can completely envision doing every night of my life. I try to steer away from any bad thoughts now; it's just another step to fixing my head. Life would be perfect if the face I was looking at was staring at me first thing every morning.

"Hey, what are you doing?" Alyssa said in a groggy tone, I almost thought it was 'Troy'. Oh, shit, was I talking out loud? Did she hear me? Holy shit, I am not prepared to come clean with any of that. She has a life and I am not really a part of it, on an emotional level, anyway.

"Will, were you staring at me?" Alyssa asked.

"Can I lie?" I said, immediately going back to the Jersey snow day out the bay window as my face turned red. The snow was still not doing anything.

"No." She said, wiping her eyes.

"You just looked very peaceful. You needed the sleep."

"There was more to it than that." She moved herself up and sat Indian-style on the 'Troy'. There are so many ways to say how she was sitting that would be socially and politically acceptable, but who cares? People are too fucking sensitive. This is what I knew and I never gave a flying shit about being politically correct so Indian Style it is.

"Not really. I'm just kind of lost looking out the window." I said, pretending to be in a daze.

"Do you want to come over and sit on 'Troy'?" Alyssa patted the bear's head.

"As bizarre as that sounds, no. But thank you. I've never had the urge to sit on a 'Troy'."

"Are you okay? You seem a little lost right now." She said.

"Yeah, I'm just thinking. Trust me. You don't want what's in my head. I don't want what's in here."

How bad can it really be?" She asked.

"There are things in there that I don't think I'll ever tell anyone Alyssa. No offense but I am not opening anything up right now."

"No offense taken. Just promise me that when you feel like it you'll come to me."

"Don't hold your breath." I said.

"You should stop being so negative, Will. It *is* Christmas."

"Did you call home and let them know when you'll meet up with them?" I always used home as the word for her life outside of me. It kept things impersonal and easy to walk away from.

"Yeah, don't change the subject." She said.

"What, Christmas? Screw Christmas."

"You're a dork."

"What? Christmases never quite lived up to the hype. Do you have any idea how depressing it is to be let down after six months of prep time? It's not worth it emotionally."

"Listen, you are a nice guy. I wouldn't be here if you weren't. You can't hold onto that thought all the time Will. It's just not healthy. Why don't you let people know how nice you are and maybe you can make someone else's Christmas better. Wouldn't that help yours?"

"Um, no. They can find their own way. I am done being people's crutches. I've been doing it for too long."

She looked at me with those brown eyes and I swear I just ripped a part of her heart out. Was she telling me I helped her have a better Christmas by being here? Am I reading too much into this and she's pissed she's all the way in Alaska, trapped with a prick for a boss? Who the hell knows but that look drives me mad and not knowing why I am getting the look drives me even crazier.

"Someday a light will go off above you and you'll see. But don't come running to me to thank me." She looked into the fireplace.

As soon as Alyssa turned, a heavy object crashed into the roof of the cabin. It was accompanied by a red light, which flashed brightly into the window and quickly streaked into the woods. Alyssa and I jumped nearly into the fireplace.

I just stared at her, dumbfounded by the coincidence. "Now you can tell me someday I am going to be hung like a porn star and cash is going to flow out of my pockets." I paused, looked at my crotch and patted where my pockets would be. I was still hung like I normally was and still had no cash. "What the fuck was that?"

"I have no idea but I need another drink. Do we have anything stronger than wine?" Alyssa zombie-walked to the kitchen and started her hunt for alcohol.

# Nine

The inside of the old red brick building looked deserted. Uncle Frank stood outside staring into a frost-covered window, looking for any signs of life. He knew that The Herald was still in circulation, he caught an issue last week, but he would never know it judging by the lack of life inside the building. It was a good little newspaper that struggled for a while after the power was switched to the power of greed in the North Pole. No reporter-angel knew what to cover when the old ways went out to make way for the new, faster paced world they now lived in.

The original elves, who were now in seclusion about a mile out from the border of the Pole, helped build this little newspaper to be the one binding entity keeping harmony in their little desolate part of the Earth. Now the paper has everything under the elusive sun to write about, not that anyone cared to read.

All of the corruption practically writes itself but doesn't turn any heads. Nothing is ever answered, just questions upon questions to temporarily raise an eyebrow of whoever bought the paper in the first place. It wasn't like the media around the world where you can buy people to back up your left or right wing conspiracy theories. Your hack theories went on as reading fluff with absolutely no merit whatsoever.

The one and only reason the paper does okay is the comprehensive racing form that's in it daily to help the poor gambling bastards down at the Douglas Fir Memorial Track win back their lives. A lot of dreams were made and destroyed betting on the Reindeer Games. In a way this paper almost helped the little city to become a duplicate Las Vegas minus the class. All of the success up here spawned from the success of that track.

Through the Herald's door Uncle Frank heard a loud snap of power, followed by the familiar steady hum and click-clack of the ink rollers. Whoever was in there was going into production on tomorrow's paper. He knew that the angels have a red light in the press room for any deliveries, so he breathed in real deep and pressed the doorbell. He couldn't hear a sound other than the mayhem of the printing press in the back firing up to spit out the next issue that a few people may read.

A moment later Dawn came to the door dressed in her angelic white robe. Her wings were standing steady, sprouting outward from her back and up about a foot over her head.

"Well, if it isn't Frank Foster. Come on in, it's been ages." Dawn said.

The angel winked at him as he entered. He didn't even hear the door close behind him. For that matter, he didn't see her feet as she floated towards him.

"I still don't know how you never get ink on your robe, Dawn. You never cease to amaze me." Frank gave her a stupid smile. "How's business?"

"You know, it could be better, could be worse. What brings you to this area? I thought your charters died down after the buyout."

"There was no buyout, you know that. Jack Frost and his ridiculous form of a shipping company pulled the strings all the way through. I don't live by his rules and I never will. Plus, I have a good thing going with the Alaska travel people and I shuttle wounded animals to the vet clinics."

"Yeah, well Mr. Frost insists that we are the only business that doesn't have to pay him rent once a month if we print what doesn't hurt him. I hate being me and falling victim to extortion." Dawn floated over to a chair and effortlessly meshed into it. There must have been accommodations for her wings or they folded up, Frank Foster never had the balls to ask.

"Well maybe that's because you have the best tip sheets going for the active gambler. He'd lose more money than he would be getting from you. Isn't that a moral dilemma being an angel? You know, aiding and abetting?"

"The rules are far gone, Frank. It's not like it used to be. These little streets were filled with pride once. They were filled with happiness and love. Now it's all neon, hookers and gamblers, not to mention the youth on the streets addicted to that Humbug stuff. It's just one of those things. You either roll with the punches or get your wings sliced off and remain human in this miserable place. For whatever reason humans are still a little freaked out by a winged woman, so we have a slight advantage when it comes to being left alone. Believe me, it's a gift. I remember the days when people would believe in us, now they'd hunt us down and display the wings on their wall." Dawn shrugged. "I used to know God's plan but now I'm not so sure."

"Speaking of "we", where's your partner in crime?" Frank started looking around the front office.

"Oh, Eve took a leave of absence, she's on assignment undercover. She also had some things that needed to be done in the first choir. Gabriel's been going absolutely insane over the past three years, I'm sure you can imagine. Needless to say it's been a real mad house around here. I have only three girls on location, two anchors for our television spots and me running the actual paper."

"What if I was to tell you that things are going to change? Would you like a heads-up on the story of the year?" Frank wasn't smiling. He didn't want this conversation to have a high school reunion feel to it, where they would catch up, pretend to be listening to each other and then go off and forget each other again until ten years later. No, he wanted her to take this story.

"And what kind of change are we talking about?" Dawn asked.

"I am talking about giving the Pole back to the original owners."

"Oh that fruitless human talk, Frank. You can't possibly think that I would even entertain the thought that it may even be possible. Do you have any idea how much money Frost has tied up around here? He owns pretty much everybody and everything. I mean, for Heaven's sake, he has a poker tournament and a billiard tournament the day before Christmas Eve. They say it's going to be one of the highest rated sports television shows in history, not to mention the winner gets an escort for the remainder of their stay and five million in cash."

"When I find out the asshole who claimed poker was a sport in the first place I'll kill him myself. It's one of the reasons the Pole is all out of whack. No one finds pleasure in actual sports anymore. It's all about the big quick win. Hell, even athletes don't play for the game anymore, they take the signing bonuses and produce their own stats and leave when the going gets tough and cry all the way to the bank. You know they pre-empted a school shooting going on because it was more important to discuss a football playing ego-maniac who accidentally took a few pills too many? Now that's news for you."

"Please don't say the fire word, Frank." Frank shrugged. "You know the aitch-e-double hockey sticks."

"Oh, I'm sorry Dawn." Frank put his head down, ashamed that after he offended every human woman he's seen, he actually found a way to offend an angel. "Will's coming up here."

"Will the nephew? What's he doing here?" Dawn asked.

"He's coming up with a woman. She insists they're not together, but you'd be really odd if you didn't think so. Anyway, he has something that may help."

"Listen, Frank. You don't want to get caught up in this. It's way too dirty. I at least have to get my wings ripped off first, and then I get a second chance. You don't. Do you remember Frosty? Frost melted him a few days back. He's said to be in a jar on his desk. And by the way even if you can do something, Kringle is still in the institution and will be until it is confirmed that his mind is officially turned into mush."

"And Frost was his defense attorney, right?"

Eve nodded, not knowing where he was going with this.

"Frost is a good attorney." Frank said coldly. "There would be no reason in the world that a jury would find that Kringle was insane. Unless, of course, they were all bought by Frost. Father Time was the judge correct? I have a feeling that he was bought too."

"Can you prove this?" Dawn was officially intrigued.

"All you have to do is print the alleged allegations. His ego will do the rest. I just need a diversion to get Will and Alyssa into Old Town and eventually into the casino. Oh, and did I mention they have the Christmas Crystal? What's been left of it anyway."

"No, you seem to have neglected that fact. That's puts a new spin on things." Dawn sat there and thought to herself for a minute, tapping her petite angelic fingers on the desk. "You know where the outskirts are, right?" Frank nodded. "Okay, the elf in charge of production in the old days, Oliver Winkle, lives there with his family. He's keeping the community alive and in good spirits. You can go to Ollie. He has elves on the inside that can get Will and Alyssa wherever they need to be."

"They actually have a network?" Frank couldn't help but laugh.

"Yes, and it would put anything to shame that you are accustomed to. The CIA and FBI couldn't be as clever as the shamed elf community. Remember, they made reindeer fly and humans still need metal tubes in the sky to get around."

"Thanks, Dawn." Frank laughed. "We'll be in touch. Expect Will and Alyssa here within an hour or so. I have a scout waiting for them when they arrive."

"Good luck, Frank." She smiled at him with a brilliantly hopeful glow that she hoped would stay around for a while.

"Thanks. We're going to need it."

"Oh, and by the way, we're actually working on a piece that will destroy Jack Frost and everything he's created. It was top priority, but we can actually call it a contingency plan now. I'll make sure Eve is notified that everything is in motion."

Dawn smiled to herself as Uncle Frank left her building. A soft glow surrounded her, something that hasn't happened to her in years.

# Ten

Alyssa was staring out the window, looking like one of those hot women out of a science fiction movie from the fifties. Her mouth was open as she tried to figure out whatever was happening.

"Will, did you see that light?" "What do you think it was? You think it was Uncle Frank or Gus?"

"There isn't a plane anywhere near here that would fly that low to generate that much light, especially Gus' piece of shit. He's crazy but he wouldn't test it by ruining his plane. We should go outside and see what it was."

"Do you think it has anything to so with this ring?" Alyssa asked. The ring on her hand was pulsing blue, sending waves of cold through her body.

"I have no idea what my uncle has planned for tonight but I don't like it. He's always doing some sort of practical joke crap and I stopped liking it when I was around fifteen. It was hard to bring girls around with my family."

Alyssa ran past me and up the stairs and into the bedroom. She emerged as quickly as she left, holding her orange corduroy jacket. She quickly flipped it on and pulled her hair from inside it and ran to the door. She was the only person I know who could pull off wearing that color, not to mention she only had her flannel sleeping pants and a tank top on under it. I was going to say something about the nights in Alaska in December, but thought it would be funnier to watch it unfold in front of my eyes, not to mention that a tank top in the snow could be visually beneficial. Like I said, I am a selfish bastard.

My leather jacket was on the back of the couch so I grabbed it and threw it on. Luckily, I never get ready for bed until I am almost comatose, so I was still almost fully dressed. I ran and followed Alyssa to the door after slipping on my sneakers.

"Will, what time is it?" Alyssa asked, flipping the front door open to the zero degree weather outside.

"It's about eleven o'clock." I said.

"Crap, I forgot to take my pills." She said, looking around the house like a maniac.

"I told you a long time ago, I don't think you need them." She started taking anti-depressants a long time ago. For whatever reason, I was trying to get her to quit taking them forever now. If there was ever a person that didn't need to be cheered up it was Alyssa. She could get herself caught in a rut all the time but she always found a way to laugh her way out of them. Hell, she said that after her twenty-ninth birthday she was going to remain twenty nine forever.

"I can't just stop, Will. Plus, I need my fish oil."

"Take them when we get back." I ran out first and gave her no choice in the matter. I have never been like that. I don't remember ever caring to take the lead. I don't know if I was trying to impress Alyssa or myself. It just happened and I really didn't like it.

Alyssa quickly followed me outside, opting to lose on the pill issue in lieu of staying in the cabin alone in the woods.

It was so dark outside except for the moonlight but the naked trees all over the place cut the moon into blue window blinds all over the snow. It was like running through a strobe light situated in a poorly made haunted house. When we left we were in such a rush to get out there into the mysterious light that we forgot to take the flashlight. I can blame the wine for Alyssa, but I guess I'm just a jackass. Luckily the moon was full so it was relatively easy to see out here once your eyes acclimated.

We walked about fifty yards away from the cabin where there was a clearing in the trees. Our feet were loud as they crunched the snow beneath our feet. We were going in the direction the light was traveling when we saw it, so this was the only logical place it could be, even though logic flew out the window of Gus' plane earlier today. Alyssa was holding onto my jacket the whole time, trying not to lose her footing in the knee-deep snow.

"Are you cold?" I asked her, sounding completely retarded considering the weather out here and her wardrobe. It wasn't like I was going to give up my jacket any time soon.

"Oddly enough, no." She answered. The ring on her hand was pulsing a deeper blue than before. I reached back and grabbed her hand.

"Your hand is freezing!" Her hand felt like I was like holding a block of ice. My skin almost stuck to it.

"I swear I am not cold. This is comfortable to me right now. I have no idea why, but it just is." Alyssa said.

"Alyssa, you used to get cold when the air conditioning went down to seventy when we were at work." I was more pissed that there wasn't going to be a show in the snow.

"Will, I am telling you that I am not cold! Now just shut up and let's find this thing."

I shook my head and continued on, shivering for the both of us. We walked North about another fifty yards to the center of the clearing. The moonlight was so bright that it was like walking at noon. The only difference was the blue color all over the place.

We didn't say a word the whole time. Alyssa's hand was still in mine, cold as hell. All you can hear in the air was the snow still crunching under our feet. It was so loud in the silent night that it echoed through the leaves.

As we reached the center of the clearing I stopped and motioned for Alyssa to stay quiet. I told her to listen in whatever hand gestures I remembered from all those SWAT movies I have seen over the years.

She stood silent behind me. There we were, just the two of us, standing in the middle of a snow field in Alaska. She was barely dressed and tipsy, and I just wanted to go to bed, with her if possible. It was these moments that made me want to disappear from the living world in the first place. Not end my life, but live it in seclusion. There were way too many scenarios that it made my head hurt. It was so romantic but as fate would have it, the timing sucked.

About five yards to the North of us I heard a weird sound off in the distance. It sounded like the crunching of the snow but was much softer, like someone tip-toeing up to us. That was soon accompanied by what seemed to be the smacking of gums and some light snorting.

There definitely was something, some big animal eating right in front of us, we just couldn't see it. I just stood there frozen and ready to piss my pants if I didn't think it would freeze my jeans to my leg. This figures, I was going to be eaten in the middle of nowhere by a sasquatch or something. At least Alyssa could run while my arms were being consumed by this mystery beast. Maybe I could beat it to death with one of my freshly cut limbs.

"Is there anyone there?" I asked. I always yelled at the television screen when someone said that stupid shit and now I was that person. Each second I am here I am turning into more and more of a hypocrite. "We are not here to hurt you. We are just wondering if everything is okay. That is, if you're human and can understand me."

"You're a dork." Alyssa started to laugh at how silly this all was. You're *human* and I'll never understand *you*."

As she said that I turned around to do something as adult as maybe sticking my tongue out at her when I saw the red glow on her face. The red glow accentuated the shocked look on her face, again making her look like the scream queen heroine in the vintage horror movies of the fifties. Her mouth looked like it was trying to form a word but her brain forgot how to send the message to the lips to do it. She motioned for me to turn around, slowly circling her finger around towards the sky. I thought for a second that I really didn't want to. I mean, why would anyone want to look at the thing that causes such a look of shock? Again, I would yell at these people in the movies. It's like smelling something awful and asking someone else to smell it for verification.

I turned my head at what can only be described as slow-motion and couldn't believe what was in front of me. It was way too odd to be shocking. The only thing I felt was that I was dreaming. That was all. I fell asleep in the window seat. I never told Alyssa anything and I was asleep thinking about sledding in Goffle Brook Park. I never stepped in moose shit before. This was all a dream.

"What are you looking at?" The thing in front of me asked. The only thing I can see was that it was a reindeer. Not just any reindeer, but THE reindeer. The red bulb for a nose gave it away. His voice was tiny and child-like, but I could tell he could rip me apart if I made fun of it.

"I'm looking…at…Rudolph!" I said, not being able to believe that I was talking to a reindeer. Worse than that, he was talking to me. "But you…don't exist! You…you…you're a story! A Christmas story! My uncle must have put you up to this! No, you're Gus in a well-made reindeer suit!"

"I don't think so." The little elf said as he walked in front of Rudolph. He was only knee-high to me and sounded like he was toking off of a helium balloon for the past hour and a half.

"Who the fuck are you?" I asked, getting really pissed that my uncle would stoop to this level to give me some holiday spirit. Where he found a little person to go through with this humiliation, I had no idea.

"The name is Wedge. I am Rudolph's trainer. I am terribly sorry about the roof. I will arrange to have it fixed as soon as I can." Wedge said as he was smiling.

"You're not real!" I said, not able to stop looking. Alyssa was still frozen in shock, her face still reflecting red, blinking on and off.

Wedge looked at me angrily and ran up, kicking me in the shin with his pointy shoe.

"Jesus! You little son-of-a-bitch!" I yelled. "What the hell did you do that for?" I was really starting to get murderous feelings towards my uncle and this deranged little freak.

"Something not real wouldn't be able to kick you, now would it? Now, I know this isn't something that you're normally used to seeing but you're going to have to get over it pretty quick. We are here to show you the way."

"The way to what?" Alyssa said in a complete monotone. She sounded like she was reading a cue card that was out of focus.

"Your uncle Frank told you about the Nine?" Wedge asked.

Alyssa and I both nodded.

"Well, if you remember the song, there were eight reindeer, right? Well, who do you recall was the most famous reindeer?"

"Rudolph is the Nine?" Alyssa asked, putting two and two together. This was a commendable act under the circumstances, considering how much wine she had.

"Trust the Nine." I said, shrugging. It should have been the ninth but who was I to proofread elf logic.

"We are here to show you the way to the portal, Will and Alyssa. So you best put the 'strange' factor behind you because the things you will be seeing will exceed this in so many ways."

"What were you doing out here?" I asked.

"We were training. You see at the Douglas Fir Memorial Race Track, Rudolph here was never asked to be in the Reindeer Games. He is the fastest by far, but the other reindeer won't let him join."

"Why the hell not?" Alyssa asked, obviously irritated that he was left out. Hell, every kid in the free world in any faith knows he was never allowed to join in. I can only blame the wine for her asking such a ridiculous question. I have nothing to blame for me wanting to hear the answer to it.

"The Douglas Fir track is a betting establishment." Wedge said. "All of the other reindeer are favorites against the South Pole team. They think because of Rudolph's size he'll never place so they don't let him try. And the odds against him are a hundred to one. Frost doesn't want the odds stacked that high."

"So, you're telling me that you're training him so you can bet on him to win and collect a hundred to one." This was too surreal to even contemplate.

"I just want to do it to show the rest of my brothers and sisters that I can hang with the big guys." Rudolph said through helium as he looked down, looking like he was starting to cry.

"Plus, Frost won't let me in as his trainer because I owe him a hundred large. I am lucky to just be alive so I clean the stables and sneak off to train him." Wedge looked like a broken elf. He looked like he wanted to win just to show everyone that he wasn't a hack. "If he wins at a hundred to one I can pay Jack back and go on with my own miserable life. But then he'll be pissed that he lost that much cheddar."

"Frost?" Alyssa asked, wanting to get all the pieces of this demented little puzzle that was unfolding in front of me.

"Jack Frost." Wedge said.

"Oh, I see." I said, nodding that this makes complete fucking sense to a patient at the *Arkham Asylum.*

"Please, Mr. Foster and Ms. Witt. Your uncle recommended you to help us. The North Pole is in trouble and has been for a few years. We need your help to turn this around so we can all be with our families again for the holidays."

I turned around to Alyssa, who was still holding my hand. "What so you think? Do you want to see this crazy shit out to see what the hell my uncle is up to?"

"I would say yes, just because I am really intrigued and partially inebriated." Alyssa said.

"Alyssa, you have a fiancé to go home to and a family that you care about. Think about what you're doing for a second."

"Will, I am in the middle of Alaska, dressed in sleeping pants, a tank top and a jacket and I am not cold. I think it's the ring. As crazy as all of this is sounding right now I think it's real. I mean, look at Wedge's ears. I think those points are authentic. No one does makeup that well."

Wedge pulled on the points on each ear to prove that they were in deed authentic.

"But if anything happens to you, I don't think I could live with myself. You have a lot more to lose than me." I said to Alyssa.

"Are you worried about me Will?" Alyssa smirked at me, giving me goose bumps again. I swear it was like we were married.

"I'll be worried about you until the day I die. That's just the way I am with you." I said.

"Will, I'll go if you will. You are the one that turned off his feeling to the rest of the world, so I will understand if you don't want to see this all the way through. But I don't want to rest my fate on a cynic who's going to leave me when the going gets tough. I just don't know if I can rely on you so if you're in you need to be in it all the way."

"Fair enough." I said, turning her phrasing into the perverted things I wanted to hear. "I am not letting you do this alone and it seems like there's no way we can back out of this. I want to make sure that you know that I will have you back to your family by Christmas. That's a promise that I will never break."

"Fair enough." Alyssa said, smiling like I just proposed or something. "We need to get supplies first."

"Wedge, can we get some stuff before we go?" I asked the shin-kicking little freak. He was getting the reins together to lead Rudolph behind us.

"You may need the light. Let Rudolph lead." Wedge said, patting Rudolph on the head. Rudolph responded by blinking his nose twice.

"Not a word of this to anyone." Alyssa said to me as we filed in behind Wedge and Rudolph. "People know you're crazy, but I don't want people to start believing that I am as well."

"You know, a lot of people think I'm crazy but it's cute when you tell me I am." I smiled at her to mask the fact that I just really needed a drink and a mattress to crash on.

Wedge looked at Rudolph and rolled his eyes.

"You know, Rudy? I could swear that these two have been married for years." Wedge said. "Thank God I'm not human."

Rudolph smiled and walked to the front of the pack, shining his red light brighter than ever.

# Eleven

The walk back to the cabin seemed colder than it did on the way up to the clearing. Alyssa finally started to shiver so I gave her my coat. It wasn't much farther anyway so I figured I can handle it. Hell, brownie points never hurt anyone.

Rudolph and the shin-kicker were about ten yards in front of us.

"I decided that I'm not going Alyssa." I said as we finally reached the side door of the cabin.

"Why the hell not?" She asked, losing her cool in every sense of the term, temperature-wise and attitude-wise.

"Look, this is all too surreal for me. I have no idea what the hell my Uncle cooked up but I am not falling for it again." I opened the door and went inside, motioning for Rudolph and his aggressive little friend to stay outside. Alyssa followed me and at this particular point I wish she was with the freak show outside.

"Will, I think this is real. As completely retarded as all of this sounds, how can he make a deer do that? I mean, he has a fake bear rug to avoid activists! Do you think he'd staple a red light bulb on a deer? And why would he have a little person shipped here to make the illusion real? Do you think it's just to mess with you? If you think that than you're an idiot!" She slugged me in the arm really hard. "Why are you so private and selfish? Why so you always think everyone's out to get you?"

"I told you. I don't want to talk about it." I said.

"Well, you better think of something because there are about four different things that can happen right now and all of them end with you cold and alone. Not everyone is out to get you but right now, I'm starting."

"Listen. I am only going to say this once." I said. "I grew up as a minister's son. I heard all about the ways people steal from the church, taking from the collection plates. I was there when my dad was fired from counseling years later for having Parkinson's Disease. He gave and gave and what do you think happened to him? Everyone that should have been behind him just spit on him instead. Not to mention I wasn't allowed to be myself growing up. Oh, no, the people at the church couldn't see me doing this or doing that, blah, blah, blah. So I learned early on that no one really gives a shit no matter what you give so why bother giving? It's all just about making people believe that you're a certain way, like a cult. I couldn't talk to anyone the way I wanted to without being judged as the son of a man of God so I kept it all in. And you know what? I still do. Because when it all comes down, no one, including you, will be there to pick me up if I fall. So I avoid falling in the first place. The only person I have to impress now is me. I don't have to impress friends, family or even God. It's just me and it's perfect that way. Take it or leave it. Thou Shalt not Judge is all horse shit. All the people that subscribe to that way of thinking are the most judgmental bastards on the planet."

The long silence and then, "How much do you have in that pig head of yours?" Alyssa asked, looking concerned or pretending to be.

"Plenty and I am taking it all to the grave. You do not want to know why my mind works the way it does. I've been trying for years to get some things out of my head and it's been working okay."

"You know what your problem is, Will?"

"No. Enlighten me." I said.

"You are one of the most genuinely nice people I have ever met. But you are the most sarcastic prick I have ever met and it's done in a funny way so you can get away with not offending anyone. But the real problem is that you do great things all the time. You'd help anyone with anything. The difference now is that you expect praise for them when you're done. Great people do great things knowing that there may never be anything said or done about it. You're not one of those people, Will. Your nice things wind up being motivated by self-worth, which is only doing something good for *you*. The people you affect are only the vessels to get *you* to where *you* need to be."

I knew she had it in her to talk me down; it just took five years to do it. I just stood there, not saying a word and staring right into her eyes.

"Well, that was the nicest speech if I ever heard one." Mort the elf said, standing in the hallway behind them, decked out in a pinstripe Armani suit, complete with sunglasses. Stan was next to him, wearing a stained tie-dyed shirt and bow tie. Mort was holding a hand-held crossbow with what seemed to be an icicle loaded in it. Alyssa and I were staring at each other like a Clint Eastwood showdown that it didn't even phase us that they were there.

"What the hell do you want?" I asked, getting irritated at my life in general right now. The two killer elves didn't help much.

"Boobies!" Stan yelled, staring at Alyssa.

"Okay, that's not going to happen, you little pervert." Alyssa snapped like it was rehearsed. She closed both jackets over her chest.

"We want the Christmas Crystal! Hand it over!" Mort looked like the Incredible Little Hulk, freaking out on command.

"And if I say no?" I asked in my trademark smartass tone. I looked at Alyssa and told her with my eyes that yes; I was going on this terrible journey now.

Without a word Mort shot the icicle, shooting it through the air and through the sleeve on Alyssa's left arm. The shot knocked her back and stuck her into to mantle over the fireplace. Her left arm dangled freely over the fireplace.

"You little freak! I am going to kill you!" She yelled, looking at her arm as the icicle started melting from the heat of the fireplace.

"How? I just stapled you to the wall!" Mort started laughing like a complete idiot.

"You shot me into the mantle over the fireplace, you mutant." Alyssa shook her left arm free. "Not the smartest one, huh?"

"Stan, get boobies!" Mort yelled, prompting Stan to run full speed at Alyssa. If I could slow him down I could swear he was drooling all over his bow tie.

Stan looked like a cartoon. He seemed to run in place waiting for his little feet to get some traction, and as if on cue his feet met the ground below them and he sprinted towards Alyssa at full force. Well, considering his size I guess it would be considered running at half force. The sound effect as Shaggy and Scooby tried to run ran through my head as he did it.

He ran completely around the couch at what looked like Benny Hill's fast forward and Alyssa froze in horrific anticipation that this little pervert was running so fast to cop an easy feel. This was way too bizarre to even try to comprehend.

As Stan approached Alyssa she crouched down, resting her hands on the floor, looking like a linesman on a football team. As Stan came closer, she bounced a little like a cat ready to pounce on dinner. She looked at me and smiled, ready for the kill. Either that or she was telling me that this is what happens to actual guys try it. Either way I thought she was the hottest woman in the world.

Stan was about two feet away now and as he took his final step, he looked at her position and readjusted his attack. He leapt into the air, hands completely in front of him, like a fleshy little torpedo. Stan was in such slow motion it was like watching The Matrix completely blitzed off your mind.

He gained inches and inches until he was face to face with Alyssa. As he flew in front of her, she grabbed his midsection, standing up at the same time and holding him over her head like she was playing airplane with a pointy-eared kid.

"So you want to see my breasts, huh?" Alyssa said in a total mocking tone. She pulled him down and held Stan in front of her, staring at the creepy little man.

"I think you have nice boobies." Stan said, laughing.

"Well, you're out of luck." She turned him around and was getting ready to toss him away when Stan reached his hands back behind him and gave her the biggest titty-twister that I have ever seen.

"Ouch! You little son-of-a-bitch! That hurt!" Alyssa tossed the elf down and held her chest. "Will, we have to get out of here. This is really starting to freak me out."

"We will leave if we can have the crystal." Mort said plainly. "That's all he wants, so that's all we want."

"Who is 'he'?" I asked, having no clue who the hell was involved in this madness. "No deal until we know what we're in the middle of."

Mort came across the room and stood right in front of me. He strained to move his head enough to look up at me. At six-foot-four, it was quite a task for a three-foot man with a crossbow.

"That is privileged information. I cannot disclose it." Mort said, still looking straight up at me. For three-feet tall he wasn't going to back down.

"Mr. Frost needs an update, Mort." Stan popped in from somewhere behind him on the floor. Mort rolled his eyes. How he got partnered with him he'll never know.

"Mr. Frost?" I asked, more confused.

"You mean Jack Frost?" Alyssa chimed in, still rubbing her chest. Under different circumstances that would have been nice to see.

"It's no business of yours!" Mort yelled, punching as hard as he could directly in front of him, hitting me square in the balls.

"SHIT! You little bastard! You didn't tell us anything!" I squeaked out the last part before the stars in my eyes accompanied me to the floor. It felt like my testicles were lodged in my throat. I did the three second countdown of testicle pain and as I hit zero, the real pain came through and I screamed at the top of my lungs.

"We only want the crystal and we know you have it. So just hand it over and we'll leave. We promise. We have better things to do than mess with two humans on their honeymoon."

"We're not on our honeymoon!" Alyssa yelled, keeping her distance from Mort and myself, trying to keep Stan from getting ballsy again. Between the jabbing pains at my testicles and the lump in my throat, I can almost start to get pissed that she was so adamant that we weren't here on out honeymoon. Was I really bad looking? Is she upset that I can probably never put the 'boys' to good use now? No, I was pissed that my nuts went to live in my stomach.

Mort paced around for a moment or so before his stubby little leg made contact with my face. I rolled over and screamed again, feeling violently ashamed that I am getting my ass kicked by an elf. In front of Alyssa no less. I wouldn't go on a honeymoon with me either.

"I told you, we don't have it. My Uncle never gave it to me." I had no idea what to say. The nose that I always thought was big felt like it was broken and my balls hurt. If they stayed any longer someone was going to be killed and by the looks of it I was in the painful and shameful lead for that honor.

Outside, I heard Rudolph's hooves on the ground, pounding on snow like he was ready for flight. Hell, it might have been my head but it gave me something to think about. I completely forgot they were out there.

"Wedge!" I yelled, almost passing out. "Wedge, Come in here, now! Rudolph, we have a problem!"

Mort looked around frantically, not knowing what the hell I was yelling to. His look squared on me again and he gave me one more kick, this time to the stomach sending my nuts back down to where they should be sitting.

As Mort reared his leg back for another kick, the front door slammed open, breaking the glass all over the floor. The red light was blinding as Rudolph busted into Uncle Frank's cabin. Wedge seemed to be in slow motion as he started rising up on Rudolph's back like William Wallace in *Braveheart*.

"Leave the humans alone, Mortimer." Rudolph said in a deeper voice that anyone was used to hearing. "They don't have what you're looking for. Even if they did, I wouldn't allow them to opportunity to give it to you."

"Well, if it isn't little pansy Rudolph." Mort straightened himself and walked over to Rudolph. "What's the matter? Your brothers and sisters won't let you race at the track so you have to come here and mess with humans? Do you think these bastards will give you any respect? If they don't have the ring, then why are you even here in the real world?"

"They are my friends, Mortimer. Leave them alone." Rudolph stood there. He was slamming one hoof into the floor and shooting air through his snout with authority.

"You know, you'll never race at the track." Mort said. "Odds on you would go for three hundred to one, but you'd never finish. You should face it now. You'd be better off sticking that forty-watt nose of yours up someone's ass like you've been doing so well for a hundred years."

"Good idea." Rudolph kicked Wedge off of his back. "Wedge, make sure he can't run. Will, Alyssa, if you can hold the little bastard in front of me."

Alyssa and I ran to Mort, each one of us grabbing an arm. I more or less hobbled, wondering if the boys were ever coming back down from my stomach and if they did, where exactly they were. Mort was faced against the opposite wall, Rudolph to his back.

The red light disappeared for a moment somewhere within the back of Mort's pants and before you knew it, Mort was sailing up at such a velocity that he broke through the ceiling and got stuck between floors. Rudolph looked straight at Stan, his bulb growing brighter by the second.

"Have a good night!" Stan said, laughing. "That was funny! Drive safe Mr. Reindeer!" He picked his nose and sat Indian-style on the floor, staring up at Mort's backside hanging in the living room.

"Will, Alyssa, there isn't a lot of time." Rudolph said. "You need to get to the portal as soon as possible. Once Mort gets down, he's going to call for backup and you'll have the whole elf mafia on your ass quicker than you can say the word 'shit'." He walked out of the cabin with his head held high.

My sight was coming back to me enough to make eye contact with Wedge. "He kind of talks like a sailor, huh? Far cry from anything I have ever been shown."

"He's not allowed to do anything so we sit and watch movies. He's particularly fond of *The Godfather Part Two*." Wedge smiled at Rudolph. "The real version, not the chopped up remix."

"Yeah, that makes complete and total fucking sense." I wanted to use my last breath and see what mind games heaven had in store. By nature of things it had to be at least more peaceful confusion up there.

"You have no idea what kind of things you are about to see Mr. Foster. I have a feeling you and Ms. Witt will have a new understanding of things, to say the least." Wedge followed Rudolph outside.

"Oh, and what the hell is with all the kicking? Is that all you elves know how to do to someone?" I rolled my eyes and followed Rudolph and Wedge into the snow. Alyssa was somewhere behind me, but right now, trying to walk a straight line was enough to worry about.

"Where is this portal?" Alyssa yelled over me as she walked through the door.

"It's an old fisherman's outhouse three miles up the slope!" Wedge yelled back.

"Did he just say an outhouse?" Alyssa asked me.

"Does that surprise you, Alyssa? I mean, come on." I started to laugh a little as I hobbled to keep up. "Is there any question now as to why I hate this holiday?"

Alyssa glared at me like she was going to kill me as she continued walking. I have a feeling this is going to be an incredibly quiet trek to the shit shack.

# Twelve

Kris Kringle stared out into the snowy plain with emptiness in his eyes. It's been years now that he's been in here and the view hasn't changed at all. Through the rusty bars in his room the snow drifts only moved occasionally and the lights of Jack Frost's city bounced off of the snow constantly and never dimmed. He could have sworn he heard music on some nights, but he was in an institution after all, who knows what the hell is real anymore? The repetitiveness would make you mad if you weren't there already.

The heavy metal door behind him clanked open with the familiar sound of about fourteen keys in the multiple locks on the door. Having lost enough weight to be down to a meager one hundred ten pounds, the man who was Santa Claus couldn't, or didn't want to, muster up the strength to turn around to find out who it was.

Within a moment, Kristine Kringle had her hand on his shoulder. She stood there for a moment to see if the orderly was going to leave. He was a burly looking elf, huge by miniature-people standards and Kristine felt no use in setting him off, but privacy was something they both needed right now.

"Can I have some time alone with my husband?" Kristine asked the man-elf.

"He needs his shots." The man-elf shot back with a deep voice usually reserved for humans over six five.

"He doesn't need any shots. Look at him, you're killing him!" Mrs. Kringle pleaded.

"Lady, he's been hearing voices since Thanksgiving. We upped his doses of clozapine and they seemed to go away. Now if you'll excuse me, I have to give him his shots. If I have to listen to his insane conversations for another minute I'll shoot him myself."

"I thought you had him on thorazine? Why wasn't I told about the switch in his meds?" Kristine asked as she stared at her husband's ratty beard which was heading for a length near four feet. "And what about shaving him?

"We thought you were notified." The elf-man said. "It must have been a paperwork snafu. Either way, he needs his shots and I don't shave anyone. And he needs rest. With clozapine we need to test his white blood cell count every two weeks."

"You people are unbelievable." Kristine said, feeling absolutely helpless and defeated. "Just give us some time, okay? I'd like to see him before you inject him again."

"Five minutes, lady. That's all." The Man-elf closed the door loudly behind him as he left the room.

"Kris, we're going to get you out of here. I left my amulet with your old crew so soon we'll figure out how to get you out of here and back to your old self again."

"You know?" Kris was speaking clearly. "That medicine does nothing for me. I don't even feel it."

"Because you're not sick, dear."

"I am sick, Kristine. I lost all of my spirit. Well, most of it anyway. I see life going on over there that is completely different than what it was for the past two hundred years or so. And the worst thing about it is that I am going to die knowing I couldn't do anything about it while I was locked away."

"You're not going to die." Kristine was holding back The Hoover Dam behind her eyelids, ready to burst at any moment.

"Those voices that the elf devils are trying to get rid of, the ones he said I was hearing, do you know what they are?" Kris asked his crying wife.

"I have a feeling." She said.

"Those are the remaining children that believe in me all over the globe. If you think in the terms that if a child started believing at three years old and it is three years later right now, after this Christmas I may lose them forever. I can't take that anymore, knowing that I could be making them smile and helping them not forget what it's all about."

"Frank Foster has a plan this year." She said.

"Frank Foster? He's still around? He's a good and decent man. He's been real nice to my people over the years."

"Well, it seems that he has a nephew that has lost himself somewhere along the line. From what I understand he is a fantastic writer but lost his way with people and lives in his own head. Anyway, they are on their way to the Pole tonight."

"I'm sure they'll win big at the slots." Kris said coldly.

"Will has the Christmas Crystal." Kristine stared at Kris as he continued to stare out the window without a hint of emotion. "He is going to see Ollie when he arrives."

"How will he find his way?"

"Frank arranged it all. It seems like your favorite little reindeer slipped away to train in Alaska. I wonder what he would need that light for." She smiled to herself, reminding herself that Rudolph always came through in a clutch. She never cared much for the other reindeer. She thought of them as self-centered and rude but Rudolph stood his ground no matter what. "You may want to look into some new reindeer though. They've all turned."

"What do you mean they've turned?" Kris finally turned to face her, hearing that his beloved team was gone.

"We'll explain that later. For now, just be a good patient and do what they say."

"They have elf-tossing in the basement, honey. The human orderlies do the tossing and they all have bookies. I have a feeling that things are too far gone to be turned around. Can you imagine? Elf tossing! That's not the world that I know anymore."

"I fell in love with you for your never-ending optimism. Please don't let that go away now. We're in the home stretch."

Kris nodded. "I love you too."

As Kris uttered those words, he looked out the window as a shooting star blazed past the window. Tonight, for the first time in a long time a smile cracked the skin of his face as the horizon seemed a little brighter. And for once it wasn't because of the lights on Jack Frost's little empire. It was the light at the end of the demented little tunnel that Jack trapped him in. Maybe this was the time, at least he had something to look forward to outside the rusty bars.

# Thirteen

Jack was sitting on his couch, still in his silk robe, smoking a cigar and drinking a glass of Jack Daniel's Black Label. He was staring out of his window, looking out on the birth of a new day in his own little metropolis. The money was going to be pouring in again, just like everyday, but the horizon was a little brighter today knowing that the world was soon going to be under his complete control.

"Mr. Frost, you have a call that I think you should take." Sugarplum called in on the intercom, making Jack jump a little in his seat. Some Jack Daniel's spilled on his robe.

"Tell them I'm in a meeting. I'm celebrating." Jack took another swig of his whiskey, swallowing the burn with a wince on his face.

"Sir, its Mort. He's got a confirmation on the errand you sent them on. He says he doesn't have long to talk." Sugarplum sounded irritated. Jack knew she hated being blown off so he made it a regular thing to keep her sharp.

In the confusion of everything that was happening, Jack almost forgot about the Christmas crystal. Not like it was going to do any good, things were too far along in his favor to be reversed the traditional way. No matter what, he wanted them taken out of the equation, loose ends were never good. Just ask Hollywood, the loose end always fucks things up. He picked up the phone and hit line one.

"Mort, its Jack. This better be good."

"Mr. Frost, we caught up with the two human people in the pilot's cabin. They kicked our asses and ran." Mort said, out of breath.

"Where are they now?" Jack asked loudly into the phone.

"I don't know. Rudolph and Wedge were there helping. I think he's bringing them to the portal."

"Oh that's fucking fantastic!" Jack yelled into the phone.

"Yeah. We're following them right now for the ring."

"Okay, I want you to kill them, I don't care how. You get that ring and bring it back to me. Just don't hurt Wedge; he makes me a lot of money, even though he's a damned liberal shit head."

"You got it, Mr. Frost. I'll call when it's done." Mort said as he hung up.

"You call anyway." Jack said before the line went dead on Mort's end. "You and you're little shit friend fucked up in the cabin and now you're ruining my morning. If you don't get them I will make sure they're dead and you two will be joining them. Understand? And it won't be pleasant, I can assure you."

"Yes, Mr. Frost." Mort said after an awkward silence.

Jack hung up the phone and hit the intercom that patched directly through to Sugarplum. It took a second to get through.

"Yes, Mr. Frost?" Sugarplum answered, obviously faking her cheery disposition. Jack never caught on.

"I want you to get Olaf on the phone at the track. Try him at home; I need to speak to him immediately. And get everyone who was in the meeting last night. I want to see them in here right away. They're going hunting."

"Right away, sir." Sugarplum clicked off the intercom.

Jack sat there, the anger boiling inside of him. He grabbed the copy of the Herald that was sitting next to him and looked at the front page. He loosened the grip on his glass that was half full of whiskey, dropping it to the floor. Glass and whiskey smeared the carpet under his feet as he gaped over the headlines.

"How the fuck did this get out?" He thought to himself. "God DAMN IT!" He threw the paper into the window. He was asking himself why this was happening right now. More importantly, how it was happening. He owned everything and never gave clearance for any of this. He bit into his lip thinking of who was capable enough, or had the balls to, fuck with him.

It wasn't that anyone could do anything about it. The wheels of progress were in motion and really couldn't be stopped. It was the fact that if this shit kept happening, the people would start to find out that the casino was rigged, the reindeer were on steroids and the fabric of everything that was started up here would unravel strand by strand. The sheer fact that Jack had no way of slowing it down was what Jack found most infuriating.

The blood started creeping into his head as he thought of his alleged credibility being thrown out to the public for dismantling. He's worked for way too long and planned this for the past fifteen years and he wasn't willing to let all of that hard work go. He was hanging on the hope that all of the money he was paying to the crooked people up here would keep things quiet for a while.

# Fourteen

To say that this was the most baffling experience in my life would be an understatement. This went well beyond that description. It's almost like I was stuck in a bad drug episode, things just getting more absurd as the night wears on and knowing that you'll soon be paranoid that you'd stick like that forever. It felt like everyone was looking at me even though there was almost no one around. I was on a weird high that I couldn't share with anyone.

On one hand, I was almost killed by Santa's elves that were dressed like James Bond and were really pissed off at me. On top of that, the drooling one had a thing for breasts. On the other hand, I got the rare opportunity to see Rudolph kick one of them in the balls. And the weirdest part of all was Alyssa going along with it like it is some sort of a joke that she's in on with my uncle. And to put the icing on the proverbial cake, the more I see her, the more beautiful she becomes. Neurotic, yes, but for now, just to see that sparkle in her eye I would play along as far as my sanity would take me, which was only a couple of more exits up the road. Maybe the alarm clock will go off and I'd be home by myself, thinking up this weird shit instead of living it.

"Okay, I got all the stuff we'll need." Alyssa popped out of the cabin while I was trying to avoid eye contact with Rudolph and his shin-kicking master. "All your uncle had in the fridge was beer and rice pudding. He's a little weird, huh?"

"Look behind me, Alyssa." Wedge was polishing Rudolph's nose. "I'd take beer and rice pudding on any day of the week. I've never had rice pudding so you'll probably be eating all of it."

"You've *never* had rice pudding? You have the most bizarre taste I have ever seen. It's all peanut butter and marshmallow fluff sandwiches, right?"

"Don't forget the cereal."

"Oh, yeah. You actually have a holy trilogy. Count Chocula, Franken Berry and Boo Berry. But Boo Berry is only sold in certain places and at certain times during the year, right?"

I nodded and smiling.

"You really are a dork, Will." She said. "You'll eat the pudding with me. Oh, and look behind you, Will. You're crazier than all of them combined."

"It's scary how much you know about me." I said back.

"I spend the majority of my whole waking life with you. Not my family, but you. So I think I have a say in these things." She had all of our needed supplies in her arms. "I think we should go so we can get whatever it is done before its too late."

"I'll follow you, since you're in charge, Queen of everything." I rolled my eyes, wanting to stay far enough behind that they lost me.

"Rudolph will lead and we'll hang back and talk to kill the time." Wedge pulled on the reins a little bit, nudging Rudolph to light his nose.

And so begins the greatest journey in the history of the world. Never mind Joan of Arc or the Crusades. George Washington crossing the Potomac and creating our country has absolutely nothing on us. Even the Boston Tea Party paled in comparison. Maybe the JFK assassination would come close.

Now following Rudolph to an old Eskimo shitter in the middle of nowhere? It was no contest. This was truly legendary. I would roll my eyes all night long if it wasn't for the imminent headache and dizziness that seemed to be plaguing me right now.

# Fifteen

It seemed like we were walking for days. It was freezing out here; our breath was coming out in streams of steam like locomotives. Rudolph finally stopped at a clearing and looked back at me. Wedge was kicking the toe of his little shoe into the snow impatiently. I have no idea if he had a pebble in there or he had the burning desire to kick me again and was just winding up for the moment. He was creepy no matter what he was doing. I just want to be as far away from that little freak as soon as humanly possible.

"The outhouse is up the hill." Wedge said.

"Well, aren't you guys going first?" I asked. "We've never done this and have no idea if we're even going to be alive on the other side."

"No, we have explicit instructions for you two to go first." Wedge said like it was scripted. "If we do and you back out of the deal we're all screwed. Nothing personal, it's just that humans are a little unreliable when it comes to responsibility. We'd need to go through a lot just to go back through to drag you back, and in fact, we don't have that much time." Wedge was adamant about this and clearly wasn't going to fold until we jumped in.

"Who gave you the instructions?" I asked.

"I can't tell you." He said. "Just get in the crapper."

"I am not going anywhere until you tell me who is giving you these instructions. Because as of right now, you're in America and I have the right to know what I'm doing."

"I am not at liberty to say. I can be punished if it was found out. And you can tell whoever you want. You try to make someone believe that a reindeer and an elf made you jump into an old outhouse and let's see how sane you look."

He has a point. No matter what I was stuck in this demented carnival attraction so there was really no way that I could successfully reason my way out of it.

"From what I understand, if we succeed than you will not be the asshole that you are now, right?" I asked Wedge. "You'd go back to making your toys and being all jolly? Maybe you want to stay like the little assassins back in the cabin and be miserable. So if we don't go in there we can screw up who you are, so I suggest that just this once you put your little ass on the line and tell me something about why I am doing this. Because as of right now, Alyssa and I are the only ones going in blindly for any of this and we aren't getting anything in return but stubborn bullshit. Face it, little man. We are the only hope you have so you better be a little more fucking understanding."

I have a point too. Take that, crazy elf!

Alyssa stared at me like I was going to punt Wedge into the farthest reaches of the woods. It wasn't a bad idea, but all I wanted to know is who the hell sent him here to get us in the first place.

"Mrs. Kringle sent me out here." Rudolph said.

Wedge was going to explode. "You dumb ass! They're going to kill me! Don't you comprehend this? It's crap like this that makes your brothers and sisters hate you."

"Why?" Rudolph asked. "You didn't say anything, I did. I'll take the heat. Stop being such an asshole, Wedge. And don't pull on my reins so hard, it strains my neck and I have a hard time stabilizing."

"Don't talk to me like that, Rudolph. You ain't nothing in the Pole. I am the only one you've got." Wedge seemed a little hurt.

"My eight brothers and sisters have hated me all their lives and still tease me all the time." Rudolph stared into the snow, his nose dimming. "I clean up all of their crap while they're racing, Blitzen's cigars, Prancer's scarves and ascots, you name it. I have nothing to lose. They're still going to hate me when everything gets fixed anyway. They have to or the song would need to be rewritten. You are going to change, but my fate will always be the same, so shut up and get on my back or I am leaving you here."

I looked at Rudolph and smiled, wondering when this little boiling pot was going to explode. He was always the cute little reindeer but now he looked to be a disturbingly twisted maniac with a crack head's voice.

Alyssa and I had no idea what to say. I have never seen anyone in my life stand up to anyone like that, no less a reindeer to an elf. I decided at that moment, that I was going to hike to the outhouse so I wasn't the one getting punted in the woods. I also decided that no matter what, I would always make *Rudolph the Red Nosed Reindeer* my number one Christmas carol. He's earned my respect out here. Whatever respect I actually had that is for a trash talking reindeer with a bulb on his nose.

"What do we do when we get in there?" I asked Wedge, who stared at Rudolph for what looked like permission to speak. "Wedge, we're all a team here. I don't like it either but we all have to be honest with each other from now on. No secrets."

Wedge stared at me with a sad, defeated face. "When you get in there there's only one seat, so one of you is going to have to be on the other's lap."

I stared at Alyssa and smiled.

"Have you seen my hips?" She asked, smiling back. "One too many bagels in there Will. I told you to not let me eat like that."

"I can handle it. Don't ever do anything to change it, Alyssa." I said, creating an embarrassed look in her face that I had grown to love giving her. She loved compliments secretly; she just hated me giving them to her all the time. Well, she hated that she really liked them.

Wedge rolled his eyes. "You two have to think of the fondest memories you have of winter and pull the plunger. That will open the door and you'll be off. Just hold on to each other tightly."

I looked at Alyssa and averted my eyes up the hill. I immediately started walking, Alyssa close at my heels. I didn't know what to do but turn and wave once to Rudolph, almost saying that I didn't know if I'd ever see him again. If I didn't, at least I left it on a bright note, no pun intended with the nose. Who the hell knows what's in store for us when we flush ourselves.

We finally got to the top of the hill and stood outside the wooden box for a few minutes. We just stared at the faded Eskimo structure, silently unanimous in not knowing if we really should be doing this. For all we know, no one cleaned the thing out. Hell, a little humiliation wouldn't hurt much at this point.

"This is the last chance that we'll have to turn around, Alyssa." I said, hoping that she'd choose to turn around and run.

"Will, there are elf assassins in our cabin. One of them was fascinated with my boobs and the other was just crazy in an Al Pacino-*Godfather* kind of way. A reindeer is down there, angry at the life he's lived, with an owner that has a habit of kicking people in the shins. If we made it back to the cabin, we'd be too hurt to fight off the other two. The only way to get out of this now is to go all the way with it."

"Why did you say 'our' cabin? Are you feeling like we're married now or is it just me?"

"I did not." She smiled.

"Yes you did." I just rolled with it like I usually do. "They say people that work together usually end up together. Add in the fact that people in stressful or traumatic experiences usually have a great bond later and we're as good as husband and wife. You have to admit, this situation is weird enough to fit the bill."

"Get in the toilet, Will." She rolled her eyes at me, but I could see the curl of her lip as she tried to hide her coy little smile.

I always knew when to stop with her so I just opened the old wooden door and stepped inside without saying another word. She followed me in, holding her hand over her nose to stop the inevitable outhouse smell from making her sick. I took a big whiff and smelled nothing but wood.

Looking around I noticed that this place was barely used, if at all. There wasn't a normal toilet seat but just a metal ring with a hole in it sitting on top of a box of wood, which could have been normal, I don't like using these things so I wouldn't know.

There was a hole under the meal lid that looked to be iced over. Maybe this was an old fishing shack that had everything built in. Behind the toilet was a sign that said in neat handwriting, "If you sprinkle when you tinkle, be a sweetie and wipe the seaty." I laughed at the thought of some Eskimo placing this sign in here, or saying it at all.

I sat on the ring and stared at Alyssa, trying to adjust my ass to the immediate cold it was sitting on. "Alyssa Witt, party of one? We have a seat for you."

"You're a freak." She laughed a little bit. She didn't want to admit it but all of this was as crazy as crazy got and she was with the Mayor of Crazy Town. At least she knew the locals would relate to me.

Alyssa walked over and sat on my lap. I wasn't used to the weight, which was normal, by the way, so I shifted a little on the ring, which was making her a little self conscious of her body again.

It's been a long time since I learned that lap dances were a waste of money so having someone on my lap for any reason was a shot in the dark. Hell, if she weighed in at three-fifty, I would have loved having her on my lap. She reached her left arm around me and clasped her right hand with it in front of me. I couldn't stop smelling her hair if I tried and I couldn't help but notice how perfectly our bodies fit together. I was in the most uncomfortable place in the world and I have never felt so comfortable. I didn't want to flush, I actually contemplated sitting in the outhouse for another hour.

"Are you thinking of a memory, Will?"

I didn't answer right away. I didn't want to get anything into my head that would destroy the thoughts of her that were floating in there right now. The butterflies in my stomach were killing me, making me thankful I was on a toilet.

Alyssa leaned in to adjust herself and our lips came to about an inch from each other. I had that one feeling that everyone remembers, the one that matters the most. The feeling of wondering how her lips would feel against mine. How we would breathe with each other. How she would moan slightly, not knowing if we should stop it or continue. Not wanting it to end as the goose bumps erupted all over and not wanting it to continue for fear that it wouldn't be the same after. I wondered if she was an aggressive kisser or slow and passionate. I wondered if she connected with me the same way I felt a connection to her. Ah, there was nothing in the world like a first kiss. There was nothing like losing time and being frozen in that one moment that just feels so right.

"Will, are you thinking?" She asked, interrupting the latest chapter of the romantic novel in my head.

I was wondering why she was born with a voice.

"Yeah, I am. I'm sorry, Alyssa."

"You don't have to apologize. This is kind of nice." She said.

The comments like those are the ones that make men crazy. She's like the cartoon that would paint a black archway into a brick wall and just laugh when you run into it at full speed.

"Okay, I am closing my eyes and thinking." I said. "We should both put our hands on the flusher thing." I said. I really didn't want her to break her grip but I didn't want her to get hurt either.

"I am not letting go of you, Will. I don't want to be killed."

Paint that archway you crazy toon. I'll get the application to Acme.

"I won't let anything happen to you. I promise." I said sincerely.

"Thanks, Will."

"Alright, I'll pull it when I am ready."

I just closed my eyes. I didn't have to think about anything in particular. Having Alyssa on my lap triggered great memories of things other than women named Roxy Dunes and their patented stripper spray that you smell two days later.

I remembered sledding down the hill on Goffle Brook with my friends. I remembered listening for the fire house horn in the mornings telling me that there was a snow day and I didn't have to go to school. I remembered all the snow ball fights, snow angels, building snow caves that I would play G.I. Joe in. I remembered going home with frozen toes, just to cuddle up with some hot chocolate for the night. I loved the smell of winter in New Jersey, the air so crisp and clear. I loved it when the sun went down early and the moon reflected on the snow. Everything was quiet, eerie, peaceful and beautiful.

Alyssa squeezed me again, thinking her own thoughts. As she did it I thought of a girl I used to see. I remember she came over to the house; she was in her twenties, like I was at the time. We didn't know each other that long so we didn't know what to get for each other so we agreed not to get anything. Dinner was fine. I remembered when she looked at me with her beautiful eyes and kissed me. It was our first kiss and was just like sitting here with Alyssa. The rest of the tragedy that ensued didn't enter my mind at all, just the feeling of the nervousness of that first kiss between two people.

I didn't realize I was doing it, but before I knew it I pulled the plunger. It didn't make a normal flushing sound but hissed like it was letting out some steam. The box we were sitting on expanded around us and extended to the ceiling, creating a much wider shack within the one we walked into.

The ring under me turned morphed into a solid sheet of metal, a disk sled that my mother never wanted to get me. I always wanted to rub the wax paper all over it and sled to speeds unheard of in the neighborhood.

A panel in the wall opened in front of us. Inside, a small colored screen flipped on and a woman elf was staring at us. She was wearing a telemarketing headset and was made up like a girl's doll.

"Welcome." She said in a tour guide kind of way. "Please keep your hands and feet away from the sides and enjoy your trip. Once there, please feel free to check out the casinos and local restaurants. Just mention me and you will receive comp dollars towards your stay. My name is Trixie." She nodded once. "Now I am commencing the countdown. If you are pregnant or suffer from any heart conditions, do not ride. If sudden shocks create dizziness, please exit the portal now. And as you can assume we are mostly elves so the normal height requirement does not apply." She stopped for a moment so we could assess our bodily capabilities, Trixie blankly rotating her head left and right as we made our assessment. "Great. Countdown will be commencing on five."

"Five."

"Four."

This was going to get crazy real fast.

"Three."

I felt like I was going to piss my pants.

"Two."

What the hell did she think of?

"One."

I never want her to let Alyssa go.

"Launch." The little elf pushed a button on the console that must have been somewhere in front of her.

Within a second, Alyssa and I dropped into oblivion with a whooshing sound that was louder than hell. I had no idea where we were going or when we were going to get there. All that I know is that this is a ride I will never want to forget as the cold wind whipped us in the face. I hoped silently that it would last for hours.

# Sixteen

The moment that we dropped, my stomach crept into my throat and begged me to spit it out. Alyssa screamed in my right ear until it felt like it was bleeding from its core. Out of my left eye, I saw the ring on Alyssa's finger start to glow, slowly growing brighter and brighter until it created a cocoon-like bubble around us. Without realizing it, I was rubbing Alyssa's hair like I was curing colic, silently hoping she would not scream again.

I looked to my left and outside the bubble I saw nothing but stars all around us. It was a completely black sky filled with stars like I was flying out into space. Alyssa noticed the calm in me and looked in the direction my head was looking. She calmed down a bit, feeling that under us it seemed like we were floating to the moon. The vertigo was starting to get to me with the absence of normal surroundings.

"Will, this is crazy!" Alyssa said, the little sound making my right ear drum scream out in pain.

"Look under us, Alyssa. Just don't scream again."

She looked under us. She noticed the same thing I had noticed when we started dropping. The disk we were sitting on became translucent, enabling us to see a giant strip of snow that seemed to wind itself into a sci-fi worm hole. There was no depth to the snow, just enough of a strip to make a track for us to slide down on. She noticed the speed of the snow as it passed under us, her mouth opened in amazement.

"Will, this is insane. Where are we going?"

"If I was going to say anything, I would say to another dimension. If Rod Serling is standing there with a creepy little speech, I think I'll piss myself."

"Is there another dimension?" She asked.

"How else would you explain a little strip of snow that we seem to be sliding down in a protective bubble? I mean, look around! There is nothing out here but stars. There is no ground! It's like we're flying through space! It's almost like Richard Dawson sent us down in that *Running Man* thing."

"I think I want to take on the crazy little elves now." Alyssa said as she buried her face in my chest.

"You had your chance, Alyssa. Now we have to go through with it." I was so overwhelmed by all of this over-stimulation that it started making some sort of sense to me. "Remember in *Ghostbusters* when Dan Aykroyd had that thought at the end? You know the happy thought?"

Alyssa shook her head. "No, I don't remember all the little things in every movie like you do."

"Well, he thought of marshmallows he had when he was at camp and it resulted in them being attacked by the Stay-Puft Marshmallow Man. When you were told to think of something, you didn't happen to have the end of Willie Wonka in your head, did you? Because if this bubble is like that crazy-ass elevator I am going to kick your ass."

"You're an idiot. I just hope there's not a wall at the end of this thing." She said.

"Like the Running Man." I repeated.

"Stop with the movies!" She yelled.

"I think like that when I'm nervous. Sorry. I don't think that Rudolph and Wedge would let us go through all of this just to hit a damn wall. They're a little mental but their not sadists. Aren't they coming down behind us?"

"I guess you're right." She looked around at all angles of our descent. "How fast do you think we're going?"

"It looks like well over a hundred."

As I said that, I saw a blue sign planted in the strip of snow that resembled a sign planted on the interstate. On it were the words: *Welcome to The North Pole. Visitor's Center...One Mile! Yule Have a Great Ol' Time!* I dismissed the thought that Fred Flintstone and Barney Rubble would be down there with limo signs that had our names on them.

I had no idea why I was able to read that at the apparent speed we were moving, but then again, I wouldn't be at all surprised if I looked at my hand and had thirteen fingers. Everything was so absurd that it seemed normal. Alyssa on my lap, on the other hand, was something that felt so normal that it was absurd. Her warmth was very comfortable.

The ring on her finger started fading and the bubble started disintegrating around us.

"Will, what the hell? This is really scaring me!"

"Hold on, Alyssa!" Even if she didn't need to, I figured, why not? "Like I said, I won't let anything bad happen to you."

Alyssa gripped me harder than I ever dreamed that she would, popping a bone that was either a rib or a vertebrae in my neck. My ear was killing me and my legs were numb. She wasn't heavy but the dips in the strip made the weight move at such sudden forces that my legs weren't used to it. Hell, all of the strippers I was used to only weighed in at ninety-five pounds plus silicone and the chair I was on never moved.

The front of the disk lifted in the gust of wind as we hit the incline. The strip of snow seemed to morph into an off-ramp on the highway with no destination in sight. Within seconds, we were flying out of control. We quickly busted through some sort of energy field, populating the open space with snow banks and sled cars and moonlight. They were coming closer and closer to us as we careened towards them from what seemed like a mile above. As they got bigger the squeeze around my neck was tighter, Alyssa's face starting to dig into my shoulder. The pain was coming more frequently in me, the white hot shards getting bigger and bigger.

I held Alyssa's head and shut my eyes when we felt a slight spray of icy cold snow on our faces. We slid to a stop without feeling the sense of even slowing down.

"Are we dead?" Alyssa asked, not looking out from my chest.

I looked above me and saw the huge *Welcome* sign. Under it in the distance I looked straight into a white-brick building with maps plastered to it. There were vending machines and acetate holders full of free brochures for the attractions up here.

"Only if heaven has a visitor's center. If it does, the gift shop should be pretty cool. All of the robes to buy."

For whatever reason I started howling in laughter. It was either the rush of the weird slide through time and space, Alyssa grabbing on to me for dear life to the point of my own death or the fact that the North Pole had a Visitor's Center in the first place.

Slowly Alyssa came around and joined in my laughter at the crazy shit that just happened.

# Seventeen

From the time that Alyssa opened the huge glass door my eyes started to burn. We walked into the lobby of the Visitor's Center and the ammonia was so overbearing that I started to tear involuntarily. Alyssa didn't seem to be affected, but on second thought, she wasn't the type of person to show enough emotion to produce tears. Hell, I only saw it once and that was because I insulted her. Not on purpose, I just went too far with a joke. From then on, dry as the Sahara.

"Oh, Will you're crying! That's so sweet!" Alyssa said in a child-like mocking tone.

"It's because I'm so happy to be here on our honeymoon."

"Shut up." She said.

"You started it."

I looked down and saw the reason for the ammonia. They were in the form of two custodial elves, scrubbing everything like they were in fast forward or had yellow jackets coursing through their little bodies. The only thing missing was Benny Hill's theme to accompany them.

They obviously did a great job, the lobby was immaculate. The all-white tiles were completely white to the point of glowing. The white grout between the tiles was almost as white as the tile itself. Whoever was contracted to do this was a genius or at very least very dedicated. The walls were as white as the floor making it very difficult to see the separation between the two. Scattered in between, elves were milling around in casual business attire, traveling to and from the Pole on whatever business deals they had going. Some elf men had human women on their arms and as we passed, I saw one gently tap her in the ass as they walked. She responded by putting his head between her breasts, smiling. Shit, even elves do more speed boating than me.

The building itself was almost the identical twin of any run-of-the-mill rest stops you would see on I-75 in Florida. There was the big framed map of the Pole in the middle with a big red arrow stating "You Are Here". There were vending machines in an alcove over on the left side, creating the only depth perception the room. On the right side were the bathrooms, men on the right, and women on the left. Straight ahead of us was an information counter with an actual human standing behind it. She was wearing a tight white body suit and a red scarf. Her blond hair was pulled back, leaving only a resistance of bangs hanging down the left side of her face.

I nodded to Alyssa, motioning her to follow me to the counter. As we approached, the blonde smiled at me like she was waiting all night for me to arrive. I could only wish to be that lucky.

"You're my wife, Alyssa." I whispered to Alyssa out of the corner of my mouth. She grabbed my arm and stopped me about two feet from the counter, spinning me around quickly.

"Will, I have a fiancé. I don't feel comfortable being your wife."

"Alyssa, remember when you had the muscle strain in your right butt cheek?" She nodded. "What did I do? I called the ask-a-nurse hotline and said that my wife had a pain in the ass."

"Yeah, and his name is Will."

"Nice. What I am saying is that I don't mean anything by it. I'm not pathological, Alyssa. I'm slightly neurotic but I'm not psychotic. Have I thought about what it would be like being married to you? Yes, who wouldn't? But I don't get my kicks with pretending that I am your husband. The nurse wouldn't tell me anything if we weren't married and you wouldn't call so the problem was solved. It's the same thing here." I waited for it to register. "Think about it for a second. A male and a female going to the North Pole as friends with no purpose would seem a little odd, especially since those crazy bastards tried to kill us. People are going to be looking for us here to kill us for that ring. I think it would be wise to pretend we're here for a honeymoon. We don't want to look panicked."

She stood there for a second and looked at the ring on her hand. It was almost transparent on her finger.

"Can I help you?" The blonde asked through her mannequin's smile as the happy couple had their first public fight.

"Yes." Alyssa said, grabbing my arm and walking to the counter. "Where's the best place to spend our honeymoon?"

"Oh, that's so sweet." The blonde said. Her gold name tag said her name was Holly, making me roll my eyes. "What do you plan on doing? Seeing the city? Nice dinners or do you plan on not leaving your room?" She winked and smacked her gum.

"Somewhere that's off the beaten path." I said, trying to stay away from all the craziness that we were going to be walking into.

Holly looked around at something that wasn't visible to us. She was obviously going through the mental files in her head instead of using the computer on her left.

Holly smiled and laughed like she was high on something. "Well, my first fiancé and I stayed at the Casino hotel. He drank so much at the tables he couldn't perform. You know a wet noodle? Hmmm. It's a shame, he had a nice noodle." I tried to keep the shocked look off my face as this women just poured all of this out. Plus, I'm a guy so I started to imagine her trying to work the situation after the binge drinking. "Then I was on a date that ended at the Garland and it was beautiful. He was my second fiancé."

"What was beautiful, his performance or the hotel?" Alyssa asked, almost as shocked as I was.

"The hotel." Holly blurted out with a valley-girl laugh, nearly spitting her gum in Alyssa's direction. "The fireworks went off before I lit the wick in that department." She laughed and snorted. "Just my luck, huh? Two fiancés and about a minute of fun." She cackled her valley-girl laugh again, followed by what seemed to be her trademark snort.

"Well, I don't have to worry about that, Holly." Alyssa said. "He's known to go all night and he's built like a damned horse."

"Oh my God!" Holly yelled. "That is *so* awesome."

"Thank you, Holly. Where is the hotel?" I just wanted to get the hell out of there and take a nap. I played with the idea of dropping my room number to her but this just wasn't the time. I stopped drinking and my wick is fine for God sakes, especially since Alyssa talked it up. It's always the sure thing that pops up when you can't do anything about it.

Holly turned dead serious. "Okay, you're going to go down the strip until you get to the end. On the corner, you'll see the Yuletide Inn. Watch out in there, there's a lot of Humbug dealers and hookers, unless you like that sort of thing. It's a very scary place so have the driver drive fast when he's going past. When you get to the corner, go left and you'll see The Garland down the road about a mile."

"Why couldn't we just ask the cab driver?" Alyssa just plain wanted to leave or beat this girl for being a cookie cutter bimbo. "And how do you know all of this? Maybe you'd have better luck with men if you didn't pick them up at the Yuletide. You should aim higher."

Holly didn't seem phased by the obvious insult. "Most of them are regulars of the Yuletide. They like to go in there with all the other cabbies and have a few, you know? The only reason I know this is that they work with us all the time. They tell me everything when the traffic in here is slow." Holly kept smiling. I don't know if I was crazy, but I could swear her breasts got larger as she talked. They almost jumped out at me. "So if they are drunk, I wanted to make sure you knew how to get there. I can call and make reservations for you, if you'd like."

"Yes, please." Alyssa said, not at all amused anymore. "Kelly McCormick. This is my husband Patrick."

I shot her a glance, asking her with my eyes what in the hell would make me look Irish? Maybe my black hair and dark features, I guess.

Holly dialed up on the phone and was talking to the clerk at The Garland. The smile never left her face as she stared into the phone and her tone didn't change.

"Don't even think about having sex with me." Alyssa said. Finally she had some negativity towards all of this. Unfortunately it was all because of me.

"Nah, we're married. I left that fictional thought at the fictional altar at our fictional wedding." I smiled like the wiseass that the world wouldn't mind shooting. "We have to send back the toaster that your fiancé sent though. I don't feel right about keeping it."

"You're a jackass." She said as Holly hung up the phone.

"And you told the girl I was hung like a horse. Did you do anything to me while I was asleep?"

"Shut up, honey. We'll talk about this later." Alyssa said through her clenched teeth.

"You're all set." Holly said through her big toothy smile. "There is a taxi stand out back. I hope you enjoy your honeymoon. And don't drink. Trust me on that one; you don't want to be destroying such a fine thing with alcohol."

"Thanks, I'm sure it'll be great. I plan on rocking her world tonight." I said as Holly smacked her gum and twirled her hair. "And I won't drink, I promise."

As we turned Alyssa smacked me in the arm again.

# Eighteen

The cab we were in was designed like an outdoor sled you'd see in Central Park in all of those Christmas movies. It was actually pulled by a reindeer that looked even more pissed off than the drunken elf driving. I passed him an extra twenty to blow by The Yuletide without stopping. He grunted but realized he can get even more tanked after he dropped us off, so he skidded by it without even slowing down. His head however, turned towards it as we passed, cutting off an oncoming sled. We swerved and came within an inch of clipping his bumper.

"What happened to Rudolph?" Alyssa asked under her breath to avoid the drunk from hearing her.

"Probably went back before he was found out. I haven't seen them since the toilet ride. They were behind us and then gone."

The sled came to a stop in front of the hotel. A suped-up Honda drove by, the spinners on the wheels glinting in the lights from the hotel. The bass in his car was making the trunk rattle terribly. Inside, a teenaged elf was slouched down to his right as he drove, his hat tilted to the required thirty degrees to be in the cool club.

"Thishh ish the hotel. Garland! Have yourshelf's a good one!" The drunken elf spewed out as we hopped out of the sled. "Watch yourshelf's, thish plathe can be dangerish if you don't know where you goin'."

"Thanks." I said, not looking back at him. "How much do you need to destroy that car that just passed us?"

The driver looked at me with glassy eyes and sped off to his date with the bottom of a bottle somewhere in the confines of The Yuletide.

"Shall we, Mrs. McCormick?" I said, smiling like a seventies porn star with a horse's manhood.

Alyssa just sighed and started walking up the driveway. She placed her arm in mine for no reason and just walked with me all the way up. I wasn't asking questions, it's been a rough night.

The inside of the hotel was beautiful. It looked like it was all dipped in gold and had its name engraved all over the place. Garland was strung all over the place in an artistic way, making it feel like we were walking under a huge Christmas tree. Alyssa kept staring up into the circular ceiling that went up at least six stories above us. The building itself was circular and completely symmetrical all the way up.

Before we knew it we were up to the front counter, flipping our heads down right into the face of an older elf man in a crushed blue velvet suit. The amazing romantic factor in the lobby just went down a notch.

"Mr. and Mrs. McCormick?" The elf asked. "I am Mr. Feeble. Welcome to The Garland." We nodded. "Real quick I want to tell you that the Pole itself is climate controlled at sixty-five degrees with no wind. So during your stay you will not need to overdress because of the snow outside."

"How do they do that?" Alyssa asked.

"It's a North Pole secret." Mr. Feeble said, smiling. "I gave you room seven-seven-seven."

"The angel's number. That's nice." I said.

"It's interesting that you should say that, Mr. McCormick." Mr. Feeble said as he handed me an envelope. "Your keys are in there."

"Don't you need anything? And why was that interesting?" I asked.

"It's taken care of. Enjoy your stay." Mr. Feeble smiled until we walked away.

"Who took care of it?" Alyssa asked. "I don't like all of this *Mission Impossible* crap, Will."

I opened the envelope and gave Alyssa the room keys. Inside was a note on an index card. It read: Will, you and Alyssa take a nap and rest. Meet me tomorrow morning at the Douglas Fir Race Track at nine sharp. Ask for Wedge. He's the reindeer trainer you already met. He should be in the stables. Thanks for coming. Uncle Frank.

"That means that everyone here knows what we're supposed to be doing except for us, is that right?" Alyssa sounded like she was starting a panic attack. I hope not. She likes to smack things when that happens.

"Yeah, I think we're in way over our heads, Kelly."

"My name is Alyssa, dork. Our marriage is a lie."

"Aren't they all?" I said as I walked to the elevator. "But that shouldn't stop us from having some great imaginary sex."

"That's all you've had, Patrick. You should be quite good at it." She smiled and walked to the elevator with me wagging the tail between my legs behind her.

# Nineteen

Sugarplum was sitting behind her desk in the reception area, chewing nervously on her fingernails. Her back was itching and aching, making her contort to extremes in an attempt to just ease the pain. She was randomly trying to scrape her back on her chair, flipping all around her little corner of the penthouse section like she had a spider in her shirt.

She hated the name Sugarplum. It was never her name and despised it every time the word slithered out of Jack Frost's mouth. She despised him enough, but having him not know who she really is was killing her. Out of all the nervous ticks she has ever exhibited, biting her tongue was the one that she practiced most.

Her name was Eve. She was one of the two remaining angels in service, the other being her sister, Dawn. They, in particular were chosen solely on their names. Being that both of them had names representative of something new, they were deliberately chosen as a sign that all of the world would need their help to bring back order to the world. Eve had her wings concealed completely within her to work undercover since this all began and the only way she remembered they were there in the first place was the pain that has told her that her services were needed right now.

"Mr. Frost, I have to leave for a little while." Eve said into the intercom, trying not to sound like she was in any pain at all.

"Is it an emergency?" He replied, as cold as he always was.

"I think I deserve enough to leave if I have to, with all of the crap that I do for you on a daily basis." She snapped back.

"Is that attitude that I hear?" Jack scoffed.

"It's my time of the month, Jack, and I have a family emergency so unless you want me to come in there and rip your head off, I suggest you let me leave for a little while. Do you understand me now?"

"Be back in an hour. One minute later and I will find someone to replace you." Jack said with no emotion.

"I'll be back when I'm done and no sooner. Oh, and by the way, I'm irreplaceable. Don't forget it."

The pain in her back was excruciating this time. She hated to this day how she was made way back when. The concept was simple: extraction meant pain, to remind all of the angels to never take peace and tranquility for granted. They must occasionally feel pain to understand what it was that they were representing. Right now she thought of it as a real seriously flawed design plan. She clicked off the intercom, grabbed her purse and ran for the stairs.

As she passed the elevators, she saw that it was climbing to her floor and the doors were about to open. The only people that had passes to get up here were herself, Jack and Manny, the head elf in charge of casino security. Manny is never up here unless he is escorting someone up to talk to Jack and the only people she could think of were the five gun-toting maniacs that he called on before. She really didn't need to be caught jumping into the stairway when they came out into the hallway, the questions she would have to answer would surely blow her cover.

The doors opened and she stood there, waiting for the arriving party to come out into the hallway. She was right, the five runners were walking in front of her, Manny holding the door open.

"Are you going down Ms. Plum?" Manny asked, holding the door for them.

She stood there knowing that Jack knew she had to leave. If she said no to Manny, it would definitely get back to him that she didn't get on the elevator and would still be here. Her cover would be blown or there would be a lot of questions either way. She couldn't afford either one right now. If she did, she wouldn't be able to have her extraction on street level. It would be seen by too many people. She would have to get to a rooftop and just didn't have the time, or the energy. Her wings felt like they were going to snap her in half. "Yes, Manny, hold the door for me, huh?"

Manny nodded.

Eve looked at the group of gun runners, trying to see if they were armed. Four of them definitely were concealing, she couldn't find anything on any of them as they walked towards Jack's office. The smaller woman, she thought she was French, had a forty-five tucked in her pants on the small of her back, she noticed the bulge under her coat. Eve still had a thought in the back of her head that these weren't just any gun runners, these people were mercenaries. If she didn't get the hell out of there, things were going to get from bad to worse real quick.

She strolled up to the small woman, quickly moving past her, brushing into her as she made her way to the front of the line.

"I was on my way out, so I apologize, let me let you in." Eve made her way up to the front, opening Jack's door and letting them in. After the little French woman entered, she closed the door and ran back to the elevator, holding the forty-five.

"Sorry for the delay, Manny, thanks for waiting." As she walked into the elevator Manny stared only at the instrument panel. He was very serious about his job and treated it like he was in the armed forces. Before his finger jumped off of the "door open" button, Eve took the forty-five and hit Manny over the head with it, dropping the little machine of an elf to the ground with a thud that probably echoed down the elevator shaft into the casino. She wiped her prints off of the gun and dropped it next to Manny's head. She jumped away from it, fearing that it would go off suddenly. She was familiar enough to know where the safety was but had too much to do to worry about it right now.

The doors started to close and she slithered between them back out into the hallway. She straightened her dress and quickly ran for the staircase. Eve was in so much pain that it was difficult for her to make the three flights of stairs to the roof. With a heavy hand and spent breath, she hit the bar and the door slammed open, the cold, crisp wind hitting her in the face.

She stayed near the doorway as she removed her shoes, dress and blouse, stuffing them all in her purse. She snapped it shut and stuffed the purse itself into the slats of the vent near the doorway. Under her clothing flowed a brilliantly white silk robe that has been hidden since she went undercover. She made it a habit to keep it covered while at her apartment, to make sure she wasn't compromised by any of the nosy neighbors.

She loosened her hair and walked to the middle of the roof where the wind followed the circular pattern of the building. The funnel of wind force was enough to blow a helicopter off the roof, no less an angel. The white silk and her flowing hair seemed to be weightless in the beauty of the wind.

Water streamed down her cheeks. If the pain was supposed to remind her, she would never forget it. It felt like she was being stabbed by a hundred butchers at the same time. She screamed in pain as she got down to one knee and curled her aching back upward to the sky.

With a loud snap, the skin broke open on her back, the tips of her wings emerging from her skin. She screamed hell into the wind as her back opened up, stretching the gash from her shoulders to nearly her hips. There was no blood, the pain was to be interpreted by each angel as it happened and was to remain in her mind alone. There was never to be any remains of it, it was simply there and then gone as quickly as it arrived, which seemed to last longer with each extraction.

Within one painful, tear-filled minute her wings were straight up to the sky, wet from all of her body fluids sticking to the feathers. She twitched her back again, her head jolting up to the sky, screaming at it at the top of her lungs. This is the part that hurt most, expansion. The weight pulled on the open skin and was known to make angels lose consciousness when they were suppressed for so long, the pain too great for anything to bear.

The wings started expanding to the width of hers arms which were fully extended outward to the sides. From top to bottom, all angel wings were exactly the same height as the angel and the width was always the exact size of the angel from fingertip to fingertip. They were designed for motion and fluidity and just plain, visually beautiful symmetry.

As the expansion finished, her skin healed itself and the pain subsided, the feathers cracking and breaking themselves apart into individual pieces.

Eve dried her tears with the palms of her hands and stood up as straight as she could. As she stretched out her arms to her sides again, the wings mimicked her every move. She stood like that for a long moment as the wind started to pick up around her. The tornado circled her until it caught her wings, pulling her up into the sky, slowly spinning her around. When she reached about twenty feet off of the top of the roof, she was clear of the wind and finally ready for flight.

She floated in the air for a few moments to get her bearings, staring down at the people down below as they scurried about. It's been a while since she's been free and almost forgot how to do it. She almost forgot how much pain was involved. She closed her eyes and let the wind take her wherever she was needed, thankful to be a part of the sky once again, to be out of Jack's company. No matter how painful this was every time, she wouldn't have it any other way. Why she was needed so urgently she had no idea, but time was getting thin and the window to complete and total freedom was closing.

# Twenty

Jack sat at the head of his conference table, which was made out of a polished slab of ice. It was cooled from beneath, made from the same design work that was used to make all of the ice in the rinks around the world in hockey arenas. The chairs around the table were made of frosted glass to give the illusion of ice but keeping the comfort level intact as he entertains a lot of humans from time to time. He drummed his fingers on the ice slab as he measured up the company he was in.

Around the table Jack assembled the dirtiest crew in the world. They were all arms dealers or gun runners, as the powers-that-be liked to call them, and were people who you didn't want to cross if you intended on keeping your lungs in working order. Yes, it was true. Jack single-handedly took over the North Pole and managed to put Santa in a sanitarium. He even toyed with the idea of re-labeling the asylum The Santa-tarium, but thought that was going a little far, even by his terms in living in, and mocking the world.

Jack had some big shoes to fill, taking the place of the grand jolly one. He had to replace the values of what Santa stood for to what he was convinced that the new concept of values was. He was a slick snake-oil salesman and maybe the best of them, quickly turning the world into his necessity and profiting from it all. Manufacturers were coming to him for product advice on what would sell the best in which markets, and in turn, he would get a great back end on the deal with them having to use Frost to get the product he endorsed out to the world.

A world without global shipping is a world where everything would die, as he put it. There would be no more great deals at any stores, no products to buy and no import or export taxes. Just the fact the he alone could cripple the economy of the world just by stopping the freight for a week reinforced his belief that he was, in fact, the new God.

Even with the world in the icy palm of his bluish hand he was still nervous as hell about taking it to the next level. He eyed each armed salesman as he bounced ideas through his head on how to start the whole thing off without being shot.

"Ladies and gentlemen," Jack began, standing up slowly. "I know you're all wondering what you are doing here in the North Pole."

The five runners nodded, looking irritated that this was taking so long and that they had to travel so far to meet with him. Hell, time was money and they got no information about what this whole thing was about.

"And I trust your accommodations are to your liking." Frost said with a polite hotel-owner smile.

"Would you please get on with this?" The tall runner said in a thick Arab accent.

Jack cleared his throat. "As you know, I have worked my way up the corporate ladder to own the biggest shipping company in the world. I have put the competition out of business and since we are not on any map, this area is completely protected from the International laws that prohibit the rest of the world from profiting. They do anyway, I just decided to brag about it and stop denying it."

Jack looked around the table for any reactions that resulted in him getting killed right now. Luckily everyone was at attention but he could tell that their patience was wearing thin.

Jack continued. "I do not have to abide by the regulations of the United Nations, I have nothing to do with any trade embargos and I am basically untouchable. I am going to ask you to look around you when you leave. I have elf women turning tricks and kids addicted to Humbug and I pull a profit on all of it from all over the world. I have tourists from everywhere who have the twisted fetish of fucking an elf or have the sudden urge to get high on a drug they can't find anywhere else in the world. We produce it here, keep it here and our happy little world goes on. You can gamble in the biggest casino system since Las Vegas and stay in the nicest hotels in the world, making money that you do not have to claim because we don't exist to the rest of the globe. It's a win-win all the way around. Well, except for the sick bastards emptying their wallets, that is."

"Where are you going with this? What the fuck does this place mean to us?" The Arab runner piped up again. He was either a really big prick or the other four nominated this asshole as the spokes-dick. Either way Jack found it hard to resist shooting the mother fucker in the head.

"Up here, you have a safe haven." Jack said as the runners all stared at each other in a skeptical stare. "I have no idea who you are as I decided that anonymity is a must unless we agree to do this."

"Do what, exactly?" The Arab guy asked. He was like a fucking heckler at a stand-up show.

Jack just shrugged him off and kept talking.

"As you know already," Jack started, "the company that supplies the American military with all of its weapons has just lost their CEO. He made his money and up and quit. Nice, considering he is a prominent figure in the American government, right?"

Heads were bobbing up and down around the table.

"The world is in the middle of a fucking war that they start and then they pull out of the supply business. Shit, if I were those soldiers I would try to fucking swim home. Anyway, I have a contact there that has gotten a great deal on ten thousand MP-5's, as many tanks and copters that are needed, RPG's, Glocks, Berettas, and M-16's, you name it and I can get it. Hell, I have a warehouse here already full of them."

He stopped and waited for the Arab to compute the information and talk himself into being confused enough to ask Jack something. Luckily he saw where Jack was going with this and stayed quiet.

"Being up here," Jack continued, "those supplies just disappeared off the map and off the radar. Now, what I have in mind is this: The governments are so fucked up with the oil thing that they are making a God-damned killing on the prices and taxes from the people around the globe. My shipping company raises the price due to the gas increases which, in turn, raises the prices of the things I ship, from vibrators to DVD players. You raise the prices there's more taxation. The taxation goes where? Military spending on the war over the oil that started the vicious circle in the first place, that's where. It's all price gouging for votes, my friends. And where do you think they will spend their money for the military?" He looked around the table and saw five small smiles on the faces around him. "That's right, gentlemen, The North Pole. You will still do all the dealing around the world like you do now, but will come back here when you're done. I will ship the merchandise and take care of all the paperwork to make sure it's all untraceable. The only thing I ask in return is twenty percent of each deal."

"That seems really fucking high, asshole." The Arab yelled. Jack knew he'd sleep better that night knowing he finally found a way to piss him off in the first place.

"Asshole?" Jack slammed his hand on the table, hard enough to crack the ice. "Asshole? Listen, what is the one thing you don't have you stupid bastard? Security! You go through day in and day out wondering if this is going to be the day that someone shoots you with a nine millimeter round to the fucking head. You wonder if this bitch you're sleeping with will be the last woman that wets your dirty little dick because the guy you just scammed found out and sent her to kill you! I can give you that security. I can assure you that under the Pole Protection that you will be safe. I can get any whore around here to wet your dirty little dick at a moment's notice. This is fucking Shangri-La, asshole, and I think that twenty percent is pretty fucking generous. Oh, and if you let me finish, when we broker the deals we up it twenty percent for those pesky gas issues. You make your full pay out and I make the twenty. So shut your fucking mouth and do not insult me again or I will God-damn well shoot you myself. Nod to me if you fucking understand me!"

The four other runners nodded and smiled at the idea. The Arab sat for a moment before nodding his head. He smiled at Jack, who in return just stared directly into him, wanting to plant a bullet into his smug little face.

"Chaos, gentlemen." Jack paused in an attempt to try to calm himself down. "Whether it's a Christmas gift for someone and you fight like hell to get it or it's a gift for a militant people just to fight like hell and change the world…it's all profitable for us." He looked around the table again. "Merry fucking Christmas, gentlemen. We didn't create this; we're making the best of it. We will re-convene tomorrow to go over the details."

"Why are you doing this?" Another runner asked. "It seems to me that you have everything you need to sway things your way anyway. Why involve us and what we do for a living?"

"That's a good question." Jack looked around the table again, slowly looking into every one of them. "If I have all of this, I need people who know how to unload it. I'll ask you this. What is the one emotion that is spread worldwide right now?"

Nothing but blank looks stared at Jack from around the table.

"Is it love?" Jack said. "Is it sympathy? Some of both of those emotions are evident in the world, but what one emotion tops them all?" Again, five shrugs around the table. "It's fear. Ninety percent of the governments around the world rule in fear. Fear is what makes you all of the money that you have in your possession right now. That ritzy little lifestyle that I'm sure you like living only lives in people's fears. If everyone loved each other, where would we need guns? Where would we need to buy gifts for people when we can 'make something from the heart'?"

Five nods.

"Turn on any news station." Jack continued. "You tell me how many nice stories are on there. It's all kidnappings to crime sprees to military fuck-ups and conspiracies. You at least get about ten minutes of sports updates, which is corrupt in itself."

"I don't understand the connection, Mr. Frost." The woman said, shaking her head a little bit.

"The connection is this. You sway the public into being the slightest bit paranoid about the way that they live their everyday lives and perceptions of what is right and wrong go out the window. It gives the government free reign on what they want to do to benefit them. Take, for instance, Louisiana. I'm sure you are all aware that it is in the United States and parts of it are still in ruin. Now take the football team in the area and ask the government why the hell it's normal for the league to pay an athlete sixty million dollars on a contract when there are thousands of people with no jobs or no place to live. It's all tied together in one elusive theme of 'the rich get richer'. Television news deals are all mixed together and they all sway whatever information they want for the desired result of the highest bidder with product placement and all of that other electoral bullshit. And that desired result is…money to make the economy stronger, even though it doesn't go to who needs it."

Jack cleared his throat. "You are no different than the governments that hate you because you can expose them all for being in on the deals in the first place. The governments utilize you and then deny you all at once. And the common people are being duped by the news, by sports, by anything and its all okay. There are valid reasons that the world is the way it is, so they tell us. But the truth is that chaos makes people money. It makes elections happen. Chaos is what the rulers of the world created for their gain, chaos is what I am creating. The world's priorities have become fucked up, ladies and gentlemen. I think it's our duty to make sure that all of what happens in the world comes from one place, and I see no reason why that place can't be up here. I am doing what everyone else is doing. The only thing that's different is that I am a hell of a lot fucking better at it."

Jack smiled with his pointy teeth. "One set of bosses is a lot easier to deal with than over a hundred who don't agree on a damn thing. The governments don't trust their people and their people stopped trusting their governments. No one has faith in anyone, so it's a win-win all the way around."

Jack smiled again as he realized that somehow he won these people over. He was never one to organize his thoughts into anything comprehensible. He didn't think this was, but he miraculously pulled it off and the last process was in motion.

"I think you have a point, Mr. Frost." The Arab man said, obviously swayed to join. "I do have one request first. We have to know that all of the merchandise is indeed up here."

"What, you don't trust me?" Jack asked, obviously surprised.

"We didn't get where we are by the theory of trust." The Arab man said. "I'm sure you can respect that."

"I suppose you're right. Let's go down to the warehouse." Jack smiled at the group, lifting his arms to motion for them to follow. "It's about ten minutes away from here, we can take the limo. Santa Claus is gone, ladies and gentlemen. And as far as Santa Claus goes, hope and faith will die along with him."

# Twenty-One

I almost had a heart attack when the hotel phone started to ring. I completely forgot that Alyssa called Mr. Feeble to ask for a wakeup call, knowing full well that she would hit snooze about a hundred times and I would sleep right through it. I rolled over to the side of the all-white couch and sat upright, listening to the ringing while Alyssa slept soundly through it. She gets all the covers and the pillows and I got my boxers and a spare pillow that was the smaller one that they put under the real one to make the whole stack look higher. Damn, my back was killing me. I'd be pissed about it but she deserved it, being doomed to coexist with me for all this time.

I walked over and picked up the phone, telling Mr. Feeble that we would be ready in twenty minutes. He politely told me that he would have a sled ready to take us to the track. Why he knew where we were going still confused me but I was too preoccupied about getting away from this bed with my morning wood in full effect. I wasn't planning on using it, but the implications of having it would be too strange if Alyssa woke up right now. Even though she is fully aware of the morning effect, I just don't think it would be tasteful being right in her face and all. That's the drawback about respecting her relationship and situation. I will always refuse to do anything that would disrespect her or her fiancé. That's just the way I am. I may be neurotic but I do have some morals, no matter how much my little counterpart says otherwise.

Alyssa woke up and started rolling over in my direction. I looked down at Will Jr. and he was still ready to go so without a thought I ran and jumped on the couch, hitting the entire length on my stomach. Will Jr. screamed in pain, making me bury my head into the cushions and scream like the devil was inside me. It was still better than having it in her face as she woke up. Hell, I'd never live that down and probably be arrested up here. I wouldn't fit in their tiny little cells.

"Will, are you okay? What the hell was that?" Alyssa rolled over in her tank top.

"Yeah, I'm fine." I mumbled into the cushions, trying not to think about the pain in my crotch. I didn't really notice the elevated octave in my voice either. "Get up and get ready. We have to be ready in twenty minutes. There's a sled waiting for us."

"Twenty minutes? I can't take a shower in twenty minutes!" She said. "Do we have any conditioner?"

"NO! You're going to have to try to be quick. I have to take one too, you know."

"Alright, keep your head turned while I get out of bed."

"No problem there." I said as I swallowed the pain. Is it possible to break it? I would put money on her actually wanting to shower with me now that my penis was broken. It's man's fate and it's been happening since I was a teenager.

Alyssa got up, grabbed her clothes and disappeared into the bathroom. I rolled over onto the floor and the blood started rushing back into my midsection, hopefully soon followed by the boys that went to go hide up there. I gathered all of my clothes and waited for my turn in the shower. As I sat there I jumped at the loud knock on the door. I grunted and hobbled over to answer it.

"Who is it?" I asked with a little pain in my voice.

"Room service." A little female voice said through the door, sounding like she just sucked down a helium balloon. I looked at the peep hole and didn't see anyone. As I looked on the door there was another peep hole located about halfway down it. I got to my knees and looked through it. I saw a little elf brunette in a blue apron on the other side, holding a pillow and some blankets. I slowly opened the door.

"Pillow and some blankets?" The elf woman asked.

"Yes they are. And good timing, I might add. My neck is killing me and I think I got a cold last night and you bring them now? Do you have comment cards?"

"Please sir. I think you could use them." She dropped the pillow and the blanket on the doorstep with a copy of The North Pole Herald. Without a word she ran down the hall, her little footsteps echoing in the hallway.

I grabbed the pile she left and went inside just as I heard the shower stop. A second later Alyssa came out, clouded in a little bit of steam. Usually women getting out the shower were very sexy, their hair wet and smelling great, but the little room service delivery took my mind to a different level that was nowhere near thinking about Alyssa naked. I felt like I was in some sort of an Agatha Christie mystery novel where everyone knew what was going on except the person involved. I was finally an innocent pawn in an international game, like I always wanted to be. I just wish I knew the objective and what I got when I won.

'What's that stuff?" Alyssa asked, patting her hair with a towel. She had on some new clothes that I had never seen before.

"Where'd you get them?" I asked.

"Oh, last night when you fell asleep. Some little lady brought up new outfits for us. You like it? Yours is in the closet."

"Oh. She brought up a pillow and a blanket. She dropped off a paper too. Alyssa, I feel like Colonel Mustard from Clue. Oh, the outfit looks great, by the way. They have good taste here."

I looked at Alyssa and she was putting on a nice pair of jeans and a dark green sweater that looked to be made of angora.

"What's the paper say?" She asked.

I flipped it open and stared at the front page. My eyes almost fell out when I saw the headlines: *Jack Frost Has Big Meeting to Control the World! Kris Kringle to Receive Sanity Test on Christmas Eve! Will He Be Released or Put to Death?"*

"Is that the Jack Frost from the song? Is he real?" Alyssa looked upside down, some water hitting the paper from her hair.

"It would appear so, just like everything else we've seen appears to be real. And why the hell would Kris Kringle need a sanity test? What the hell happened to him?"

"Will, Santa Claus isn't real. You said it yourself."

"I didn't think so until now." I grabbed the pillow and blanket off the floor to toss them on the couch. The pillow was weighted funny and fell off the side of my arm. When it hit the floor, I heard the crack of something I have heard in a hundred movies as I was growing up.

When I looked down, I saw a nine-millimeter next to the pillow. It just stared at me, just begging to be picked up and put in my waistband while I said something clever that would mysteriously make Alyssa's clothes fall off.

"Will, why do you need a gun?" Alyssa was officially freaked out.

I picked up the pillow again and another gun fell out. It was the same exact model of the gun that fell out a second earlier.

"Will, why do you need two guns?" She asked.

"Alyssa, one's obviously for you."

"I can't fire a gun!" She said. "I left my fish oil back in Alaska; my mind isn't sharp right now."

"Well, I am not carrying two of them."

Alyssa had a sudden thought and patted down the jacket she was putting on. She opened it and looked at the inside lining. There was a shoulder holster built into it.

"Yours probably has one too." She said, her voice getting more and more jittery as she tried to figure out why we were suddenly armed.

"Alright, let's get ready so we can get this over with." I said. "I really want to get you home to your family, Alyssa. Let's be extra careful and get through this because as of right now I have no idea how to leave."

"Will, I'm really scared right now."

"Yeah, me too. I think I need to change my boxers." This was the first time I actually felt scared since I was around eleven years old and didn't like the feeling. And I really needed a damn cup of coffee.

"That's really gross." Alyssa said, smiling. "Now get in the shower."

# Twenty Two

Oddly enough, everything went as planned with the sled. It was outside the hotel just like Mr. Feeble said it would be and was now dropping us off at the back end of the Douglas Fir Race Track. The place itself didn't look so nice from back here. There was just a long building that went on for at least the length of a football field and above that we could see the stadium going up around six stories, with huge light fixtures aimed down to the track behind the wall. From here it just looked like an open-air warehouse.

The sled driver dropped us off right in front of the huge double doors of a shed and drove off without saying anything. I noticed that Alyssa and I each had our right hands on top of the left side of our coats, not used to carrying weapons obviously. I at least knew enough to put the safeties on.

The large doors of the shed cracked open and Wedge slowly stepped out. Great, I really didn't need to see him again.

"Wedge, It's nice to see you again!" Alyssa yelled. "We thought we lost you when we came in!"

"Shhh! He cannot know I was away last night." Wedge said.

"Who?" I asked.

"Olaf! He's my boss and let me tell you, he's a real asshole."

"Why are we here?" I asked. I was getting really tired of asking it but it became more of a matter of habit.

"This is the farthest attraction from the strip. It doesn't open until one so I have time to take you to Old Town." Wedge stood proud, staring at both of us as we were now on his turf.

"Old Town?" Alyssa was looking all over the place, obviously paranoid that she would have to pull the gun out and start blazing some time soon.

"Yeah, Old Town is where all the good elves like me were banished when they refused to go under Frost's way of living. He's an asshole, but I don't want to live on food vouchers for the rest of my life. I have a family, you know." Wedge looked at me with some hint of hidden anger in his eyes.

"No, I didn't know." I said. "Does this have anything to do with the paper that was laid on my doorstep this morning?" I didn't dare mention the guns. I had no idea what anyone knew and who to trust. For one, Wedge was not on the top of the list.

"Yes, you will be briefed by Ollie when we get there. We're just waiting on your uncle. Come inside and help me feed the team." Wedge said as he waddled his way back into the shed.

We followed him into the long, smelly hallway. It was dimly lit and very cold. The temperature must have dropped about thirty degrees and as we walked I felt the packed snow crunching loudly under our feet. On each side of the hallway there were eight stable stalls. At the far end of the hallway there was one more stall with a smaller door attached to it.

"Hey, who the hell are these people?" The reindeer in the first stall said as he poked his head over the stall door. The door went up around four feet but had an iron gate welded to the top, probably to prohibit the reindeer from flying out. He was obviously floating up to see what was happening. I couldn't believe my eyes when I saw that he had a cigar hanging from his mouth.

"It's none of your business, Blitzen." Wedge said. "Just shut up until Olaf gets to your shot. And what did I say about smoking in the stall? It lights the hay. You already burned your stall three times last month."

"Come on, little man!" Blitzen said. "Let me out of here and I'll kick your little ass to Kingdom Come! You stick me with that shit again and you're a dead man." Blitzen stared as he started flying like a mad reindeer in his stall, cigar smoke flying all over the place. As he circled around, some ashes and cinders started falling down.

Wedge looked at us and shrugged. "Blitzen is undergoing anger management therapy. He's a great racer but a little unhinged. He thinks his name is from the German word Blitzkrieg and thinks it's his duty to unleash holy hell onto the rest of the racers on the track. I don't know why but he seems to think that his parents fought in World War II and sent him up here to be safe."

"He's not German?" Alyssa asked.

"No, his parents are somewhere in Old Town. They retired when he was born. Santa brought him into the team because he was just so big; he pulled most of the weight himself."

"So why does he think that?" I asked.

"Because of the steroids that Olaf keeps him pumped up with." Wedge said, obviously pissed off about it. "The other ones are okay. You only know seven others."

"You mean you take care of the actual reindeer that we've been singing about since we were kids?" Alyssa eased up a little bit, like a big kid in a warped petting zoo.

Wedge walked and talked like he was the curator of a museum. "Dasher is in Stall Two. He's the fastest we have. That's why we have to increase the steroid count in the others so he's not the only winner. Sadly, it's gotten to his head."

"Wedge!" Dasher yelled into the hallway. "Are you coming in here to massage my thigh? I have a cramp and practice starts in an hour! What are we paying you for?"

Dasher rose to the top of his stall, wearing a navy blue headband and I could have sworn that I saw a tank top. I just stared at him like I was hallucinating. I would have done that to Blitzen if I didn't think he'd break out and kill me.

"Next to him is Dancer." Wedge said proudly. "She's studied all forms of dance and really puts on a good show. That really screwed with her diet though. She will only eat caviar and drink pure water. She also insists on having classical music playing during practice. She's a real damn diva, let me tell you." Wedge was proud of his team, no doubt about it. It was sweet in a disturbingly creepy way.

"And then we have Prancer." Wedge said. "Now he's a story. Not much to tell except that he has a crush on every male Southie that comes in here. It's pretty cute how he just starts Prancing around when he sees them warming up." Wedge laughed a little bit, not knowing how we would take seeing a gay reindeer. "It's starting to get in his way though. His odds are way off because of it. Not to mention that he refuses to go out and race without that damned ascot."

"Wouldn't that be a good payout if you can get him focused?" I asked. Betting always confused me but that just made sense somehow.

"Yes, but getting them to focus is just the tip of the iceberg." Wedge continued on down the hallway, stopping at the next stall.

Alyssa looked into Prancer's stall and stared into his left eye. "You'll find someone, Prancer. I know it. Just stay focused and it will happen."

"Hallelujah, human woman!" Prancer yelled from his stall. "It's nice to know I am appreciated! Do you hear that, Wedge? Your new friend is absolutely fabulous!"

Wedge pointed to the next stall, blowing off Prancer's complimentary nature toward Alyssa.

"This is Vixen." He said. "She's slept with all of the other Southies that ever came in here and started pissing off Prancer. I'll tell ya this; it's a real God damned soap opera in these stalls. Next to her are Comet and Cupid. They have shared the same stall since they were born. They were born twins. Comet believes there's a different God up there and is dabbling in Scientology, he's only waiting until he figures out on how reindeer get accepted. He knows there's a yearly fee so I can honestly say that he's trying to win all the time. You gotta love his heart."

Wedge looked at Comet appreciatively, switching focus to Comet's stall pal.

"Cupid thinks he's Don Juan and loses all the time from staring out at the chicks in the crowd." Wedge smiled. "Hell, he even invites some back to the stable. The next one is Donder. There's nothing spectacular about her. She's a very nice reindeer and polite to everyone. Always tries her hardest to win. She has trouble associating with other reindeer. The only thing that got her going was that I convinced her that she was named after Romeo and Juliet. You know, "What *light through Donder's window breaks?*""

"That's not how it goes." I said.

"No shit. She was depressed and that cheered her up! What do you want me to do here? It's not like I have a resident reindeer psychologist next door. It was hard enough to get a copy of the play up here so I could explain it.

"What's in the last two?" Alyssa asked.

"Rudolph lives in them. He helps me clean up their stalls while they practice so I gave him two stalls. I have a cot in there too with a television. No cable but at least it cuts the boredom down a little." Wedge looked upset and stared at the floor.

"They still don't let him race in the Reindeer Games?" I asked, not realizing how stupid I sounded right now.

"They heckled him into it once. He hasn't really trained all that much, which is why we were in Alaska. Truth is I don't want him to race at all."

"Why not?" Alyssa asked. "He'd probably be really quick."

"A few reasons." Wedge said as he patted Rudolph on the head. "One, he'd throw the odds. He glows for God sake. It's very distracting for the other reindeer. Two, we will need him when you finish what you were brought here to do. Third, you've met all of the team. Rudolph is my only friend here. He stayed pure because he wasn't allowed to join their games. So it's me and him, and I can't bring myself to get him hurt. I love that little guy." Wedge started to tear.

I felt bad for him. It must be very lonely out here so far from the strip. It was so far from the rest of the world. Everyone that Wedge has ever known was turned into something else, shutting him out into cleaning stables alone. They were two outcasts that only have each other. It reminded me of being at my job for six years and being laid off suddenly. All of the people that I considered a part of my family now were not any part of me any more. When I saw those people months later, the hello even seemed like work to them so they blew it off. I really wanted to know how they were doing and wondered what they were up to, but almost every person I talked to couldn't give two shits that I was breathing on the same planet.

It was like going to prison and I don't think anyone's mind can adjust to losing that many people all at once. Visitation would come but it was all obligatory stiffness and discomfort talking through that glass. It brings your importance to this world into the crushing reality that everyone is temporary. I found out that individually I just wasn't important to many people on any level other than someone to talk to while we were being paid.

"What are the other nine stalls on the other side?" I was suddenly really curious now about how this all worked.

"Those are for the other challengers." Wedge said, brightening up a bit. "They should be here in about an hour. They shuttle them in from all over. There are some local unknowns but most of them are disgruntled reindeer from the South Pole. I'm sure you heard me use the term 'Southie' a lot? They're really mean little pricks. We usually get Blitzen super mad if we know that Southies are going to be here. Then the betting begins and we race."

Uncle Frank yelled at us from the entrance that was about a football field behind us. He sprinted to us and thank God! This was getting uncomfortable. I've never been much of a pet person and that was limited to dogs and cats. Reindeer were just plain freaking me out especially when you could picture them in a poker room somewhere, or placing a hit on someone for not owning up to their vig. In the back of my head I was picturing that painting of the dogs playing poker and pondering the fact that it may be possible that it was a true portrait.

"Come on, guys!" Uncle Frank yelled. "We have to go now! We have got to get to Old Town! Those two freaks Mort and Stan caught up with you while you were at the hotel. They'll be here in five minutes. Where's the sled? I didn't see it outside."

"The driver took off!" I yelled, not knowing why I was yelling in the first place.

"Up here, you have to tell them exactly what you need for them to do. They don't stick around because they like the cash for The Yuletide. It's a bunch of damn drunks around here." Frank calmed down a little bit, silently easing the huge vein back into his forehead. "Wedge, can I borrow some of the reindeer? We need to get out of here fast. I can have them back in a half an hour. An hour tops."

"Olaf will be back in an hour. You have them back in there by then or I'll be dead. You know how he gets." Wedge's eyes were darting around all over the place.

"I will. I want Will on Dasher." Uncle Frank said.

"No. Absolutely not. He's our number one and he's got a cramp." Wedge was defiant. I would tell Uncle Frank to watch his shins but he probably already knows.

"Okay. Will can take Vixen. We all know she's fast and loose. Alyssa will have to go with Donder, she's the safest and most effective. I'll take Blitzen. I'll be in the back of the pack in case Mort and Stan catch up to us." Frank looked at Wedge to tell him to get them prepped for an actual flight. Frank yelled to Blitzen, "Blitzkrieg, you gonna kill me out there?"

"Nah, you're okay. I just like to give Wedge hell." Blitzen said in a tone that made him sound like a scruffy looking bookie in a back room somewhere. "He used to kick me in the shins when I didn't listen! Plus, you brought me some great Cubans!"

"See, Wedge, you just have to know how to wheel and deal." Uncle Frank smiled as Wedge rolled his eyes and walked away to get them prepped.

"Uncle Frank, what's with the guns?" I asked.

"Mort and Stan are the least of our problems. It's going to be pure hell going into Old Town. They have security posts on all borders. I paid off the two on the main gate. It seems that they are rebels against Frost and are waiting for the perfect time for a revolt anyway."

Uncle Frank smiled again as Wedge returned with Blitzen, Donder and Vixen.

"This is all going to work out, guys." Uncle Frank said. "The safeties are built in. The minute that your finger hits the trigger, the safety is off, so don't worry about shooting yourselves by accident."

Alyssa looked at me with a look of sheer horror on her face. I looked back and shrugged. To me it just felt like I was strapping into a brand new rollercoaster. I had no idea what to expect but in my mind I anticipated some cheap thrills and an abrupt ending. This was all just too elaborate to be believed by any rational person. The problem with that was that I was never really rational in the first place.

Alyssa reluctantly climbed on Donder's back and asked if Donder was comfortable. Donder, oddly enough, nodded yes.

I climbed on Vixen and got ready for my flight.

"Are you comfortable?" Vixen asked.

"Yes, as much as I can be I guess." I didn't know what to say. From what I understood, the reindeer I was on preferred to be on her back, not the other way around.

Uncle Frank hopped up on Blitzen and headed us out. Alyssa looked nervous as hell and I would have shit my pants right there if I knew it wouldn't stick to Vixen's fur.

# Twenty Three

I somehow made it to the front of the line, sitting on top of Vixen. From what I heard a little while ago, she knows how to get around so he hoped she would in this case too. Alyssa was in the middle sitting on top of Donder. She was holding on to Donder's neck for dear life and bringing up the rear was Uncle Frank on the emotionally unstable Blitzen. I was nervous that Blitzen would freak out and kill us all while we were out here.

We were flying faster than a normal speed limit, from what I could gather it was around seventy or eighty miles an hour. The wind itself made it feel like we were going well over a hundred. The reindeer stayed in a perfect line, rising up in unison over the cliffs and falling in a perfect line in the valleys, the wind whipping around their bodies being the only sound. It was easy to tell that these animals worked together in the past and were well trained in staying in order. Obviously Santa had to run a tight ship, reminding me what the hell we were doing here in the first place. The only drawback was their leg movement, which seemed silly as Hell considering there was no traction. They moved their legs like they were running to nowhere and it was making me nauseous.

We were heading into a valley and the plan was to land on the strip at the bottom to make sure we were not being tailed. It was like the Tatooine scene in *Star Wars* where Luke was hit by a Tusken Raider's Gaderffi stick. The only difference was that this had winter colors and there wasn't typically any snow in the deserts of Tunisia.

As we headed straight down between the rock cliffs I think I heard Alyssa scream. It was like a roller coaster designed by a sadist, my stomach dropping at the speed of sound. Within a second we were on the ground, not even feeling the landing as we slid on it. Man these reindeer were good. A lot of them obviously had mental issues but they were efficient.

"You see anyone, Uncle Frank?" I asked, louder than normal to compensate for my ears popping for ten minutes straight. The wind was chilly and loud, made worse during our drop from Heaven.

"No, but they can't be far behind." Uncle Frank yelled back against the wind. "I'm not worried about the stupid one but Mort is one sick little son-of-a-bitch!"

Alyssa closed her jacket tighter over her chest to shield her from the cold that was coming at us at breakneck speed. "It's the stupid one that I'm worried about. He's a little pervert!"

Alyssa looked at the ring on her hand and it started flashing, a brilliant blue strobe going off from her hand.

"Will!" She yelled. "I can't stop the ring from flashing! They're going to get us!"

"Hide your hand!" I yelled, hoping that she would agree that the suggestion was as obvious as someone with a third thumb.

Alyssa rolled her eyes and shoved her left hand in her pocket, holding Donder's neck with her right as tightly as she could, even though we were already on the ground.

Behind us a rock fell from the top of the cliff, bouncing on the rock walls all the way down to the ground, smashing into little pieces. We all looked around at each other and instinctively fell silent. We all stared up to the top of the cliff like we were attached to a marionette's string just waiting to see some action. We didn't see anything for a few minutes and we just sat there frozen on top of our reindeers.

In what seemed like a fraction of a second, Dasher flew down into the valley with Mort and Stan on top of him. Mort was in front, an MP-5 strapped around him and ready to deal us some death from above. Stan was in the back with an MP-5 of his own, screaming like a Mexican soldier during a revolution. He sounded like a fucking banshee on speed.

As they approached quickly I heard a delay in the gunfire coming from them. Mort had his MP-5 set on rapid fire while Stan's seemed to be stuck on single shot. I didn't know a lot about guns, but I knew enough to realize I had a better chance with Stan. It would be real easy if I can convince Alyssa to open her jacket and flash him, he'd drool and drop his weapon. He'd be all out of sorts, but that chance was going to have to remain an impromptu fantasy.

The bullets hit the ground below us, strafing a line all the way down the line to our left. He was flying above us now shooting straight down. Little bits of ice were being chipped away by the nine millimeter bullets being forced into it. We were being showered in ice as they passed us overhead. The gunfire came to a stop as they went for a turn-around at the end of the valley that was in front of us about fifty yards.

"Guys, get your guns! Fingers on the triggers!" Uncle Frank screamed like a damn drill sergeant.

"I've never shot at anyone before! I've never even shot a gun before!" Alyssa yelled back.

"It's either you or them, so you better learn pretty fucking quick!" Frank yelled at her directly. "I am in no position to have you killed under my watch!" Whatever Alyssa found so nice and trustworthy about Uncle Frank before was now completely erased and replaced with *Rambo*. I don't think anyone had ever cursed at her in anger before. I've never seen it or tried it so it made me uncomfortable. I watched for a brief second to make sure she didn't just shoot Uncle Frank.

"I can't do this! I can't!" Alyssa was starting to panic.

"Get under me!" Donder said, flipping Alyssa off of her back and walking over her, making a shot very difficult for the two gunmen.

Blitzen flipped Uncle Frank off of his back. "She's right." Blitzen said, chomping down on what was left of his Cuban cigar. "She has the ring and we need to protect her."

"You two take care of them." Vixen said, flipping Will off of her back. "The girl does not need to fight. She needs to stay alive. They won't shoot us anyway."

"Yeah, we bring in a lot of money for that asshole Frost. He wouldn't want to lose an investment, or three of them." Blitzen said. "We'll take care of Dasher if we can."

The three reindeer stood in a wall around Alyssa and each got down on their knees. They each put their heads in the middle looking like a reindeer triangle, Alyssa under all of their snouts. Blitzen grabbed the gun from her hand and flipped it behind him, followed by the cigar that was encased in reindeer spit.

"Heads up!" Blitzen yelled.

I looked in his direction and saw Alyssa's gun flying towards me. I picked it up as it slid to my feet. This was fantastic. I was not used to holding one gun, now I'm standing here like the hero in a John Woo movie. I was not waiting for the part where me and Mort were in a standoff, holding our guns to each other's faces in that stereotypical moment of slow-motion-Asian-mercenary tension.

"Will, you alright?" Uncle Frank asked.

"Yeah, a little out of my league here to be honest and I think I just shit my pants. Is this your idea of helping?" I smiled through my gritted teeth.

"You'll do fine Will. You've fired a few times with me and you were good." Uncle Frank pulled a twelve gauge from his back. It must have been under his jacket, I didn't notice it before. It was like I was in the woods with some crazy mountain guy who thought bears were conspiring against him while his grits burned. "They would have turned around by now, keep an eye out South and I'll keep an eye out South."

"You look like Bruce Campbell from *Army of Darkness* and what the fuck does that mean?" I yelled.

"We're in the North Pole, sorry. It's all South. You keep an eye to the front of the valley, I'll watch the back. Whatever you do, do not shoot Dasher."

"I'm not making any promises. I'm about one step away from eating a bullet myself." I had both guns at the ready. They were shaking, half from cold, half from nerves but they were both at the ready. One was aimed up and the other over to the mouth of the valley in front of me. Uncle Frank looked like he was with a military resistance, standing there with his twelve-gauge, ready to open someone up in a most bloody way. I really wanted to walk home.

Without a sound, Dasher flew down almost on top of me. I would have screamed but it would have ruined my bad ass image I was displaying for the first time in my life. Mort was spraying bullets all over the place, intermittently accentuated by the single shot bursts from Stan, which were all missing the marks terribly. The bullets whizzed by my feet, shooting chunks of ice up to almost face level. I didn't know what else to do but run for cover.

As Dasher flew by me I slid on the ground, unloading a few clips in the direction of Stan's back. Mort and Stan were both focused on Uncle Frank so I had an open shot. I shot off around eight rounds, the recoil settling down after the first two, the palms of my hands adjusting to the power being pounded into them and going numb. By some stroke of luck, I hit Stan in the back of the right arm, his MP-5 falling around ten feet to the ground.

He screamed like a banshee again and turned around. He looked upset that he lost the game and all he could figure to do was hold his arm and give me a raspberry with his tongue like a five year-old.

I heard some shotgun bursts and the clicking as Uncle Frank was cocking the gun like a madman at a gas station hold up. I ran over and picked up the MP-5. It was weird and heavy but I figured there was some sort of setting for rapid fire. On the left side, I found the toggle switch and flipped it on rapid fire. I had the handgun under my arm, another in my left hand and this maniacal instrument of death in my right. I threw down both handguns and steadied the MP-5, aiming directly at Mort.

"Blitzen, how do I make Dasher buck him?" I yelled to Blitzen as Uncle Frank was opening the gates of Hell on Mort. Missing him obviously but it sounded bloody.

"Tell him he's a slow piece of shit! He'll flip out on you. He's a total jock that hates losing!" Blitzen yelled back over his shoulder. "And don't step on my cigar!"

Dasher turned around and started back towards me. Uncle Frank was reloading and took a holding position in a rock bed off to the side. I was the only person in his path and didn't know if I could handle it. All I had to do was insult Dasher, sounded easy enough if I could avoid getting a bullet to the face.

That's the one good thing and bad thing about reindeer. They aren't normally people-carrying creatures but obey orders until they are told to stop. The only way to get through to them is tell them something that would cause a reaction to stop the order. That's how Wedge trained them, I guess, like the "Donder window breaks" thing. I have to remember to kick him in the shins when I see him again.

Dasher flew at me like a bullet train. Mort wasn't firing but had the MP-5 aimed dead center at me. I didn't notice before but he had a laser light on it that was illuminating a red dot on my chest. Shit, this is the day I am going to die! I don't think I had the mental capacity to handle that.

"Hey, Dasher, you slow piece of shit!" I yelled into the air at the oncoming reindeer. "Is that all you got? By the time you get here I'm going to die of old age! Do you hear me, Dasher? I am going to bet on you later as the long shot because it'll be a miracle if you even make it to the finish line!" I had no idea on how to insult a reindeer but you had to give it to me for trying.

I saw him coming towards me. Dasher's head was starting to twitch and his lips were tightening into an angry snarl. I think I even saw smoke blow from his snout.

"Come on, you slow bastard!" I was laying it on thick, glad that it wasn't Blitzen I had to do this to. I carefully steadied my MP-5 and centered it on Mort, trying like mad to replicate a normal SWAT guy and hoping it was accurate. I had to move up and down because Dasher was going into a rage. Mort was flying up and down like a small bull rider on crack, the red light on my chest jumping around like a psychiatry test performed by a hyperactive doctor with a laser light. It was making me dizzy, figuring out where he was aiming. I let it go and looked down the sight of my own gun.

Dasher bucked one final time, throwing Mort and Stan in the air like test dummies. Dasher was aiming straight for me, three hundred pounds of pissed off reindeer coming at me to steal my last breath. My adrenaline was going haywire but I managed to keep a line on Mort. I breathed deep and squeezed off some rounds, going right over Dasher's head. Dasher ducked, lost his balance and hit the ground, sliding close enough to me that his nose hit me in the pants.

The shots hit Mort in the leg as he spun around in the air. His gun was thrown in Uncle Jack's direction. Within a second, Mort and Stan thumped to the ground. Man, I hope they were still breathing. I really didn't want anyone dead at my expense. On the other hand I was really excited that I did that in the first place without wetting my pants. It was so cold out here that it might have frozen already, I had no idea.

"Dasher, you're awesome." I said to him as he landed by my feet. "You know you're the fastest one out there. I just had to stop them."

"Damn right I'm the fastest." Dasher said, getting up on the icy floor like *Bambi* taking his first steps in ice. "And you're an asshole."

"Will, are you okay?" Alyssa asked, getting up from under her reindeer blanket of cover

"Yeah, I'm fine." I said smiling, in total denial that I just did any of that super action crap.

"Will's an asshole." Dasher said, smirking at me.

I walked over and gave Blitzen a new Cuban to smoke. "I took it out of your stall before we left. I figured you'd need one after this."

"Good times, human Will. Good times." Blitzen smiled and chomped down on the cigar. "Dasher, you need anger management more than me."

"Get these guys and bring them to Old Town with us." Uncle Frank said, walking up to the crowd. "We need some information and need to get them bandaged up."

"But they tried to kill us!" Alyssa wanted them dead and I couldn't necessarily disagree with her.

"They are good elves, just walked down the wrong path. We need their help and we need to get them some help immediately. Dasher, take them to Ollie and we'll meet you there." Uncle Frank smiled at me. "You see what you can do when you open up a little bit?"

I nodded, admiring my MP-5 and smiling a little bit.

"Oh, this is nuts." Alyssa threw her arms in the air. "I should have never agreed with Uncle Frank. I forgot that he's Will Foster's relative, how sane can he be?"

"We should go. We need to have these reindeer back in a half hour or Wedge is going to catch some serious shit." Uncle Frank said as he started loading the wounded elves onto Dasher. I got Alyssa onto Donder again, feeling like the chivalrous cowboy that saved the hot cashier from the mercantile.

Alyssa pet Donder's neck when she got up there, I guess in an appreciative way for protecting her. Who knows? I stopped trying to figure her out. It's like reading Braille with numb fingers.

Within minutes we were airborne again, almost like nothing had happened since we originally started out. The only difference being that we adopted two elves that I shot and now had pretty close to a full arsenal strapped to me. Yeah, this trip is turning into a journey that I would never in the life of me think that I would be taking.

# Twenty Four

The doors slammed open and Wedge just about jumped out of his skin. Olaf walked in and walked faster than Wedge thought he ever could towards the back of the stables. Olaf was not a decent elf, no one on the Pole thought that anything nice ever passed through his veins. His veins, on the other hand, were extremely happy to be living in Olaf's body. They were pumped full of enough reindeer steroids that it made professional baseball players look like they have never worked out. Shit, give Olaf a bat and he could break any slugging record in the history of the game.

"Wedge, where are you?" Olaf screamed down the hallway as he practically sprinted to the back. "Get the fuck out here if you are in the stables!" Olaf was an asshole enough, but to add roid rage on top of it he was a damned monster.

Wedge walked out like he knew nothing. "Is there a problem? I was just getting the mixture ready for the shots."

"That would be great if there were any fucking reindeer in here! I just got a call from Frost saying that you sent three reindeer away to help some God damned humans!" He was spitting enough as he talked that Wedge looked like he was caught in a rainstorm.

"They're outside. I thought that they could use a little air." To Wedge, this wasn't a complete lie, they were outside and did get some air, a lot of it, as they flew the humans to safety against all orders.

"Don't give me any lip, asshole!" Olaf slammed Wedge in the face with a meaty fist, immediately making Wedge's nose erupt in a stream of red.

"What the hell was that for? I told you, they're outside! Damn, I think you broke my nose!" Wedge doubled over in pain.

"I hate liars. You could cost me a lot of money! I don't need a bullet in the head and I don't need a liar working for me." Olaf kicked him in the gut like he was making the game-winning extra point. A crack of the ribs echoed down the hall.

"That's enough!" Rudolph said as he walked around from his stable with fury in his eyes.

"Oh you want some of this too?" Olaf stopped beating the shit out of Wedge long enough to turn around and stare Rudolph in the face. He stared hard enough that you could see the blood vessels in his eyes just begging to be relieved of duty.

"He's my friend." Rudolph said. "I would appreciate it if you stop hurting him."

Olaf didn't hesitate in punching Rudolph in the side of the nose, making it blink on and off like he just short-circuited it. Rudolph let out a yelp and jumped back about a foot. He shook his head a little bit and his nose came on like a basement light that clicked the filament until it buzzed to life. He tried blinking twice and it went off again. It all seemed like it was working properly even though it hurt like hell.

"What do you have to say about that, you little punk? You want some more? I'll break that damn bulb off of your face and stick it straight up your ass!" Olaf was pumping his fist getting ready for his final kill shot. "I'll make you venison by tomorrow."

"I wouldn't do that if I were you." A familiar voice said from the entrance of the stables. It echoed like death in Olaf's ears. He turned around and saw Blitzen standing in the doorway, chomping on his cigar, sending embers flying everywhere. Smoke was flying out of his nose. Dasher, Vixen and Donder were standing behind him.

"Two things: I break this cigar, I will break your legs. You hit my little brother again and I will end you." Blitzen said.

"You wouldn't dare. You're just a punk like him." Olaf wasn't prepared for this uprising and didn't know how to deal with not being in control. This was new territory for him so he did what any power-mad asshole did in situations like this: He readied his fist for another punch.

"Wedge is good to us. I'll make you pay for that either way." Blitzen snorted again. "Oh, and I didn't have my anger control shot yet."

"Oh, shit." Olaf said under his breath.

"Yeah, that's right. Oh shit. I am ready to kill something. It's been a real long morning and I'm hungry. Why don't you make us something? I'm thinking eggs benedict, some white toast and some Columbian coffee. I take it light and sweet, of course. And if you can have that Columbian guy ride it in on his donkey, well that would be…"

"…just fantastic!" Prancer yelled, finishing Blitzen's thought.

"You all work for me!" Olaf was losing control.

"You're stuck, Olaf the Asshole. You kill us and Frost will kill you. You beat us enough and we can't race and you still get a bullet in your fat drugged out head. However if I kill you then Wedge will take over and Frost doesn't have to provide you with that bullet."

Blitzen walked into the stable, followed quickly by Dasher, Vixen and Donder. Blitzen walked up until he was nose to nose with Olaf.

"I want you to apologize to our brother right now or take your final breath." Blitzen said. "It's your decision you juiced-up freak."

"I am not apologizing to a fucking animal. He works for me just like that little puke bleeding all over my floor." Olaf was standing his ground, what little ground he had left in the stable.

"We were outside on a walk for some exercise, just like Wedge said and you went all ape shit on him. I think you owe him an apology too." Blitzen said in a menacingly calm voice.

"Not on your life!" Olaf yelled. "Now get back in your stables until I kill you myself."

Olaf would not back down for anything. No one knew if it was the roids or if he just stuck to his guns no matter how demented they were. Either way Blitzen found his dedication somewhat admirable. It was unethical but admirable. Olaf smacked Blitzen in the mouth with the same beefy fist that broke Wedge into a bleeding mess. A cigar fell to the ground and split in half.

"Well, now you've done it." Blitzen said, looking at the floor. Without a hesitation, Blitzen smacked Olaf in the head with his own forehead, making a horrifyingly loud cracking noise that could possibly be heard in Old Town. Olaf hit the ground silently, the skin in his forehead split in half from the top of his head to the bridge of his nose. The pool of blood was trickling itself down towards Blitzen's feet. He looked down and picked his cigar up with his teeth before the blood hit it, placing it back in his teeth.

"Thanks, Blitzen." Rudolph said, still twitching his nose. "I didn't think you'd be back so soon."

Blitzen walked over to Rudolph and motioned for the rest of the reindeer to remove Olaf's body. He turned back and walked up to Rudolph.

"Hey buddy. How's the nose?" Blitzen asked.

"It hurts a little but it still works." Rudolph was embarrassed. Throughout his whole life he always thought of his family as looking down on him. This was more than a little awkward.

"Listen." Blitzen continued. "I know I've been rough on you since you were a kid. You had that cool red nose and I didn't and it freaked me out a little bit so I picked on you. You know why I'm the way I am right now?"

Rudolph shook his head.

Blitzen looked him in the eyes. "It's because it puts the attention on me and gets it off of you."

"So you're jealous of me?" Rudolph actually laughed.

"I used to be. Now I do it so no one else bothers you. These aren't the nicest people or animals that we deal with all day long and I don't want you hurt. That's the only reason why I insisted that you don't participate in the races. I told them I wouldn't do it if they made you do it. It was all me. The others agreed so that's what happened. It's not that I don't like you."

"Why? I'd like to race." Rudolph was being quietly defiant like a kid eager to do big kid things for once.

"And you would be damn good, Rudy. You would. Hell, you led our whole team in the old days and we all thought that was the coolest thing ever. But the reindeer games change a deer. They make them not care about anything but themselves. We make a lot of people a lot of money and have to stay good to not be beaten to death. I want you to stay pure, kid. You have the best heart I have ever seen and I wouldn't hesitate to kill anyone if they tried taking that away from you."

"I never looked at it that way." Rudolph said with a small tear in his eye.

"Kid, hang in there. You'll be leading the team again soon enough. I promise you that."

"Thanks Blitz. I love you." Rudolph said.

"Love you too kid. Now can you do me a favor?"

Rudolph nodded.

"I need you to take Wedge to Old Town to get fixed up." Blitzen said. "When you get there have Ollie call Frost and have him act like

Olaf. Have him tell Frost that he took care of Wedge and you and that the races are on like normal. He's never gonna come down here to verify it so it gives both of you a pass."

"But what about you? I don't want to leave you guys." Rudolph was almost crying out loud.

"Don't worry. You'll see us again, I promise. Like I said you'll fly this team again. I have never lied to you and I don't plan on starting now. There's a plan brewing and things are going to change around here. So go now so we can train. We have to do this race so no one gets suspicious."

"Okay, I will." Rudolph started pulling Wedge up to get him on his back. He looked to make sure he was still breathing.

"Rudolph, remember that we are all here for you and I'm sorry we haven't let you know that until now. I guess I have lied to you once but it was to keep you safe, so I think that counts." Blitzen turned away so he wouldn't start tearing, he did have an image to uphold.

"You're the best family a kid could have." Rudolph blinked his nose as he got Wedge on his back. As he walked down the hallway to the exit his eight siblings, one by one, kneeled on their front legs as he passed. That was their way of showing respect and it was the first time that Rudolph saw it. The little brother stood up to someone to save another, the right of passage of the reindeer community and for once, he passed with flying colors.

"We need to get these stables ready!" Rudolph yelled. "Southies will be here soon and we have to be prepared! And for gosh sakes, will someone mop up that blood on the floor! It's really gross."

# Twenty Five

J ack was pacing around his office, the five gun runners were nervously sitting around the table staring as they were silently wondering exactly how deep they were into this crazy man's plot. When they first walked in they were all under the impression that it would be business as normal: buy, resell and hide up here in paradise. That was all different now with the sudden ringing of the phone. It was all different after getting back from the tour of the warehouse.

With each step their thoughts certainly changed. Jack didn't even know their names yet. The contracts weren't signed yet and he insisted, for his safety, that he not know who they were until they were legitimately employed by him. They were simply named in numerals, and even more simply, they were numbered by height: one being the tallest and five being the shortest.

"Things up here may have changed a little bit." Jack started out, not knowing exactly where to begin. He hung up the phone slowly, staring at it as if wishing it brought him more favorable information. "It has come to my attention that there may be two individuals who have, in some way, the capability of destroying everything that I have worked for in the past few years. My…our imminent global dominance may be in jeopardy. We need to fix this by tonight."

"What do you want us to do about it?" Number One asked.

"Your business is weapons. What the hell do you think I am about to proposition?" Jack continued, taking a well-deserved deep breath. "I need your expertise. What I would like is the best person in the room who knows how to train someone in the ways of killing. I'm not talking about telling them where the trigger is, I want someone who can handle training killing machines. If they fail with guns, I want them to know how to rip someone's throat out with their bare little hands."

"Who are these killing machines going to be?" Number Two asked. "Little hands?"

"Elves." Jack said, smiling. "I want to make an elf mercenary army, ready for anything by tomorrow."

"You want an army by tomorrow? That's nearly impossible! We would need enough weapons and time to train each one! Tomorrow?!" Number Two was pissed to the point that his color was changing.

"Yes, by tomorrow." Jack stated, looking straight in Number Two's eyes. "I want an army ready for battle tomorrow. I need to protect my interests and your future endeavors with me."

"And you need an army to protect yourself from two people?" Number Five asked, almost laughing at the thought.

"Take a look at the jar over on my mantle behind you." Jack said, all five heads turning to the back of the room, staring at a mason jar with a corn cob pipe and an old black hat lying next to it. "That, my friends, is Frosty."

All five heads whipped around to look at him again.

Jack smiled. "He was supposed to make a routine pickup at the Yuletide and tried to pocket ten percent for himself. He said it was to feed his family. I don't give a flying fuck what it was for, it was my money!" Jack slammed his fist into the table. "The Yuletide is where I keep the Humbug labs. I have almost every teenager on the streets addicted, begging on corners just to get another bug. They're so happy when they're miserable and so willing to spend their money. They steal it and buy shit back from me! I make money on all of it: the gambling, the drugs, the guns and best of all, I make a killing on shipping it all. Christmas isn't on anyone's mind anymore. Does that sound like something that two people would be capable of turning around?"

All of them had no clue what was going on.

Jack's smile faded. "No, it's the people that would be helping them that I am worried about. Obviously all of the elves I have working for me here have been converted by many things, none of them more powerful than greed. They love the life that they live and really don't want to go back to what they came from."

"I don't see where you're going with this." Number Five stated, confused. "You don't even know our names and you're pouring out all of this on us like you've known us forever. I just don't understand."

"When we had our meeting before I failed to mention how I came into this business in the first place. I have done away with Christmas as the world knows it." Jack stood straight, fixing his hair. "The world has been losing it for a long time. People hate each other and would do anything just to pacify someone to not deal with them, so I decided to profit from it. Chanukah, Christmas, Kwanzaa, all of it is gone. The only happy people in the world are the atheists now, because they never believed in that shit in the first place. Jesus hasn't played a part in Christmas for a long time. Hell, his birthday wasn't even in December, so I put away the only man who had some sort of pull in the holiday, Kris Kringle. That fat bastard was an idiot."

"So you had Santa locked up?" Number Two stated in solemn disbelief that a world icon was in a nut house.

"That fat sack of shit, so full of fucking jolly." Jack laughed. "He's now full of fucking methadone at the loony bin. That's where our problems arise. It seems that he has smuggled a vial of Christmas spirit out of the Pole and now two people have it and want to give that shit head his power back. What I need from you is this: I need one to train the elves. I need another to make a run to Old Town to run a sweep and kill everything that moves suspiciously. Toss all of the damn houses and find them. I need one of you to check out the sanitarium. It seems that old Santa is up for his last dose of Humbug and the remainder of his mind will be completely erased and I don't want anything interfering with that. He's almost brain dead and I intend to keep him that way. Last but not least I need someone to be my personal security around the Pole since my two best elves were compromised."

"Sir?" The intercom buzzed. "This is Freddy at the craps tables. It seems that some lady called the cops when the elevator opened a while ago. I've been trying to reach you."

"What the fuck for?" Jack slammed the table again.

Freddy cleared his throat. "It seems like Manny was knocked out with something. It looked like it was some sort of high caliber hand gun; it was laying next to him. The doctors think his skull was broken and don't think he's going to make it. When they checked it, it seems like the gun was involved in some sort of a double murder back in the States."

"Oh, this is fucking fantastic." Jack yelled. "That's what I get for taking the service elevator once. Who the hell would do something like that?" Jack was about ready to slam the table again when Number Five spoke up.

"She took my gun!" Number Five said, checking the small of her back. "That little bitch stole my gun and knocked out that little shit in the elevator!"

"Who was that?" Jack asked, getting severely irritated.

"It was your secretary. She brushed passed me real quick when she opened the door for us. Said she was leaving but she would at least let us in first."

"I thought she would have been gone already." Jack said. "It won't be long before they ask for the security camera tapes. Number Five, you take Old Town, the cops never go up there. I'll arrange another firearm for you. Just don't lose it this time, God damn it!" Jack was actually starting to sweat.

"Sir, it's Freddy again." The voice broke through on the intercom. "I thought I would let you know that Manny was the only thing in the elevator when it came down."

"She's in the building." Jack said to himself. "Freddy, get me anyone immediately, you understand? You let them know to comb the entire building for Sugarplum. When they find her, I want her corpse on my desk immediately."

Jack's head was spinning.

"Everyone else," Jack said to the five people around the table, "let's go and I'll tell you where to go on the way. I want these elves ready, understand? We may have a war on our hands, so we can put what you sell to some good use. Call it a field test."

Jack turned around to Number Five as they were filing out of the office: "Manny was a friend, probably the only true friend that a person like me would have. He saved my life twice and was the only one with me from day one. So if you ever insult Manny again, or any other elf for that matter, I will personally put a bullet in that pretty little twisted head of yours. Understand?" Number Five nodded, all of the blood leaving her face. "And I won't think twice about it. Remember, I was the man who locked up Santa Claus, so having a heart isn't an attribute that's fitting in my profile. So, let's go, we have an army to build."

Jack smiled at her like he wanted to chew the flesh from her face and he licked his lips as she passed. He wanted someone to be gasping for their last breath right about now. He didn't give a shit who it was.

# Twenty Six

Rudolph got a chance to do what he's been missing for years. It was race time and he was finally in charge of something. Wedge was in no condition to be leading anyone anywhere and Olaf was in such bad shape that no one knew if he'd ever be normal again, regardless of the outcome of everything going on.

"Dasher, Dancer, Prancer, Vixen! Up front and center!" Rudolph yelled as he walked his family up to the starting gates. "Comet, Cupid, Donder, Blitzen! Get in the gates!" He smiled to himself, finally having his voice heard.

The crowd was in an uproar, waving tickets and racing forms all over the place. Elves and human men and women were in the grandstands, eager to see how much of a take they were in for. Every one of them salivated with the thought that they may be the lucky ones to topple Jack Frost's empire. Each screaming person was going to take the house and they let it know all the way down to the gates.

"Who is in favor of changing things up a little?" Blitzen asked as he entered his gate, chomping on his cigar.

"Like what?" Vixen asked from two gates over.

"Well, Dasher is the favorite right?" Blitzen stated blankly, staring up into the grandstands. "I say we let an underdog beat them and send one of those maniacs up there home with a lot of Frost's money."

"You mean blow the race?" Dasher piped up.

"I don't see it as blowing the race, Dash." Blitzen said. "I think I see it as urging Frost to do something good with his money. You know what the spread is, right? A thousand to one on a Southie named Edgar. That's a lot of green for someone up there."

"So we're encouraging people to gamble?" Dancer asked.

"Nah, just thinking of tilting the odds in one person's favor. If he loses it all after the race, there's no hope for him." Blitzen tossed down his cigar. "If everything goes down as planned this will be our last race together. So let's have some fun with it, for Santa."

Dasher stared off into space pondering the thought. He looked at Rudolph who looked like he just figured out what his place in the world was and was extremely proud of it. He knew that there was one thing that Rudolph wanted to do and thought this was the last time he would ever get the chance.

"Okay, fine. I'll do it. We let the Southie win. On one condition, though." Dasher looked at everyone as they stared at him. "We let Rudy run. It might be his last chance and he stood up for us back there. Olaf could have killed him and he didn't back down at all, just to save our asses. He's earned the right, so if he doesn't I'll win it like normal."

All of the reindeer looked at Rudolph who was in a sudden shock that he was finally nominated to race. He had no idea what to say. He looked at Blitzen for permission before he said anything. Without a hesitation, Blitzen nodded.

"I'll do it. I'll race." Rudolph said excitedly.

"Good, we got your back. We won't let you get hurt." Dasher said. "And run like hell, it would be cool if you won the damn thing."

"Oh, I think this is fantastic!" Prancer said as he fixed the ascot around his neck with his teeth. "I'm so proud of you, Rudy! This is going to be fabulous! Use the nose!"

Rudolph jumped into an open gate at the end of the line. There were a few boos in the crowd, as everyone knew that they never got the opportunity to place a bet on the lit-up little late entry. The reindeer got in position anyway. Eighteen reindeer waiting patiently for the mechanical partridge to make its way around the track seemed like forever right now. The little partridge was about a foot tall and was welded to the same metal as the pear tree it was chasing. Today, it seemed like the little motor was broken.

As it neared the gates the red, yellow and green lights on the racing stand blipped off and the doors flew open. Rudolph heard the rush of hooves on the ground as all eighteen competitors jumped into the hard dirt. They normally only took half the track before they went into flight, but today Rudolph's siblings stayed on the ground until Rudy was lifted off successfully. They ran and waited for him to clear a length in front of him before they became airborne themselves. As they lifted off, the race became almost silent. The only noise was the air flowing under them and the occasional huff and puff of the reindeer. The audience went into an uproar, mostly behind the near-silent race but also for the fact that a reindeer was running that they couldn't place on.

Rudolph was catching up to the Southies quickly. He pulled up next to a small off-white one in the back and blinked his nose, momentarily blinding him and sending him crashing into the crowd. There were many cheers as he careened into them. Rudolph smiled and continued the hunt to be the first across the finish line.

The first lap was easy. It was the second one that worried him. Different tiers of obstacles popped out from the rail at different heights that the reindeer would have to navigate through in mid-air. It was called the deer gauntlet and lots of ribs and noses were broken as a result of them. Rudolph thought it would be wiser if he stayed a tails-length away from the first in the pack to see what his movements were. If he moved up, Rudolph would to. If he hit a pole, Rudolph had time to compensate until he got to a straightaway and could get around. As he pondered his next move, the reindeer in front of him cracked his head into a materializing gauntlet pole.

Rudolph gasped and ducked once over one pole and up over the second one. He pulled up to another deer in front of him, one that he recognized. It was Edgar, the oddball that would make someone rich today.

"Hey, follow me!" Rudolph said to Edgar. "You're going to win this and I'll help. Ready?"

Edgar was panting like crazy, obviously not used to this type of strenuous exercise. It was no wonder why he would wind up a thousand to one. He didn't say a word; he just followed Rudolph like he was told.

Rudolph blinked his nose on to the brightest setting so he could see the obstacles before him, shining his light like headlights in front of him. He's seen thousands of races from the stable and knew the configuration of the gauntlet but was not used to all of the dust kicked up in the process. Not much was kicked into the stables while he stood there. Anyone could know all of the layouts, but seeing it definitely helps.

He was flying up and down through the last set of poles, hoping like crazy that Edgar didn't quit or wind up on someone's lap. He couldn't dare turning around, he could get killed, and that's the only reason Blitzen didn't want him racing in the first place. He had to make this work, too many reindeer were pulling for him.

The track in Rudolph was clear. He could see the checkered flag about a hundred yards away. He looked back and happily saw Edgar grinning like a kid with a cake in front of him, waiting for the first slice.

"Okay, Edgar. It's all you, my friend. Take it home." Rudolph made sure that there was no one behind him. It seemed like they lapped everyone, the track was completely clear behind them, except for the dust that was kicked up by the wind they were generating beneath them.

Rudolph just aimed towards the ground, skidding like crazy down the track, stopping about ten feet into the slide. Edgar panted and drooled all the way towards the finish line, his hoof crossing the checkered stripe. The crowd booed all of it but that couldn't hide Rudolph's smile. He was just like everyone else! Finally!

As he sat there, he heard a man in the crowd yelling that he won the lottery or something. He tried to make out what he was saying but tuned it out as his family came up behind him, hooves landing lightly in the dirt.

"Now that took guts, kid." Dasher said, smiling. "Why'd you ditch it?"

"You're the fastest here, Dash. I didn't want to ruin that. You worked a lot for it and we'll always remember it that way. I was just glad I could race at all."

"Well, I got the tip sheet before the race and some guy just walked out of here with ten million of Jack's money!" Comet yelled! "Now that's gotta hurt the blue bastard! Maybe I can borrow some to donate to my organization. Maybe I can get in to my faith now."

"Your organization, Comet, is full of thieves. Who the hell would want to give money to buy into a science religion? Hell, it's in the name of a damn alien! Snap out of it, huh, it's embarrassing!" Dasher stopped wanting to hear about the dreams of Scientology long ago. He had an open mind but even weird little religions like that wouldn't accept a talking reindeer, no matter how much cash he had.

"I don't care what you guys fight about, I feel great!" Rudolph yelled back, laughing hard enough to echo into the night.

The crowds threw their tickets and forms on the track, as well as some cups of beer. That didn't muffle the laughter coming from the nine reindeer sitting about fifty yards away from the finish line. For the first time all of them were getting along like the siblings they used to be and no one would be able to take that away from them.

# Twenty Seven

Uncle Frank led the way up the hill to Old Town. Alyssa and I were behind him, six feet crunching snow under us. If we had to get here in some sort of secret mode, this would probably get us killed but unless these elves were some sort of border patrol madmen I think we were okay.

"It's right on top of the ridge." Uncle Frank said, not bothering to turn his head.

Alyssa and I just said nothing. By looking at her face I knew that the desire for her to go home was growing by the hour. I couldn't blame her, this was a living hell.

"Uncle Frank," I started, Alyssa's look triggering a thought in my head, "if this is some sort of reality survival show, I'll never talk to you again." Granted, the thought was irrational, but I gave up on the notion of being rational when Ruthie gave me the ring in the first place.

"You haven't talked to me at great length for a while before this, Will. That's not really a threat." Uncle Frank rolled his eyes at the obvious.

"Good point." I said.

"How much farther is it? I'm cold and I don't want to do this anymore." Alyssa started to shiver.

We weren't dressed in more than light coats and sweaters, the things we were used to in any typical Florida winter, which never got below fifty degrees. Plus, from the visitor's center to the city it was all climate controlled to keep the tourists happy. Up here in the hills of Old Town, we were dropping a degree with every step we took and dropping farther and farther into the weather that made the North Pole what it commonly known as. Or what it was known as, for that matter.

"We're pretty much there already." Uncle Frank said. Alyssa rolled her eyes this time, feeling like the little kid in the back of the car having to pee on a road trip with her family. The destination never seemed to arrive.

We walked up to the ridge and just stopped. We couldn't believe what was in front of us. There was a main street that we appeared to be standing at the beginning of, and it stretched to what seemed like the horizon. On each side of the street stood little market shops, from coffee shops to eateries, to blacksmiths and tool repair shops. There were no lights on anywhere, even though there were strings of lights hanging from the awning of every shop.

"This is beautiful." Alyssa said, the kid in the back of the car getting interest back in the road trip.

"It's fucking weird." I said. "It's like a ghost town for little people."

"They are little people, Will. Have some compassion." Uncle Frank started walking down the road. Alyssa followed in his footstep, I just wanted to make a snow igloo and hide until this was all over.

As we walked down the street all of the shops appeared to be totally abandoned. There was no power in anything and some of the doors and windows were boarded up, giving it the appearance of a town that was wrecked by looters. It resembled a Thomas Kincaid painting without the light and taking place after a riot. The street lamps were oil-driven and long since dried up. The only light tonight was the moon.

As we reached the end of the deserted road it split off into a residential area, somewhat like I was used to in Florida; nice neat blocks evenly spaced into cookie-cutter subdivisions, the houses had little room between them. The houses themselves looked like little cabins, logs from ground to roof. Icicles formed on the awnings, the dripping sound was the only thing heard dropping into the snow like a working coffee pot.

The snow on the rooftops reflected the moonlight, creating a fluorescent looking glow in the night, making it look like mid-day with blue light instead of the yellows and the oranges of the sun. There were some candles in some of the windows but the elves that were probably in there were not making any sounds. I sniffed the air and there was wood burning in someone's chimney. Some of these buildings were inhabited, by whom, I had no idea. Right now, I really could care less.

"Is there anyone here?" Alyssa asked.

"Yes." Uncle Frank stopped and turned around to face her. "A few years back, Jack Frost closed down this whole operation. It was just like when we all heard about it. They made all of the toys for the world and lived in their own community. They were self-sufficient and didn't rely on money to live. They lived on what they knew how to do and shared it with people to make everything better."

"How many are here?" Alyssa asked again, like she was doing a huge breaking news report on some cable news channel. Throw a microphone in her hand and she'd be ready to take on any interview.

"Almost all of them. I would say in the neighborhood of a thousand. Some of them went on to work for Jack and couldn't say no to the life he guaranteed for them. The others are here, just living until things get better. That's how I know them. These are my customers throughout the winter and sporadically through the rest of the year."

"You bring them food?" She asked. She was almost ready for syndication.

"Yes. It's the least I could do." Uncle Frank said. "About two years ago, Jack started giving food rations to Old Town so they could live, but at the same time, he cut the power in the town. He wanted them to be completely under his control so they would eventually come over to the city and be his minions. He treated them like they should be living in poverty and that's what you see here. That's when I met Ethan. His family was starving and the rations ran out. He dog-sledded all the way around the perimeter of the city to the visitor's center and went through the gate."

Uncle Frank stopped for a minute to compose himself. "My friends and I, all of the other charter pilots, were playing poker back in the cabin. I remember because I still have a running feud over twenty bucks with Gus."

"I know, he told me to remind you." I said.

"There was a knock at the door and it was Ethan." Uncle Frank continued. "The only thing he said to me was this: "Our families are dying. We need help. I cannot save myself, but please, if you still have a heart, find a way to help us."" Uncle Frank started to tear up. "I had no idea what to do. I mean, I've never seen an elf before. Hell, I never knew they existed. But after one lands on your doorstep and practically dies in your arms you're changed forever. So I followed the sled tracks back to the outhouse and from that point on all of my friends and I have a silent pact that we would help them out until everything gets better. The other guys fly the food to Ruthie and I fly it here. We usually take turns."

"Then why am I here, getting into a battle with elves in a valley, protecting my editor who happens to be ducking under the cover of three talking reindeer?" I was getting sick of this shit real quick. Yeah, I can handle weird. I'm weird and the way I think is weird, but when weird can get you killed for real it becomes a real pain in the ass, especially if you have no idea why you're there in the first place.

"I'll let Ollie explain that to you." Uncle Frank turned and started walking down the street that went to the left. My guess was that all of these streets headed south so I bothered not to ask which way we were headed.

The last house on the block was Ollie's. It as up on its own hill, kind of separated from the rest of the neighborhood. It had wrought-iron fencing all the way around which was no taller than me. I guessed that it kept elf thieves out but I could have scaled it with no problem. It was like he was the doctor who bought the huge house in a shitty neighborhood just to show off that his five minute check-ups for three hundred dollars actually paid off. By the looks of it I wasn't going to like Ollie very much, just on that alone. Yeah, I was being petty but I was hungry and wanted to go home.

Ollie opened the door as we walked up to it, pulling lightly on his long, gray beard. He must have been looking through the windows for us because God forbid that we make a sound in this town. Yeah, I was really going to like him a lot. He was like the guy that owned the creepy house that everyone dared someone to go trick-or-treating at. Ring and run. He peered out like we just left some bag of flaming shit on his porch.

"Frank, it's nice to see you. Please come in." Ollie let us file past him into his house. We all had to walk hunched over to accommodate the low ceilings. Yeah, he's racking up a lot of points in the like department.

"Please follow me into the library," Ollie continued, "and don't worry, this is the only part of the house with low ceilings. That's why I am up on this hill. I had to do a lot of remodeling to accommodate humans."

Alright, he got some points, at least he was thinking ahead. He was still a creepy little thing and not a lot was going to change that.

The library was huge. There were books piled to the ceilings, which were a lot taller, just like he said. Tall enough, even, that they looked to be almost cathedral style.

"What are all the books?" I asked, just curious to see what an elf read in his spare time. The candles burning in this room weren't enough to even read the spines, no less an actual book. It was light enough to see each other but not much more.

Ollie smiled at me, obviously glad that I was interested. "There are a lot of legal books, some human resources issues and a lot of marketing strategies throughout the world. It helped with the job."

"Which was?" I asked, trying to read some of the spines as I walked past the wall of volumes.

"I was Santa's right hand elf. I was in charge of production, deadlines and had to filter through the Naughty and Nice list every year starting in January. I was also in charge of the coal mine, to make sure all of the naughty people in the world were taken care of also."

"Are you this open with everyone?" I asked. I was curious on why he would spill all of this to a guy he just met.

"I have nothing to hide. Most of it has been taken already, Will Foster. The world knows how this all works. Whether they still believe it or not is still an issue." Ollie sat in a beaten leather chair behind his desk. "I remember that you had a fascination with Star Wars toys and G.I. Joe figures as a child, correct?"

"Yes." I said, knowing that my Uncle knew that but wasn't the type of person to openly give such trivial information to anyone. Not that I was in any position to do anything to him if he did. "Don't forget the Transformers."

"You have no idea why you are up here, do you, Will Foster?" Ollie stared at me like he was going to jump the desk and kill me with his tiny hands. "I mean, besides finding that Optimus Prime figure that eluded you all these years."

"No, and no one was willing to give me a straight answer." I rolled my eyes and smiled. "Do you have an Optimus Prime up here?"

"You have a lot of hate and spite in you, Will Foster. You have a lot of contempt for life, don't you? You would like to live in solitude just to get away from all of the people in the rest of the world, yes?" Ollie sounded like he was trying to be the Yoda version of Sigmund Freud. I was just waiting for the phallic symbolism.

"Sure, Yoda." The smartass was coming out and I had no idea what it was capable of. It was a mixture of him being small, getting philosophical and the weird way he ended the question with yes that got it started. I was suddenly stuck in Dagobah! If I was going to have to do a one-handed hand stand with him on my foot, I was going to shoot myself in the head. I was in no physical shape to attempt it.

"Sounds like contempt to me." Alyssa said under her breath, not looking at me.

Ollie just looked at me. "You're here, Will, because you represent the way that people are now around the globe. Not all people, Will Foster, but most. There are nice people left in the world but they get drowned out with all the negativity. You are here to show those nice people that it can be turned around." Ollie stared at me like he was trying to pull the soul out of me like a medicated tapeworm. "You and Jack Frost are more alike than you think. That's why you are here in front of me. We need you to fix this. We need you to make Jack find himself and in doing that, we need you to find yourself."

"And how am I supposed to do that? Is there a crystal ball anywhere in here? Or maybe one of those magic eight balls?" I was looking around like a fool to prove my point, ignoring the fact that I looked like a complete idiot.

"I have something better for you." Ollie said, smiling.

Eve walked out from a shadow that was behind Ollie, her wings lined up straight out behind her. She came over to me and stood right in front of me with her white robe flowing like white milk in a commercial. I was completely mesmerized by her. I have never seen elves before and was kind of let down when I did. When I saw her, though, she was possibly the most beautiful creature I have ever seen, aside from Alyssa. She had a glow on her that was like sunset, making you want to go to Heaven right now just to sit next to her until eternity reached its end. It felt like that was going to be soon but as time slowed down as she walked, I realized that wouldn't be that bad.

"Please sit down." Eve said, sounding like a chorus all by herself.

I sat in the chair that was behind me, nearly slipping off the front of it as I did. As I did, Eve put her hands on my head. This was either going to be a strange angel thing or the best lap dance in the history of the universe.

"Close your eyes." Eve said calmly. It was like I was in a trance, my eyes just closed without thinking about it. "I want all of you to close your eyes. When this begins, you will all see what he sees. He will need reassurance that someone else in the world knows what has been trapped in there all this time."

I couldn't pull away even though I really wanted to. I wanted to but didn't want to, all at the same time. On one hand, she was a hot angel that was holding me in a trance. I haven't had a woman touch me in a long time. On the other hand, from the sounds of it she was going to steal my thoughts and broadcast them to whoever was tuned in. What kind of angel was this?

Everyone around closed their eyes, Alyssa not really wanting to either. She hesitantly closed her eyes. Our options of getting out of here consisted of doing this little circus stunt so I guess I would oblige.

"Will, angels aren't what you think." Eve whispered. "We are born in severe pain. It is the same pain that comes to us every time we spread our wings. We were created in a way that the pain that we feel reaffirms the life that we want for everyone. In turn, your pain will make you realize that there's a life for you beyond it."

"No." I whined, under my breath. I couldn't seem to find breath in my lungs. "You can't broadcast my mind without my express written consent!"

"Will, you need to let your pain be your guide. Accept it and move on. Pain is a permanent part of all worlds, not just here. You have to deal with it or it will deal with you and if that starts to happen it rarely turns out good. This isn't like playing baseball, Will. Trust me, it won't hurt a bit and you have to believe that no one will chastise you for anything that we see."

She stopped talking and started singing lightly into the air. The notes ran through my head as they did when I was a child. She was singing my favorite Christmas song, *Silent Night*. It rushed through me as everyone in town turned quiet. Outside I heard a few voices near the window, starting to sing along. My mind ran like an old nickelodeon projector, showing old movies of me in front of my eyelids. They all looked old and I couldn't figure out who was holding the camera. Why didn't I notice him or her through my whole life?

I shook my head, trying to break free of Eve's hold on me. She held on even tighter as her singing grew a little louder.

*In my mind all I saw was me. I was a little kid, maybe eight years old, I don't really remember and I can't tell by the horrible eighties hairstyle. I was up in New Jersey and it was Christmas Eve. My aunt and uncle and grandmother were there, Uncle Frank was there. My brothers and sisters were there. It almost felt like I was sitting in my old living room but at the same time I knew was at Ollie's.* Silent Night *was still echoing through my head.*

*One by one the guests started to disappear, filing out the front door at the end of the night. My mind was working through the movie quickly. I watched myself follow them out, standing in the snow, and as the cars were pulling away there wasn't a sound to be heard except for the family stereo in the house playing the same song that was escaping Eve's beautiful lips. I felt goose bumps on my arms. I always loved Christmas Eve and the odd stereo effect of the same song from two different people was very strange, to say the least.*

*I saw now my mom and dad fighting with my aunt and uncle. Later on there were phone calls and loud voices. I couldn't place when this was but I remember that they went on not talking for two years.*

*I saw my best friend, Becky, sprawled out on a couch at her house with stitches in her head. I remembered trying to recreate a Dave Winfield play from a Yankees game I was just watching and hitting her in the head with the broken bottom end of a wiffle ball bat. The jagged edge was worn, hard plastic, jutting up in jagged shards like a primeval weapon. I was apologizing to her, feeling incredibly bad for a nine year-old, having broken her head open in my back yard.*

*I saw my family leaving for another house. My dad got a job being the minister in a new church somewhere else in the state. I remember saying goodbye to the best friend I could ever have, Becky. I saw myself crying that I wouldn't talk to her again. I think I felt a tear on my cheek while I sat in Ollie's room, rolling down towards my mouth. I always thought, even at a young age, that we would be inseparable until we were old but that thought ended pretty quickly.*

*My head started shaking violently when the next image came to me. I was around eleven years old. I was with my friend who had epilepsy. He would have seizures all the time, convulsing for no reason, scaring people who didn't understand it. I saw us going into someone's house as the snow melted outside.*

*It was the beginning of spring; I had my denim jacket on and was ready for anything. The man was balding and wore big glasses, looking like a computer tech guy that had a nervous tick. I saw him bolt the door behind us. He said that he had some stuff that he wanted to give us. I remember the damned ski goggles. He said* that he had some new ski goggles and what kid in the world wouldn't want some cool new shit? I saw him reaching for my friend, massaging his neck. His hands slid down to his midsection as my friend started to go into one of his seizures.

I was telling the bald computer man to stop, yelling at him as I was trying to stop the urge to vomit. My stomach hurt and I was nauseous, like going on to a roller coaster for the first time.

I saw myself pushing my friend out of the way and inadvertently taking my friend's place. The bald man with big glasses took himself out of his pants, whispering at me to touch it. He was sweating and smelled bad and I couldn't stop shaking as he stared at me through his magnifying glasses. He whispered it again to me, closer to my ear, the air from his evil breath hitting me in the ear. His hand was wandering down into my midsection as he whispered. I was frozen in terror. He grabbed my hand and moved it towards him. He kept whispering things in my ear, each puff of air hitting me like an unwanted bug.

I didn't look at any part of him. I would die if I had to. I held my hand back as much as I could but he's strong and sadly I am a weak little string bean of a kid. The monster man was sweating like a deranged devil. I saw my friend getting out of his seizure, running out the back door. The bald man tried to stop him, running after him quickly. I ran to the front door, unbolting it and running out.

Minutes later I met up with my friend down the block. I looked down. I had pissed my pants; the puddle on my crotch went almost down to my feet! The whole front of me was wet. It wasn't in there when it happened. I know that I pissed my pants because I couldn't tell my dad. As a minister's son we were expected to be perfect kids so the consistory didn't look at him badly as a guy who raised a demon child. I was a minister's son who was just told to touch a man's manhood against his will would look really bad to My Father, his son, and the good old Holy Ghost. I didn't touch it or didn't even look at it but still, the event itself was not something that a Child of God would have done. No, a Child of God would not even let temptation get in the way to bring me there in the first place.

I didn't want to let him down so I tucked it far from my memory. My friend had no recollection while in his seizure state so my secret was safe for now. At least my friend got out of it without him being hurt. I saw myself praying for God to make it right and have that bastard hit by a bus but it never happened. I guess it was punishment for letting temptation guide me or something.

I was now looking at myself at the age of fourteen. My brothers and sisters and I were in a music video, shot by my aunt and uncle. We were all just acting like asses, singing to "I Heard It Through the Grapevine" and other classics being played by a vinyl LP. I remember that being the last time we were actually what you would call close. My brothers all went on a trip to Europe, my day was coming, and I knew *it. It never did. There was no trip except for the journey to Florida. I saw myself saying goodbye once again to all of my new friends in New Jersey, never to see them again from The Sunshine State. The pattern was beginning to unfold in front of me. The close ones always go away and the others try to steal innocence and there's no one to talk to without being judged by a higher authority. And the family that you have normally shelves things to avoid the feeling you need to share because anything that is out in the open is up for scrutiny by God and His/Her many followers. I remember continually telling the higher authority to fuck off for a long time after that.*

My tears were rolling down my face. The vomit was making a home at the base of my throat, daring me to let it out.

*I was talking to my guidance counselor in my new Florida High School. He was talking to my dad about my entrance scores on the entrance test I just had taken. I heard him say I wasn't really smart according to the State of Florida. He said I would most likely be a bricklayer for the rest of my life so he recommended remedial classes to get me by until I graduated and made my meager way in life, not living up to what he did for a living. I remember him saying, "What's the Point in frustrating yourself when you know that it's above you?"*

*It was about that time that I was enjoying my first cigarette with my friend and it stuck with me ever since. My mind switched to me smoking my first joint at the age of fourteen. And then my second and my mind was one big bong hit, a lot of pot in a lot of compacted high school hours. I had to at least numb my future of placing bricks in a foundation that I couldn't give two shits about.*

*I looked at myself at sixteen and watched as I was playing in a band, playing the bass guitar. I saw my friend Chris playing guitar. I saw him telling me that they are going with a new bassist for a little concert we were having before the talent show, the one that we were practicing for all this time. I watched me cry to my girlfriend that he was saying that she was getting in the way, which wasn't true. I am not good enough, I was told all the time! He wanted me out of the band, end of story. He was a great friend and he didn't want me playing with him. That hurt, considering that I saved up and bought a bass so he could teach me and I could be in his band in the first place.*

*Later on from that time was when I caught my girlfriend with two of my other friends, into the foreplay stage with both of them at the same time. I did play the concert though, I even sang my fist song to an audience and Chris and I became greater friends, along with Billy the drummer. We were inseparable from that point on.*

*I was watching myself drinking a lot of whiskey with a joint chaser until I got to the point of passing out. I was only sixteen or so at the time. I was passed out on a buddies couch, sleeping off a bender to end all benders. I saw me wake up with his fat fucking father trying to get his hand down my pants as he tried jerking himself off.*

*Luckily he never got that accomplished. I thought of the bald man with glasses and threw up all over his floor. I woke up and swaggered all drunk to the door, stumbling into the street. I saw me leaving, smoking a lot of weed on the way home, outside and all. I filed fat fuck with computer nerd and headed home to finish my joint in the confines of my used 1970 Ford Mustang with the black hood.*

*I saw myself drinking a lot in High School. I was smoking a lot. I was taking a hit of weed followed by a chaser of speed. They were yellow jackets, to be exact. I mean, how much did I really have to apply myself to lay bricks? At this time, I was lowly entering the fun-filled world of porn. I figured I would let them do all the fucking and deal with all of the bullshit that followed. I got what I needed from them without the feelings attached.*

*I saw me getting kicked and hit in the face until it felt like my stomach was imploding. I saw blood drooling from my mouth, spewing onto the floor of my liberal arts math class. Football players said that all around they didn't like the way I looked at them in the hallway. I didn't feel much because I was too stoned. I felt it the next day but when it happened, I didn't care. So I smoked more to numb the pain. I hid it from everyone, I have no idea how I got away with it but I did.*

*I saw myself graduating and not giving two shits about it. I only wanted to see a few people again. The rest could go to fucking hell. I saw myself in college, the same thing as before: weed, whiskey, cigarettes and speed. Every day I wanted to destroy myself. The one good thing about it was me making a film for one of my classes and getting a standing ovation for the unconventional way that it was filmed.*

My head started shaking violently again. I really wanted to throw up but didn't want to dirty the angel's robe.

*I was looking at my good friend Chris. We were finishing up a musical play we wrote at Perkins. We were well out of college and I didn't ever lay a brick in my life. At one point, we dated two sisters and were all inseparable.*

*It was late night, two o'clock. We finished and he said he was depressed. I asked if he needed anything and he said no, he'd get over whatever it was that he needed and that he would be okay. In the recent past, he was on some acid and tried to file all of his teeth out. He since had a new smile and a new outlook, so his depression seemed like nothing more than him having a bad day.*

*The next morning, I watched myself answering a phone call from my dad, who was a counselor at that point, and said that Chris shot himself in the head, my musical equipment used to tie up the mattress. I saw myself crying badly and took the best course I could. I strayed into unknown territory and bought myself some cocaine.*

*I saw myself and was looking like a mess. People were always trying to take advantage of me or telling me I wasn't good enough for the life that I remembered.*

*They always dismissed me. I was losing people around me, the ones who knew me the best, gone with a bullet twenty minutes after I talked to him. If we were there just five minutes more…who knows? Things could have been different. I could have done something, read between the lines. The people who were going to put on the play dropped out of it so it went with all of my unfinished projects with unfinished friends.*

*I saw streams of girls coming and going, all cheating on me, each one I cared less and less about as time went on. One guy actually beat my ass because he was in love with her. She took his side and I just eventually numbed over the whole thing. That's when I hopped up on some pills, not wanting to wake up in the morning. The idea was implanted in me that I was unlovable; I was something that no one could connect to. I still had a lot to give, but it was nothing that anyone wanted. Everyone that looked at me had the look that I was some sort of a freak. They looked at me like they knew all of the skeletons in my closet personally and just played around until the said skeletons introduced themselves and scared them off. That was the point where they would run for the fucking hills to get away from me.*

*I filed it all away as I got high and got more and more addicted to porn. They couldn't hurt me! They weren't real to me like that. Let them have sex and deal with it. The best part of any relationship was in front of me and I could rewind any time I wanted to. Rewind, repeat, throw out the tissues when I'm finished. And through all of this, my family thought I was happy go lucky so good times. What they don't know can't hurt them. I was fucking up for God and God alone, He or She would be the only judge, not some asshole who thinks he has a direct connection to him.*

*And then, from out of nowhere, I was sitting alone in a room. There was one light on and I was thinking that I needed to straighten myself out before I was actually confirmed dead. My family communicates by not communicating so I decided they don't need to know what I've been through. I have always had to put on a good face to not show anyone that my family was human and not so perfect mostly in the name of God, so I would keep that face on. I constructed these walls around my mental filing system and held the only key. I have always had a great sense of humor and timing, so that was the Will that everyone would get. I was starting fresh, the man with a peachy past joining society with a fabricated smile on my face.*

Eve slowly stopped singing as she took her hands off of my head. I opened my eyes and saw Alyssa staring at me, looking completely disgusted. I don't know if it was sympathy or repulsion. Uncle Frank was crying and Ollie had his small head in his tiny little hands. Eve just stared at me with sad eyes, sadder than you would think an angel would have been.

"Will, I am so sorry. I had no idea." Uncle Frank walked over and put his hand on my shoulder.

"It's not your fault, Uncle Frank." I said through wobbly tears. "I just want to be left alone for a few minutes."

The room emptied and I proceeded to throw up all over the floor, crying through each heave. Everything was leaving me tonight, not to mention the bagel I ate a long time ago. I just wanted to stay here and not see anyone ever again. If this was God's way of making me a better person, His or Her track record was not far from the gauntlet that I've been put through the past thirty years.

# Twenty-Eight

I slowly made my way to the middle of the main strip known as Wonderland. I had no idea how I made it out of Ollie's house in the first place, I don't remember doing any of it. I was wandering around in a complete and total daze. I had no concept of anything that was going on around me; it was all a complete blue-white blur in front of me. All I remember hearing was the choir somewhere behind me, Silent Night finally becoming silent again, the sole sound of crunching snow as the entire population surrounded me.

The entire Old Town population encircled me and held hands. All of the elves, Eve, Uncle Frank and Alyssa all held me in the center, most of them staring down into the snow except Alyssa. She was staring at me like she would a stranger who had elaborate ideas of hurting her. If she saw the same things that were in my mind, she's looking at someone completely different than the asshole she flew up here with. I was a completely different entity.

People seem to change when you know all there is to know about them. I had no idea why she was looking at me so differently. Hell, she wanted to know all of this back in the cabin and I knew it would change her so I spared it. How come people want to know everything and judge you later for it?

I didn't like the look she was giving me but was indifferent to it at the same time. I was somewhat used to being looked at like an outsider.

I had no idea what anyone was doing; they just held me there in the center of this crazy circle. The only thing I could think of was that Eve was mentally connected to the whole population and they all saw what was in my mind in simultaneous broadcasting. Normally I would think of it as an invasion of privacy but the strange thing was that I really didn't mind. They knew it all and they stood there surrounding me, making me feel awkwardly safe for a reason I didn't even want to contemplate. And the weird thing about it was that no one besides Alyssa seemed to be judging me.

Suddenly an elf ran into the middle of the circle, running wildly until he hit my leg, which inadvertently knocked him over into the snow.

I looked down and he looked vaguely familiar to me. When I leaned down to his face I noticed that it was Stan. I completely forgot that they were even here. It's been a weird trip since the valley.

"I am sorry I tried to kill you, Mr. Will." Stan babbled, still huddled in the snow, nestling himself in as he started to make a snow angel in the snow beneath him.

"Did you see too?" I asked, tears rolling down my face.

"We all did." Mort was standing behind me. "I too would like to apologize for putting you two through what we did."

"Why?" I asked. Were they on drugs?

"I tried not to see but was unsuccessful." Mort said. "When I saw what you were looking at again I realized how you lost your faith, Will Foster."

Mort looked straight up at me.

"I didn't realize that that is what I turned into also." Mort said. "The only difference is that greed was my reason, but it paled in comparison to what I saw in your head. I have never had any events happen to me like the ones I saw from you and it made me realize that what I was doing was pretty petty."

"Thank you, Mort." I was completely crying right now, I was barely able to hold it in.

It's one thing to have my live drama broadcast to everyone, but it's a completely different feeling when you have it become the basis for someone else to find their way or purpose in life, however it may work. It was the most flattering justification and acceptance that I had always wanted from someone. I never knew I wanted it until Mort opened his mouth. He tried to kill me a few times and I changed that just by what happened? Who could have known?

"All I wanted was for someone to understand." I said aloud to the circle, sniffing tears as they were produced. "No one ever seemed to care enough to hear my stories, no less help me through them so I stopped letting people in." The tears were coming out as if my eyes were defective garden hoses on full blast. "The stupid guidance counselor and his track team."

"You don't have to keep us out anymore, Will." Uncle Frank said solemnly, compassionately. "We will never turn our backs on you. I give you my word on that. The rest of the family is up to you, but now someone in that family understands why you are who you are, even if they don't."

"We are all behind you Will." Eve said, her skin still glowing like sunset. "You will be just fine. There are millions of people just like you and I think it's time that they found out that there still is some faith in the world and in a higher power, whatever that translates into personally. There are people who would understand, you just have to be persistent and patient in finding them."

Alyssa kept her head down, still not believing that I am the same man that she saw just yesterday.

I tried to compose myself. "Whatever you need me to do, I will. I think I understand why I am here, Uncle Frank. It could have been anybody else but I was the only connection with the outside world, through you."

Uncle Frank nodded. "That's not the only reason, Will. Hopefully you will find out when this is all over."

I looked over at Alyssa. For some strange reason I got this feeling that we would never be the same again. I respected her so much from the time that I knew her. I respected her whole family so much. But the look on her face tells me that she didn't like the Will that she saw every day. We got along incredibly well with each other. It was almost like we've known each other for fifty years but that was the "me" that was visible. Everything I am was composed of the experiences I have been in, and I could just see it in her eyes that she liked me more when she didn't know anything about me.

It was the first moment of clarity I have ever had about Alyssa. We got along like a married couple but she didn't know me at all. Her looking into the snow just told me that she had no intention of ever wanting to know more about me and it hurt but I understood. She wanted to know just to know, not to actually accept it.

My chest hurt and my stomach was in knots thinking that the one woman I would do anything for and loved with all my heart could care less about who I was or who I am. I never intended to steal the girl or anything. She has a family for God's sake. And the look on her face like I was just a creepy guy she worked for made me want to throw up again.

I walked up to Alyssa and lifted her chin. "I know you didn't like what you saw."

"I didn't ask for it!" She snapped back.

"Either did I. Well, you kind of did. Remember the cabin?"

I smiled a little, hoping she'd catch on.

"But it's there now and we have to deal with it." I said.

What I really meant was that I was going to deal with it. Her face told me that it would be forgotten once she was back in civilization.

"Listen, I need your help." I said. "Whether you like me enough to do it or you think I'm some sort of a basket case, I'll understand either way. I am going to promise you one thing though. I will get you home where you belong by Christmas morning." One last tear left the factory. "I told you that I would do anything for you and I will come through, whether I live or die doing it."

"Will, listen." Alyssa said. Her voice was so soft it was almost inaudible. "I will help you do this but I am going to need some time to figure this all out. I mean it's like the gut that I've know for so long is a total stranger. It's like dating a guy and finding out he's been a serial killer for the past five years."

"I'm not a serial killer, Alyssa." I said.

"I know." She returned.

"But it was like we were dating?" I asked, smiling.

She smiled at me. "You're a dork. You know what I meant."

"Can you figure it all out when we're done?" I asked, smiling a little bit more.

"Sure." She said flatly.

"Please, just trust me. I am the same guy as before, okay?" I knew I never would be, but now wasn't the time to tell her that.

Alyssa nodded. As she did a loud bang erupted from behind us. I heard something whizzing through the air between Alyssa and me. We followed the direction of the split-second sound and saw that Eve had a red stain on her robe, growing from the center by the second. All of the elves gasped in unison.

It appeared that she has been shot. Within seconds the color ran from her face, turning sunset into moonlight as she fell to the ground. Number Five jumped down from a rooftop and ran into the broken circle, waving her gun everywhere.

"That's what you get when you're an angel that steals a gun." Number Five yelled at Eve, who was still breathing into the snow.

"And do you know what happens when you kill an angel?" Uncle Frank asked Number Five.

"What, does Heaven open up and unleash holy hell on me for all eternity?" Number Five smiled. "That's fine. In my business, it's all just endless purgatory. I deal in death every day, so I'm doomed anyway and I know my way around."

"It's not quite like that." Uncle Frank said, popping his neck from one side to another. "What you get is a thousand screwed-over elves with nothing else to lose. They all have something in common though. The angels are their best friends and have been for a long time. So in my opinion I would run before your clip runs out. You can't kill us all or save yourself, but I'm going to make damn sure that you do not leave here with her body."

Without hesitating, Number Five shot Uncle Frank in the shoulder, sending him down in a pool of yelps and groans and blood spatter all over the snow.

"Uncle Frank!" I yelled at the top of my lungs, running over to him quickly.

Alyssa ran up to Number Five, fast enough to almost qualify it as a sprint and hit her so hard as she turned around that Number Five did almost a complete three-sixty in the air before she hit the ground.

"He was my friend, you bitch!" Alyssa stared down at her like Muhammad Ali in that famous photo, waiting for her to get up on the seven count. After seeing for herself that Number Five was not going to attempt it, Alyssa grabbed the gun and ran over to Uncle Frank, placing her hand on his shoulder. He screamed for a quick second as Alyssa held the gun firmly in the direction of Number Five's sweating head.

"I don't know what came over me!" Alyssa said with a smile as wide as a continent. "That was pretty cool, huh?"

The ring on her finger was pulsing blue as she kept it on Uncle Frank's shoulder. Uncle Frank felt the cold pulses go through him but insisted in his mind that it was merely shock. As the pulses increased, Alyssa noticed the bullet slowly climbing out of his skin.

Her mouth was open wide, not believing that she was actually doing this. Within ten seconds the bullet popped out and fell in the snow, the blood crawling back into his skin. I looked at his shoulder and the only thing out of place was the nine-millimeter hole in his clothes and the dried blood that seemed to have come from nowhere.

"What the hell was that?" Uncle Frank asked, happy as hell about cheating death but confused on the mechanics of it all.

"It was the Christmas spirit, Frank." Eve said, standing up and smoothing out her robe. "That ring holds the last of it. Is it gone?" Frank got over being alive more quickly than anyone would in that position.

"How are you walking around, Eve?" I asked Eve.

"You check on me now?" Eve raised an eyebrow. "I could have been dead, for all you knew. Man, now I'm going to have to comp the receipt for the dry cleaning."

"But my uncle..." I started.

"He's family. Instinct took over. It's okay, believe me." Eve was still trying to fix her robe, laughing a little at my expense. I guess it was angel humor, I had no idea. "Plus, due to design and divination, the pain is real but temporary. It is virtually impossible for a human to kill an angel." She smiled like a coy eighteen year-old that just conned her dad into giving her his car keys. "There should still be enough spirit left for us to finish everything."

"I think it's time we came up with a plan." I said. Time was running down and there was a lot to do before tomorrow night.

I turned to Alyssa.

"That was impressive, Alyssa." I said. "Scary as hell but impressive all the same."

"Thanks." She said to me with a hidden smile that she perfected long ago.

# Twenty Nine

Kris Kringle sat in his cell, staring out on the snow bank towards Old Town again just like every night. Through all of the years he's been sitting in here, the scenery never changed. The only movement he has seen previous to today was an elf on a dogsled heading south. Kris guessed that someone went for help because the charter plane was heard numerous times over in Old Town doing whatever.

At first he thought he was going crazy but then he realized that all of his friends, his family, were surviving. Granted not by a lot, but they were surviving. He restricted his wife from giving him any details on anything because fear, or insanity, told him that maybe the room was bugged. If not by Frost's technology, it would be actual bugs taking the information to him. This is why he demanded that she go into hiding until all of this was over, one way or another. They could kill Kris but he'd be damned if they hurt his wife.

This wasn't normally the fashion in which Kris' mind was wired to work. He was always fair and balanced in the way that the business was handled around the world, contrary to what was contrived to send him to this hell. He was wired for happiness and peace and now was consumed by conspiracies and spy work that he has become the victim of. He occasionally worried that he would never get that back if he got out of here or if he was going to be completely nuts for the remainder of his waking life. The drugs didn't have nearly the effect that sheer insanity did. They didn't have any effect at all but the scratches, clicks and pops and multiple voices that bombarded his senses seemed normal to him now, the absence of any one of them at any time made his mind flip into conspiracy theory mode.

In the hierarchy of all things related to the Christmas world, Kris was mentally tuned in with the choir of angels. They used to help him decipher the Naughty and Nice list, going back at the half year mark sometime in June. They went all over the world to make a second assessment on the population, to see if they tipped the scales the other way, either from Naughty to Nice or vice versa.

Children were exempt until the age of thirteen when legally they were regarded as teenagers. Once they are no longer children, the world starts taking its toll, swaying their minds into the pressures of life. This is generally where the lack of belief comes into play and the core audience makes way for a new generation of believers, based on what the previous generation teaches them to believe. The basis of everything he has ever done was that the children will keep the spirit alive to give to their own children.

Through the rusted metal bars he heard Eve chanting Silent Night a while ago. He would not mistake her voice for anything in the world. No matter how crazy he was to become her voice was the only true beacon of hope that he's heard in a long time, aside from his wife. He didn't flinch at all, his stare not wavering from Old Town while he crunched a cockroach under his battered black boot. He smiled grimly as he smashed the informant into an early hell.

As he listened, he heard the most amazing sound. Eve was still echoing over the vast field between Old Town and crazy town when she was accompanied by the remainder of the elves in the community, however many of them were left. They repeated the song twice, all the way through. For the first time in years, Kris felt like he was sitting in his chair, listening to the weekly caroling that they enjoyed doing throughout the year. Hot cocoa and families singing in harmony kept the spirits up when the work load became heavy due to the ever-increasing population.

On this night Kris felt human again. His ninety something pound frame felt as jolly as it always was. His beard lost all of the dirt and grime, shuffling with every move of his head. He remembered laughter, belly rolls of it, filling the night with fun and happiness for no other reason than it was the right thing to do. He laughed at himself, thinking that at least with his new look, climbing down chimneys shouldn't be a problem ever again. At least there was some light in his deluded mental tunnel.

He closed his eyes and was completely lost in the carol. He was so lost that he didn't hear the knock on the door. He ignored the multitude of keys hitting all of the tumblers in all of the locks that would bring in the enemy.

Kris didn't care that it was time for his prep. They were going to try to take his mind tonight, but for now he was going to enjoy the beauty from across the snowy field in front of him. It might be the last sound he ever hears, so he thought he would revel in it until his mind gets taken.

# Thirty

We were all standing in the cold, in the middle of the main strip of Old Town, Wonderland Road. We were congregated there for some long minutes, tossing around some ideas on the best way to get things done before Jack and his crew started to hit us hard. They wouldn't normally be scared, but trying to off an angel took something that not everyone possesses, something that no one should really want to possess in the first place. Jack possessed that and was definitely someone that I would rather not have the pleasure of meeting in my lifetime.

"We need to mount some sort of a defense." Uncle Frank said. "We know that they're coming and we need to be ready."

"How are we going to do that?" Ollie asked. "We're weak, Frank. We don't have enough to fight back against the weapons they have. We haven't eaten a good meal in weeks and I don't think we have the actual energy. Unless, of course, you find it lethal to throw snowballs at them."

"You may have everything you need right here." I looked all around them. "Listen, when I first came here, I wanted nothing to do with any of this. Now that we've come this far, I saw who you were as people…"

"Elves." Ollie corrected me.

"People." I said back to him. "We're all living creatures that walk and talk. Some of us kick others in the shins."

Wedge looked into the snow, ashamed that he had that little tick.

"Whatever the case is, you found a way to maintain." I said. "Sure, you haven't had the best luck in the world, but you stayed true to who you are and maybe that's all that we need right now. You've already stood up to this prick, so I see it as that you've already rattled his cage. The ball is in our court."

"I am not sure I understand." Ollie said.

"What is it that you all did before all of this shit started happening?" I asked, circling around to incorporate every one into my rhetorical question. "You built toys. You built games and nutcrackers. Who's to say that we can't build more of that to take him on? I mean, beat him with who you are?"

"Like we can stop bullets with wood? Are you crazy, man?" One of the elves around the circle asked, like he was starting an uprising of his own. "The toys are for children and have no offensive things on them. We're not dealing with eager five year-olds here. These are mercenaries. We don't even put shooting parts on the toys for fear of hurting the children. We don't believe in violence."

"They are mercenaries with no imagination." I said to the crowd. "It's all money and all that crap with them. They like power but lack the imagination to keep it." I replied like I had this in my head since I was ten years old. "They are easy to beat because they're a cliché of every stupid war movie I've ever seen. I'm sure they have no military training. Is there any way we can make remote control units?"

"We have no power, Will." Ollie stated so low that it was hard to understand. "There is no way we can fabricate all of that without power."

"I'm sure you can find a way." I said like a commanding officer. "What I'm thinking is forty nutcrackers, twenty feet tall, remote controlled from back here. In front of them, twenty toy soldiers of the same height. Remote controlled just the same, by the team in the back." I smiled at the cool absurdity of the thought in my mind. "And they need to fire ice balls."

"We can't hurt anyone. It's not in our nature." Ollie said. "Plus, we'll only have time to wire the toy soldiers with the people we have here."

"Then how is it possible that they could hurt people if you can't?" I asked, trying to figure out the loophole.

"I mean we could but we all took an oath that we couldn't. It's against everything we stand for." Ollie stated.

"Okay, so we need twenty volunteers to steer the nutcrackers." I looked around the group, hoping they'd take the hint. I just let it go that they vowed to never hurt anyone in hopes that they'd come around when they were actually in danger.

"I'll take one!" Stan said in his near-incoherent babble. "Ooh, a nutcracker pilot!"

Twenty other elves raised their hands, volunteering to steer the nutcrackers on the lines, jumping up and down like lunatics with too much caffeine in their system.

"Is there a way that we can make these in an hour?" I asked.

"If it's made with wood, we can do it." Ollie said confidently. He grabbed the lapels of his jacket and raised his head proud, rocking back and forth on his little feet.

"Great." I said, turning to the crowd. "I need all available elves to go to the shop and start building. Nutcrackers! There will be one for each volunteer!"

The elves suddenly scattered and ran to their houses to get their tools. They were all cheering and whistling, obviously happy to have a reason to build something again.

"I think we need to have them lined with steel plating." Uncle Frank said, turning his gaze to Ollie. "Is The Welder still living here? I haven't seen him in a while."

"Yeah, he got all crazy on all sorts of theories about governmental takeover and global warming that he's convinced that the North Pole is going to be washed away when the ice caps melt. I keep trying to convince him that it's a con job presented by Frost to sell more crap around the world but he insists. Hell, Frost puts out enough energy to melt them himself and still goes on about going green. The Welder is in a bunker somewhere under the town in case it slides away in a flood. He's gone a little crazy, in my opinion." Ollie looked away, slightly embarrassed that they had a resident nutcase underground.

"I have not!" The Welder said from behind them, wearing his face shield. He was walking down the path towards the group. "I heard all of the singing and cheering up here and I heard a gun. I just came up to see if the apocalypse was here, you guys knocked part of my ceiling down! I thought the warming was happening so I was ready to ride the planet into oblivion!"

"Global warming has been happening since there was a globe. Nothing's changed Welder." Uncle Frank said. "Except the number of people who are convincing you that you're going to die from it."

"No, we're taking it back." Ollie said. "We're taking back the Pole tonight."

"Call it fate, Mr. Welder," I said, "but we were just talking about you. We need your help. We need to plate twenty some nutcrackers with steel. They're around twenty feet tall. Some toy soldiers too."

"Now that's what I'm talking about! We're building an army!" The Welder flipped up his shield. "Call me Tig, by the way. When do we get started? I already have an ark built to save us from the melting, so this is no problem."

"Right now!" Ollie said. "Head to the shop, the rest of the crew is on their way. We only have a few hours."

"Good times, brother." Tig flipped his shield down and saluted us all in classic military form. "Can they shoot anything?" He laughed under the glass plated shield, running off to start his work. "Please tell me yes."

"Is there anything else we can do?" Ollie asked, dismissing The Welder's military pride. "How do you we get Santa out? What else do we have in addition to Nutcrackers and toy soldiers? It doesn't seem like a good defense. There has to be something else, a lot of lives are at stake out here."

"We need something that can withstand bullet fire and not get hurt. Any ideas?" I asked the remaining core if the group.

"Reindeer?" Alyssa asked.

"I don't want to get them hurt. Plus, there are only nine of them plus the Southies. They wouldn't be as effective, even though they can fly. Plus, I might need them later."

I had no idea why these things were coming to me so easily. I was excited and freaked out, sounding like a convincing impromptu general.

"What about snowmen?" I asked.

"Our intel told us that Frosty was melted. He's in a jar on Frost's desk." Ollie was upset and hurt about the loss of their longtime singing ball of snow. "Plus, we need the magician to make his hat magic again. Problem is that the magician has been missing for years after stealing all of the hats from his family."

Eve piped up for the first time since she was shot. "There's a magician who works the casino. He's modeled himself to be like Criss Angel but is far from a Mindfreak. If we can get him we can put the spell on anything we want. We would need Frosty at the same time though. But, Frost's office is impossible to get into. There's only one way up and you need clearance to get in. Either that or you need some serious reason that you need to go up there quickly. I can't do it, they're already after me. My cover is completely blown. Plus Manny wouldn't let me in, considering that I knocked him out earlier." Eve looked directly into the snow.

"We have no reason to get up there." I said, grimly. I just started this, but it was long enough to be pissed off and slightly disappointed when some part of a plan didn't make sense.

Stan walked up behind Alyssa and pulled on the bottom of her jacket. She jumped a little, not fully trusting him since he tried to assault her chest. He pulled on her jacket again like a kid waiting for her to buy him something from a toy store.

"What?" Alyssa snapped. "I thought you were going to drive a nutcracker. You still want to do that, right?"

"Oh, yeah. I just have to say that we were sent to find you." Stan said. "Boobies! We were sent to get you and bring you to Frost! Sorry about trying to get your boobies!"

"What is he saying?" Alyssa snapped. She wasn't mad. She just couldn't understand how his mind worked and somewhere in her mind didn't want her chest to be attacked again.

Mort jumped to Stan's side. "What he's saying is that Frost has no idea that we aren't working for him. We could bring Alyssa in and get her in that office." Mort put Stan's head in a head lock and gave him a nice brotherly noogie. "Good job, kid. I knew you had it in you."

"Stan, I owe you dinner." I said. "Is there any way I can get to Santa?" I asked the rest of the group, probing for ideas.

"Whoa, what if Frost kills me?" Alyssa asked, pissed off to the furthest degree that she would have to step in this deep.

"He won't." Mort said. "I won't let that happen. Plus, if Will has the ring, he will use you to get to him. Trust me, we've done this before. Not to mention that I think Stan would take about nine bullets to keep you safe."

"That's what scares the shit out of me." She said, deciding not to fight anymore. She was in this no matter what the consequence. If she bailed out now, she would be letting down all the hard work suddenly happening around here. She wouldn't let me do that before and she sure wasn't going to do the same thing now. I wasn't either, regardless of her lack of personal feelings for me.

"The only way I can figure is getting some ID from a doctor to get you into the hospital." Ollie said. "All you have to do is get past the nurse at check in. After that, Santa is no problem."

Ollie was still rocking on his little feet.

"We know an elf working the casino." Ollie said. "She's a hooker named Candy Cane. I could tell you why she picked that name, but I'm sure you could figure it out." Ollie smirked at his joke. None of us were in the mood to get it. "She pulls tricks with doctors and lawyers all the time. She can swipe one from you, but you'll have to pay her."

"I am not sleeping with an elf hooker." I said. "I may be neurotic and watched a lot of porn in my life, but an elf hooker just isn't my thing."

"When you see her, tell her 'take the Pole back'." Ollie said, not embarrassed at all that he even knew this lingo. Maybe there was more to Ollie that met the eye. "That's the code phrase we use when we share intel. It's not my thing either, Will Foster, even though we are the same kind."

"Share intel?" Uncle Frank looked at him like he watched too many movies about the CIA and FBI. This wasn't the same elf that he knew. He has morphed into a small version of Hannibal from the *A-Team*. My guess was that he loves it when a plan comes together.

"Okay, I'll handle getting Santa out. Where do we need to go?" I asked, not knowing how to reverse this whole thing when all was said and done.

"Peary's Point." Ollie stated. "Robert Peary was the first person to discover the North Pole back on April sixth, nineteen hundred and six. Later, Frederick Cook challenged Peary, saying that he found it first. In nineteen hundred and eleven, the United States congress gave the credit to Peary because he actually was the one who found it. Luckily for us, Frost didn't follow up on the outcome from Congress, or merely forgot about it."

"So Frost is not technically on the North Pole?" I asked, wondering where this was going.

"His casino is on Cook's Pole. Rumor has it that he fell a little short of Peary during the whole development thing. So, all in all, his casino technically isn't on the North Pole. He's a little south. Every Christmas the North Star shines a beam of light onto the actual North Pole, where we would generally draw our energy for our global deliveries. No one knows about that but us, so if you please, can you keep it that way?"

I guessed all of Ollie's reading paid off. After all of this was over I intend on sitting down with him for a nice conversation about whatever crossed our minds.

"So why didn't you draw the energy from it before to give you power here?" Uncle Frank asked, wondering why he was shuttling food to them when they have a natural power source about a half mile away.

Ollie cleared his throat. "The energy from the star requires a balancing element. It is no good on its own. It needs to have a reactive agent to make the energy effective. Not to mention we would rather not call that much attention to it."

"Is it Christmas spirit?" I asked, stating the suddenly obvious.

"Yes." Ollie said. "The stuff that's in the ring as well as the spirit that is in Santa's bloodstream. Those mixed together should do the trick."

"Is there a contingency plan?" Uncle Frank asked.

Eve piped up again. "My sister is running a story in the paper. I've been feeding her inside information on all business holdings, mergers and guidelines that Frost has set up around the world for the past three years. She is doing a first-ever worldwide telecast to show this all in the event that we fail. Either way Jack Frost is going down in the eyes of the world. If not like Eliot Ness would have it, then he'll be tried like Al Capone. He may think he's impervious to all of the world's forces but when they find out how he put them all out of business, they will all come hunting for his head. You can take my word for it."

"But if we miss tonight he gets put away but nothing changes. The world will feel the effect but everyone here will be lost. Jack Frost has been their only lifeline even as an insane asshole. They need the prick." Uncle Frank said. "No matter how much they want to deny it."

"We won't miss tonight." I added, more enthusiastically than I anticipated. "I made a promise to get Alyssa back to her family and I don't plan on letting her down."

Goose bumps. I was starting to hate them. Alyssa was looking at me and questioning me silently about all of my motives. Little does she know that my only motive that she was happy…no matter what happens to me throughout the course of it.

# Thirty One

I was walking with Mort and Stan up the tackily-lit main strip to the casino. I had on a nice suit that the elves somehow owned in my size. It was even a little long but it was okay for this one event. Alyssa was ahead of me with Mort and Stan, walking in the middle of them with her hands tied in front of her. I found it odd that no one was looking at them, just passing by as if this sort of thing happened all the time in this city. It probably did.

As I followed a good ten feet back a young boy came up to me. He was dressed in a loincloth and methodically banged a drum that was held by a strap that was around the back of his neck. He had a darker complexion so I couldn't place where he was from. My first guess was South America, maybe Portugal. Alyssa had some Portuguese in her and this kid's skin didn't resemble hers so Brazil even crossed my mind. He just banged his drum with the same monotonous beat, pah-rum-pum-pum-pum. I repeated it in my head until it hit me like a bag of bricks being thrown at my face.

"Are you the Little Drummer Boy?" I asked, bending down to his face level to talk to him, and at the same time trying to take that drumstick.

"My name is Eddie Drummer and I'm not little. I'm looking for my family." The Drummer boy replied. "I haven't seen them in two years."

I had no idea how to handle that. "Have you been to the police?" I asked, not knowing what else to say.

"They don't care. All I have is this drum. I play it sometimes to get money to eat, but mostly this one song. It's all my dad taught me."

"What song is that?" I asked.

"It's *The Little Drummer Boy*. My dad wrote it for me when I was born. He couldn't think of some words though."

"The pah-rum-pum-pum-pum?" I asked.

"Yeah. He said he could never get anything to fit in there, so he hummed it. Well, I have to go mister. I have to find my parents. And I have to find some food, I'm starving."

I didn't feel comfortable leaving this little kid out here, practically naked and banging a drum. It was just plain weird. I looked at him as he walked away and had to reach out to him anyway.

"Eddie?" I asked as he walked. He finally turned around.

"Listen," I started, "I have some things to do in the casino and I was wondering that maybe you can use my room. I won't even be in there but you can watch television and order anything you want to eat. It's on me."

I don't know if he knew what pedophile meant, but I didn't want to give him the impression that I was one. Nowadays you can't do anything nice for anyone without them thinking you're a stalker, child beater or pedophile or all of them rolled into one. You help a kid; you're suddenly a sicko in jail so the parents can sell the rights to the news or write a book about something that never happened in the first place.

"And while you're up in the room, I will be looking for your parents. Is that something you'd like to do?" I told him.

"I guess. I shouldn't be talking to strangers." He shrugged like the kid who just agreed with the parent because it was the right thing to do, no matter what their true intentions were. "I have to let The Wise men know where I'm going. They look after me. They're right up the street on the corner."

Alyssa the prisoner was out of sight by this time. I hoped she would be alright. I grabbed Eddie's hand and held it as we walked up the street. We passed a lot of people begging on the curbs, mostly with signs that said they'd work for anything without the intention of getting a job. We were on the deep end of the strip where the real culture of the city was, just as it is in every city. Washington D.C. was the same way. It's beautiful when you see the sights and the city, but drive five minutes more down Pennsylvania Avenue and there are bars on the convenience store windows, hookers and thugs all over the place. It just goes from beautiful and historical to scary as Hell in a flash. I thought it was ironic that the laws to ban those things were made right down the street and it seems to be so common.

Eddie and I walked past a boy in a blue jacket and knickers. It was the first time I have ever seen anyone wear knickers or pantaloons for that matter, so I just kind of laughed to myself. The boy had a crutch under one arm and was missing a leg. Even I stopped my laughter as I noticed it.

"Hey, Eddie, did you just pick that guy to be your father?" The boy laughed at Eddie Drummer. From the looks of it, Eddie was probably teased a lot by this little kid.

"That's Tim. He's a little asshole." Eddie said.

"You shouldn't curse." I told him. "And don't call him names, it's very rude."

"Yeah, you talk to him every day and not call him a prick." Eddie said defiantly.

Eddie changed directions so slightly that I had no idea we were moving in a different direction. We were moving towards the curb in front of a restaurant. As we got closer to it Eddie walked right past Tim and smiled widely. Eddie casually swept his leg up on the curb, knocking the crutch out from under him, sending Tim into a wobbling frenzy as he tried to maintain his balance.

"Don't make fun of me again." Eddie said. "I will find my parents. You will too if you can stop being so mean." Eddie reached down and picked up the crutch, giving it back to Tim. "You do it again and I'm taking the crutch and making you hop out here, got it?"

"That was incredibly nice of you and real mean all at the same time, kid. Well done." I was impressed at this Drummer kid. He was street smart but made his points to the world by disrupting things and then setting them straight again, all in one shot.

"He has a lot of balance for being tiny. Most of that crutch stuff is done for pity and money." Eddie continued walking to the three men sitting up the street. I looked at the hand-written cardboard signs and resembled ZZ Top sitting there.

The tall man's sign said 'Will work for Gold'. The middle guy was willing to work for Frankincense and the third on the end was willing to work for Myrrh. To this day, I have no clue what the hell Frankincense is or what Myrrh does but I would have to be blind not to see who these guys were. They all traded in their beautiful robes for fedoras and sunglasses. It was like an older version of *The Blues Brothers* was standing in at the nativity scene.

"These guys look after you?" I asked.

Eddie nodded. "Yeah, they're good to me. They're very nice, just down on their luck is all. Their last names are Wise, they're all brothers." Eddie nodded again and turned to the three men. "This man is going to give me some food and a place to stay for a day so he can find my parents. When I get out I'll bring you some food, okay?"

The three Wise men nodded and stared at me, telling me silently that they'd be watching to make sure Eddie was okay.

"Is it okay to buy them dinner or something? They're like family." Eddie looked up at me with huge saucer eyes. This kid was something else. I nodded and Eddie smiled back.

"You know, if I do what I have to do correctly, I have a feeling that everything is going to be okay real soon." I said.

Eddie looked at me like I was his baseball hero and it gave me chills that I never expected. I was out of my league before but I realized I was just in the wrong ballpark. I just graduated from the minors to the big show and it was time to play ball. "Eddie, we gotta go. I have things that need to be done and you have plenty of room service to order, compliments of Jack Frost."

# Thirty Two

I had somehow caught up with Mort and Stan, with Alyssa still in custody as their prisoner. I don't know how Eddie and I did it. I gave all the credit to the youthful bounce in his step and the melodic beat of the drum as we walked. There was no other reason why we were able to make up so much ground.

I was in front of the casino, standing in the front entrance area behind the car port. The blue lights had an icy look to them, complimenting the blue ground that I was standing on. There was a lot of blue neon involved, surely making people excited to get in there and open their wallets without knowing why, considering the color was mainly used to calm people down. I know that because it was having that effect on me. It just looked literally like a very cool place to hang out for a while if I wasn't a target and a pawn in a world takeover.

Mort and Stan disappeared through the casino as I stared through the doors into the lobby. The check-in counter was on the right, all of the people working that counter, luckily, were humans. Maybe at the very least they would have some sympathy and understanding towards Eddie and not give me any shit about me getting him set up in a room. You never know what Jack Frost implanted in them but I was hoping anyway. It didn't help matters much that Eddie was barely dressed in anything substantial.

As I stood there waiting for Candy Cane to come up, a limo pulled up in the little lane devoted to it. It was a pale blue limo with a paint job that made it shimmer under any light. To me, it looked like a rolling sheet of ice. The windows were even tinted blue. As the door opened a man popped out with a frazzled look on his face. His hair was a whitish-blue and stood straight up in the air. The blue suit he was wearing was made of a material that looked like it could be water. His slightly bony face was scary as hell even though its demeanor was calm. He looked like he could suck your soul through your eyes like he was shucking an oyster.

At first I passed it off as another high-roller coming in to try to clean out Jack Frost's casino with his talent. When I looked at him harder, I realized his talent was very different. His talent seemed to be that he was the real Jack Frost. Shit, just looking at him I could see that this was a man who knew everything that was going on everywhere. Not only here, but the track, the streets, the hotels and anything else you could think of up here.

"Eddie." I leaned down to him before Jack heard me. "Bang the drum and walk around asking for change. We can't be seen together by that guy."

"Who, Jack Frost?" Eddie asked.

"Yes. Later, I want to know how you know him, but right now I really need for you to act crazy and broke. If he thinks anything is weird the whole thing is blown. Your parents and the world will never change."

Eddie didn't say a word. He just broke free and started talking about the end of the world and how he really needed a bowl of chicken soup for his soul's last meal. He was acting like a little crazy person. I think I heard something in there about his loin cloth needed cleaning and he had to buy new clothes.

This kid was a genius like Bart Simpson. He was an impromptu opportunist just waiting to happen. I have never seen anyone walk into an unknown situation and use it to his advantage so fluently. I impulsively checked to see if I still had my wallet. Who knows, maybe he was a pickpocket and kept his winnings in the drum. Either way that kid earned himself a big dinner.

Jack breezed by Eddie, pushing him to the side. At first I thought he was just trying not to get Eddie's street stink on his cool blue suit, but as I looked at the intensity of his face he was in a severe rush to get in the door. As he passed me I pulled out a fake cell phone that Ollie put in my breast pocket and started babbling about some medical terminology that I had picked up on *Nip/Tuck*. Granted, other shows use those terms when their altering someone, *Nip/Tuck* uses them to figure out how to make them superficially beautiful. I was banking on the hope that they didn't get that show up here or Jack himself had no idea what he was talking about because no one near me was dead. I certainly am not the actor that Eddie Drummer is.

Jack looked directly at me as he walked by. It was almost in Jon Woo slow motion, like one of those ultra-cool action movies that are so action packed that they slow down the best parts for effect. He was John Travolta and I was Nicolas Cage, and this was definitely a *Face/Off* on its own terms.

"Eight million dollars?" I said into the fake phone. "Yeah, put a bid on it and I'll take it when I arrive. If anyone else bids, outbid them. I don't want to lose this house! And by the way, can you call Mandy and let her know the price for the second upgrade is ten grand, fifteen if she needs lipo again." I flipped the fake phone shut and slipped it back into my breast pocket. "The house I want was just put up on the market!" I told Jack as he stared at me. I was sweating in under my clothes in the cold air as I tried to lie to this man.

"It must be a nice house." Jack slithered through his teeth, staring at me like he caught me in a lie. "What do you do?" Jack stopped and talked to me from about three feet away, his right hand resting tightly on the casino door.

"I'm a cosmetic surgeon. I've always been a breast man. You know how it is." I laughed like the cocky fake boob doctor that I was trying to be with my fake phone. I was trying to find a reason to have a fake call on my non-existent call waiting.

"Oh, I know how it is." Jack smiled back, his teeth like little points. "There are lots of them in there. They are all in perfect pairs and all perfectly huge. So save some of your money so you can give it to me." He laughed at his inside-casino humor, hoping to see me trading up at the windows after a long losing streak at the blackjack table. "See you again soon and have fun, Doctor." He opened the door and disappeared inside.

I breathed a huge breath and squeezed my butt cheeks together to avoid shitting my pants again, especially in this suit. Eddie ran up to me, banging his drum to every footstep he made on the blue floor with his bare brown feet.

"Man that was awesome!" Eddie said to me. If everything goes badly, at least I know that I impressed this little kid and made him smile. "Where did you come up with that stuff? Are you really a doctor? Do you really touch...hoo-hoos?"

"Is the end of the world really coming and is soup really going to help you?" I asked, smiling at him. "And how do you know about hoo-hoos?"

"Oh, you're good, tall guy. We can make a lot out here. Are there hoo-hoos inside?" Eddie looked like he found his calling, and found a partner to help him with his little larceny.

I turned around and found an elf standing on the edge of the car loop that fell just a little past where the awning ended. She was wearing an all-white corset, red gloves and red leather boots that zipped up a little past her knees. My guess was that she was Candy Cane based solely on the colors.

I had no idea on how to proposition a hooker. You can see a thousand pornos in your life but they just went straight to it for no reason. They never had decent hooker themes in them. The actresses just got a check when their scene was over. Hi, I'm Mary. Nice to meet you, let me unzip your pants. I don't have a license, officer. I just have these beautiful heaving fake airbags and dirt on my knees. Do you want to see them deploy? If I was going to endure that kind of stupid sex talk, I planned on running.

"Candy Cane?" I asked her, completely embarrassed.

"You can lick me all night and wind up sticky." She said, like it was the tag line for her business. "I can take care of you without sitting down. You want it, it'll be a grand."

"Okay, that was a little too much. I was just wondering how much it was to take back the Pole?" I was trying to stay at a distance for fear that she would smell of work from an hour ago. Not to mention I was scared that she was literally going to try and take back my pole.

"Oh, that. That's free, sugar. Room three-twelve. Ten minutes." She said, checking everyone else out for business reasons. She was avoiding any eye contact with me, making me feel even more uncomfortable.

"You have your own room here?" I asked, secretly wanting to pry her for information on the business side of hooking, just out of sheer curiosity of the unknown oldest profession in the world.

"Yeah. What's it to ya?" She asked. She sounded like she was from Boston. I loved that accent, it was rough and right at you but it was a complete turn-on. "Get the fuck inside. I blow a lot of things but I'll be pissed if it's my cover that I blow."

"Fine. I just have to get Eddie here a room and I'll be right up." I was always nervous around women. Hookers were just damn intimidating.

"Don't be late, I'll be losing money. With the kid, the fee goes up two hundred dollars, American. I ain't no currency exchange but I don't discriminate either." She was still looking around like a crack head checking for undercover cops.

I grabbed Eddie and quickly walked into the lobby. For the moment I wanted to get as far away from that lady as possible. I could never be a john, the women are just plain fucking creepy and disassociated with the real world.

# Thirty Three

Mort and Stan arrived at the elevator with Alyssa in tow. She wasn't being hurt but had to make it look like Mort made her pay for him chasing her all over the place. They put makeup around her eyes and cheeks to make her look bruised. She had already given Will the ring so it would not end up in Jack's hands. If he had any wind of what Peary's Point could do he would destroy everything for himself.

The elevator doors slid open, Manny was standing at attention at the controls. He had a large bandage on his head that was red in the center, dried blood caked under the gauze.

"Manny, you okay?" Mort asked.

"I'm really getting sick of this shit, Mort. Good to see you again." Manny looked relieved to be talking to someone he knew that was on the same level as him in Jack's little world of chaos. "It was that Sugarplum bitch. She hit me in the head with a gun. They said it cracked my skull but thankfully they were wrong."

"How bad do you want to keep doing this crap?" Mort asked, pulling Alyssa and Stan into the elevator.

"What, having a good life?" Manny sounded like he fished that out as the only thing to say when you didn't have the nerve to admit anything else.

"What about having your old life back? No more of this elevator. No more getting hit in the head with guns and Jack breathing down your neck." Mort said.

"What are you talking about? Does this have anything to do with the human that you're dragging upstairs?" Manny asked.

"My name is Alyssa. I'd shake hands but their tied." She shrugged like a smartass prisoner.

"Maybe." Mort was sizing up Manny. "Remember when we were back in Old Town and we used to get together for poker every Wednesday?"

"Yeah, I miss that." Manny said distantly. "I can play all I want here but it's not the same. There's always a camera over you so you feel bad about having a good time. Plus, I lose a lot of my paycheck in the process."

"Yeah, we used to laugh a lot." Mort said. Alyssa was hanging her head to keep her charade going, but was watching Mort struggle with his conversion attempt.

"But I have things I never would have had if I was still back there, Mort. I have a car, I have money and I have a different woman every night in the event that I would want one." Manny was glazed over, not taking his face off the control panel.

"Well, we're turning things around, Manny. It sounds to me like you may want that to happen." Mort waited for a response.

"Let's put it this way." Manny said. "I don't want to die. If it changes, I'll be happy about it; if it doesn't then I will live like I'm living."

"With everything in the world you could have ever dreamt of." Mort looked at the floor and waited.

"Yes, with everything I have." Manny fixated on the elevator buttons.

"There's one thing that's missing though." Mort looked at Manny and he actually broke his trance and looked back. "Respect for yourself, Manny. You have no family here. All the things in the world can be at your disposal, but what good is it if you have to lose yourself in return?"

Manny stared at him and a tear rolled down his cheek. He was at a crossroads that he knew would be approaching, just had no idea that it was going to be this soon.

"If there's anything I can help with, let me know. Like I said though, I don't want to die." Manny looked like he genuinely wanted to help but was scared to do it.

"You won't. Just keep the elevator up here with the doors open." Mort pulled out a neatly folded duffle bag from inside his jacket. "Keep this in here. When you see Stan, fill the bag and go to the third floor. There will be someone to get it."

"What am I putting in the bag?" Manny asked.

"A snowman." Mort said. Alyssa was smiling under her hair.

"Oh, shit. This is going to end up being very loud, isn't it?" Manny rolled his eyes as the elevator reached the top floor.

"That's all you have to do for me. Then you can sit back and relax and enjoy whatever life brings. But as a brother to me I really look forward to beating you next Wednesday night over some Texas Hold 'em." Mort put his hand on Manny's shoulder.

"I'll make my famous dip." Manny smiled as the doors opened. "See you in a few minutes, huh?"

"Oh, by the way." Alyssa said. "I am not a prisoner and that lady who hit you with the gun is an angel. She's been undercover this whole time."

"Are you kidding me?" Manny asked.

"That's why you're not dead." Alyssa said. "All that we ask is that you turn a blind eye and let us do whatever we need to do."

Manny slowly turned and looked at Alyssa, nodding in his state of sudden confusion.

# Thirty Four

I was standing in front of room three-twelve, hesitant about knocking. If Candy Cane answered the door naked I planned on running. With a heavy hand I reluctantly rapped on the door three times. I tapped my shoe on the thick blue carpet as she unbolted all six locks on the other side. I noticed there was a peep hole in the door almost directly in line with my crotch, wondering if this was to size up business or just a height thing like it was at The Garland. I didn't even care to know right now but I cupped my crotch anyway.

The door clicked open and Candy Cane stood there in a Casino robe. Her hair was wet; she must have had enough time to take a shower. She looked at me funny when we made eye contact. Not in a 'so what's your pleasure?' type of way, but wondering how I was mixed up in all of this. I really wished that I knew.

I walked in and sat on the chair set up near the complimentary table. Jack obviously spent his money on the casino portion of the hotel. There was a plasma screen television, but other than that it looked like a traditional hotel or motel that you would stop at when you made the Interstate exit.

"Did you get the boy his room?" Candy Cane asked, not sounding like she was Boston anymore.

"Yeah, you sound different." I couldn't believe the transformation. She was a whole different person. I didn't even see the hooker clothes anywhere in sight. I wanted the Boston accent back for some strange reason.

"It's because I am. I am not a hooker, Mr. Foster."

"You know my name?"

"Everyone associated with Old Town does. Seems you needed to find yourself along the way? I hope everything came out okay. Well you wouldn't be here if it didn't I suspect."

"What? What are you talking about?" I asked.

"You see, to make this all work we needed to have someone that belonged in Jack Frost's version of the world, only in actual civilization.

The way you have seen the world is exactly like Jack's vision now. It's all good things sold out to make him money so he can spoil himself. You're not like that in the money sense, but the way you view the world is the same. And no one here can change it because we are in it. Someone that this actually affects in the real world needs to change it."

"That's what we're trying to do. I already know all the details on that so if I can just find out what's next, I'd appreciate it."

"The only way to change it is to make the change in your self first. Look inside yourself, Will Foster. When this is at an end, look into the person that has changed you and that will change the world."

"What the hell does that mean? Do you all speak in riddles? It would save a lot of time if everyone just said what you mean. Like I said before I already know all about that and it's done. I need to find out what to do next."

"Is that the attitude that you live by?"

"Well, sort of."

"Then I have said enough to you. You are here for some ID?" Candy asked.

I just nodded. Talking to elves was starting to get real annoying. It's like watching cable news shows. They just spin around one thought and twist it into so many different ways that you actually start to believe fourteen versions of one idea. One thought creates fourteen different issues and all of that is just to cover the fact that they have no fucking clue what's going on in the world from the first suggestion. If you had enough money, the news people will tell it like you want them to.

They can sway people's attention from one thing to another and fuck everything up in the process so no one gets the real truth. I had the sense that Candy Cane was one of those people. She had a specific mindset about what's getting done that she was slanting it to lean in the only way she knew how…in her favor. I didn't trust this woman in the least bit, hooker or not.

"You're going to the sanitarium, right?" She asked.

She sounded like she knew too much. It was possible that her ear was so close to the ground here that she knew it, but that was a stretch. Was I finally going mad? Did my contempt for the way the world works actually make me snap once and for all?

"How did you know that? Was it Ollie?"

"I have a lot of connections." She responded.

"Like who?"

"Look, I know you don't trust me." Hit the nail right on the head. "I wouldn't either. I have been working undercover for years as a hooker to get as much information as I can. I work for the local police."

"Police, here?"

"Yes. When Old Town was shut down there were job postings at the precinct. I applied for it and was turned down, so I really became a hooker. My first night on the job, some junkie gave me cash for an hour and was all strung out on humbug. Before we got to the room he got into a fight and shot another guy in the head. It was some bigwig from the casino. There were no other witnesses, I ran like hell to get away, but I saw it. So I was asked if I wanted to be a CI for the police. Most of them are paid off by Frost, but my bosses are cool. They actually try to clean up the streets even though it makes no difference and no one cares. They like what they're doing."

"So how do you do it without sleeping with anyone?"

"Spike their drinks. It's not lethal and I was approved to use it. They drink and think they had a great night when nothing actually happened; I just tell them we did it. So I did that last night and got you an ID. You're a psychiatrist from Los Angeles in charge of a mental institution. Talk about luck, huh?"

She opened a drawer and gave me the ID. He kind of resembled me but his nose was actually a little bigger than mine, which I thought was hard to do. Mine wasn't that big but I was self conscious about it anyway. I could probably pull this off.

"Thanks." I said.

"Oh, and I had a friend change the name of Santa's doctor order to reflect the name on your card. Like I said, I'm connected."

"I have to know. Why the name Candy Cane? I heard your little spiel, but is that the only reason?"

"Candy canes are great. You hang them on a tree, pull one off, unwrap it and lick it maybe twice and set it down somewhere. Most everyone does. So I decided to use that to translate into me being fast. I had to come up with something that made me look like a neurotic hooker." She smiled at me like she was trying to be my loving wife. "So, you have your badge, be on your way. You have a lot to do."

"Yes, I guess I do. And thank you, Candy."

"My name is actually Mindy. Now go." She shuffled me up and pushed me in the direction of the door. "You, of all people, can't be late for what you have to do. Tell Santa I said hello."

# Thirty Five

"Well, well, well. Look who we have here." Jack said in a creepy old-man-trying-to-bed-a-teenager kind of way. He curled one finger through Alyssa's bangs. "You sure are a pretty one for being in such a predicament."

Under normal circumstances Alyssa would have been embarrassed by the compliment. She would have pretended that it mattered, but right now the thought of it merely made her sick. "Thanks." It was all she could think to say to avoid getting a bullet directly implanted in her brain.

"You don't look like the type to hurt me." Jack said, reaching down to untie her hands. "If I let you go do you promise not to lunge at me? Unless, of course it's to knock me back on the bed." She nodded. "Because my teeth can bite through your skin so fast that I will be using your bones as toothpicks quicker than you can say merry fucking Christmas. Your skin looks very delicious though."

He seemed satisfied enough in her response that he untied her hands from in front of her. He didn't notice that they were barely tied in the first place. Mort was determined that she make it through the night without a scratch, at Will's insistence.

"It's a nice place you got here." Alyssa said, looking around the home-office.

"Let's cut the bullshit." Jack's voice turned from mock friendly to that of the devil quicker than Norman Bates slipped on his mom's clothes and wig. "Where is the ring?" He asked, walking within two inches of Alyssa. His pointy nose tapped her on the tip of hers and it was colder than death itself. "Where is the remaining Spirit?"

"I don't have it." She replied.

"Well, who does?" He insisted, not moving an inch. "You answer me now or I'll break the nose right off of your fucking face. Pity, considering you're incredibly pretty for a human woman. Now what is the name?"

Jack rubbed the back of his bony hand on her cheek, licking his lips in the process.

"You tell me his name or I will make sure that the next hour of your life is the most painful and humiliating hour you have ever had."

"His name is Will Foster!" Alyssa yelled immediately, not wanting any part of Jack's sexual tendencies.

Will has always thought that Alyssa was an opportunist caught in her own little world. She had her own friends and needed no more, no matter what Will tried to incorporate himself into her existence. And for all the trying in the world, his reward was her selling him out to Jack Frost and possibly a strafing of machine gun fire that he'd never live through. Mort and Stan looked at her like they were shot by the same gun that was gunning for Will.

"Hmmm." He said, finally backing up. "And what is his next move? Trying to rescue that fat piece of shit from crazy town? Or rescue you even though you just engraved a bullet with his name? He must be really proud to have such a self-centered girlfriend."

"He's not my boyfriend." She said quietly, knowing in the back of her head that she just killed the man who would do anything to keep her safe.

"Well that makes it worse." Jack said. "Boyfriends and girlfriends eventually do wind up selling one or the other out, but friends? Friends shouldn't do that to anyone."

Alyssa started to cry with her head down.

Alyssa just stood there and said nothing, not wanting to incriminate Will anymore than what was already done. Will was never going to believe that she had the best intentions anyway. If he lived at least she'd get to apologize to him. She just wanted to see her family no matter what the cost. Even if that cost was named Will Foster.

"I'll tell you what." Jack said. "I want you to be my date tonight."

"Where are we going?" Alyssa had a shake in her voice that she never placed there. She had no idea what the hell this madman had in mind and didn't care right now. She just wanted to leave all of this behind, Will Foster included.

"Oh, it's a little party." Jack said. "You could call it that anyway. You see, it's Christmas Eve. The casino usually has a party to celebrate wealth and laugh at the people who don't have it. It's part of society, really. You're American, so you understand that people are more interested in what people are wearing at the Academy Awards than what needs to be done with themselves. This is the same concept except you'll be on the runway with me. It's my event, so if some hack says the gown you're wearing is too roomy, I'll kill them on the spot."

"You're an insensitive prick." She said.

"Not really. People can change if they want. Put the remote down and do something with yourself, not worry about who is having babies that aren't yours in Africa and what the ex said and who fucked who in some fancy hotel and all that shit. People bring it on themselves, my dear. You may call it insensitive, I call it good marketing." Jack smiled and bared his pointy teeth. "Oh, and we are going to have a little skirmish in a little while. I am positively sure of it. Most of your friends in Old Town are going to die with you watching. And best of all, I want you to pull the trigger on this Will Foster."

"I won't do it." She said.

"Yes you will, my dear. It's in you. He's not part of your world. You shouldn't have any problem with it, considering the fact that you turned him out quicker than a pimp with A.D.D. If you do have a problem with it I will kill both of you and be back in time for my after-party. I have a good deal with the major television networks, sweetie. You'll be famous, dressed in a million dollar gown that'll look fantastic to all the people in the world that can't afford it. I'm so excited, now follow me. I'll get you ready for our eventful evening."

Jack pulled Alyssa away, slowly going down the long part of the office towards the front near the reception room doors. Mort and Stan stood there, just waiting for the door to close to his sleeping room. They hadn't said a word to them since they came up and saw that as a good thing even though they had a few choice words for Alyssa right now. Any words can come out shaky which would give them away.

Mort ran over to the mantle and grabbed the glass jar containing the liquid that was Frosty. He grabbed the black hat, corncob pipe and the two pieces of coal that were sitting next to it in the dish. There was also a button that he swiped; not fully remembering if Frosty came equipped to smell things. He gave all the components to Stan, who was pulling his shirt out at the bottom and piling things in so they wouldn't fall out, making a fabric basket for all of the items.

"Give this to Manny in the elevator!" He whispered loudly. "Be real quiet up front, Jack is up there in his room. Come back when it's done!"

Stan ran with all of the parts of Frosty swishing around in the jar on his stomach and within a minute he was back, panting like a burnout teenager in track class. Mort looked down and saw a piece of coal.

"Crap." Mort said. "Put that in your pocket or Frosty's going to be looking like a pirate running around in circles. We have to get out of here. I'll tell Jack we got a lead on Will and that should free us some time to get the hell out of here."

"What about the nice booby lady?" Stan asked.

"She'll be fine." Mort said. "But I won't be disappointed if she gets hurt along the way."

# Thirty Six

The elevator door opened as Mindy was standing there impatiently waiting for it to arrive. It was the third floor and she was right where she needed to be. Mindy checked her watch again and saw that this was the precise moment she needed to be here.

"Shit, Manny. What took so long?" She asked, grabbing the duffle bag from his nervous little hands.

"Never mind. Good luck." The elevator doors closed. Manny disappeared as quickly as he arrived.

Mindy ran quickly down the hall to the stair cases. Bolting down to the first floor was no problem for her. Mindy's legs were well conditioned from being on her feet for so long every day for her cover. When she hit the landing on the bottom floor she swung the door open, running into Eddie Drummer.

"Kid, what are you doing here? You should be upstairs." She was scolding him like his long lost mother.

"He needs my help, ma'am. The nice man was helping me and I know he's in trouble so I want to help him now." He banged his drum once. "See, it's hollow."

She smiled, knowing that no one looked at this kid as anything but a crazy, near-naked orphan so no one would assume anything of him. She nodded as he opened the top of the drum. She stuffed all of the smuggled articles inside quickly, snapping the skin back to the top.

"Okay, this need to go to an elf named Ollie in Old Town. Or ask for Frank Foster. This needs to be done ASAP, okay?"

"The Wise men can bring me." Eddie said. "They were from up there and know the way. I'll be fine. I can handle myself."

Mindy smiled at the boy with sadness on her face. No one up here had anything to look forward to in a long time. The thought of the change not happening was sad and frightening for everyone but seeing the sheer optimism on that kid's face, knowing that his life may never get better, almost made her cry. That was the new Christmas. High hopes and possible disappointments on the horizon.

"Kid, be careful and take the basement exit through the kitchen. You're going to have to run like mad so by the time the cooks see you, you're long gone. And I hope you find your family." Mindy let a tear out and watched Eddie as he disappeared without saying a word, the key to their future lying in his drum.

She heard the beat of the muffled drum going down the stairs into the darkness. She took a breath, hoping that this was the last time that child would ever be walking away alone.

# Thirty Seven

Above all else, Jack Frost had a reputation to uphold. He had millions of people and millions more in dollars coming into this casino, especially at this time of year so he thought it was in his best interest to don on his arm, not a wanted woman but a classy woman who everyone wanted to be near. As he stood on the elevator, he looked at Alyssa and smiled, like he imagined it was their first anniversary.

Manny looked at her and smiled, reminding her without words that she was merely an actress. About a half hour earlier, she was in her dirty jeans and sweater. The woman he saw before him now had her hair pulled back, some hair hanging in front of a perfectly made up face. She was wearing a shiny blue one-piece dress that looked like it was shrink wrapped around her hourglass frame. Manny would have never guessed by the clothes she appeared to wear all the time, but this woman was an absolute knockout tonight.

As they exited the elevator Jack took it upon himself to be a perfect gentleman, something he was only used to being one time during the year. Even to the woman he was going to kill later in the evening, regardless of any outcome. He scooped her arm under his, turning both of them around to face Manny.

"I need my limo up front, Manny. I have to go to the casino theatre and make sure that the show goes on as normal. We have some business to attend to later, so make sure you are here when we get back."

"Yes sir." Manny said. As Jack turned towards the casino floor, Manny mouthed the words good luck to Alyssa. She smiled through her beautiful, nervous face. "With any luck I'll never see you again, dick head." He whispered to Jack, under his breath. Seeing Alyssa swayed his mind to its final resting place…peace and the long-gone poker games played by him and his friends over some caroling and hot cocoa.

As they arrived at the theatre, Jack and Alyssa walked through back doors that lead to the dressing room area. It was a small hallway with doors on either side. They followed the stale gray hallway all the way down to the main talent room which was the permanent home to the human magician named Johnny Turtledoves. Jack owned the place and paid his salary so it was only fitting that he walk in without knocking, no matter what Johnny happened to be doing.

"Johnny boy! You see the crowd tonight?" Jack yelled into the empty room. As he walked in a few feet farther, Alyssa in tow, he noticed the shower was running. "Johnny, are you ready? Showtime is in about half an hour!"

There was no answer.

Alyssa looked around the room with curiosity all over her face and saw various articles of magic scattered all over the place. There were five golden rings, seven swans, six geese, a cage full of four calling birds, a makeshift, homemade pen with three French hens, and near the shower door were two turtledoves. Obviously he made these disappear and reappear, with the exception of the rings, which were probably just an illusion to lock them together and unlock them with a twist of the wrist. Alyssa wasn't a huge fan of magic and by the looks of it, this guy had no originality. She made a guess that the human factors in the remainder of the twelve days had their own rooms and assisted in the show, but she could care less about ever finding out.

Jack left Alyssa there to stand among the weirdness as he walked into the bathroom. As he opened the door he saw the glass shower completely empty, only the water falling on the empty tiles below. He bit his bottom lip and growled, opening the shower door. He looked on the shower head, seeing only the glimpse of a candy cane hanging from the shiny metal water pipe.

"Your friend will die tonight, regardless of who pulls the trigger." Jack screamed.

Jack stormed back out of the bathroom and returned to the middle of the dressing room, coming face to face with Alyssa.

"And you will be soon after if this shit goes bad." He said, a little too close to her face for comfort. Jack flipped out his cell phone and dialed someone who was presumably in charge of the act.

"This is Jack." He said deeply into the cell phone. "Johnny is too sick to perform tonight. I need you to put on The Lords of the Leap. Got it? No refunds, it's a schedule change. If they don't like it, kill them for all I care."

Jack flipped the phone closed without getting a response. To Alyssa: "Your boyfriend is fucking with the wrong person, human. Not only has he succeeded in kidnapping my talent, he's becoming a pain in my blue ass."

"He's NOT my boyfriend!" She yelled at him.

"Sure. Keep telling yourself that. Either way you'll have to ID the body."

Jack roughly grabbed Alyssa's arm and escorted her out of the dressing room. Within seconds, Alyssa heard music on the stage off somewhere to her left. It was an upbeat, Broadway-type of show with a fast tempo. She was curious to see what was happening, just being backstage for something was exciting given the circumstances. As they passed through the wings of the stage, she stopped for a second to tray and take a look.

"There's no time for this." Jack said, pulling her away.

"Listen. You are going to shoot me later, I know this. You would have done it already so I know now is not the time. You got me all dressed up for my own death, can you at least give me a minute to enjoy it? Why don't you just pull the trigger right now? Oh, I forgot, you are respected here, whatever the hell that means."

Jack looked at her with pity in his eyes. It was definitely going to be a shame killing this beautiful creature. Maybe she'd stay up here with him when she sees the lifestyle that she'd be in on. Hopefully Munchausen's Syndrome would work out for him.

"Okay, just one minute. Anything longer, you'll get the bullet you asked for." Jack said.

"Is that all you do? Threaten people?" She asked.

Jack just shrugged and nodded.

Alyssa blew it off and looked on the stage. It was a beautiful set piece, especially since Jack just ordered it thirty seconds ago. There were eleven pipers piping, ten lords were leaping to the beat provided by the eleven drummers in the back line of the stage.

Nine ladies danced with the pipers in square dance fashion. It was like an old western concept complete with eight singers dressed as French maids milking cows. It was a neat looking show, too bad she couldn't see where all of it was going to end. A tear went down her face, knowing that these people on stage were being forced to do this and still had smiles on their faces for the crowd. They were truly talented and beautiful creatures and were considered nothing more than a well-orchestrated stage show in a true-to-life hard knock life. If only the people in the audience knew that they weren't acting.

"Why are there only eleven drummers?" She asked as she started doing the math in her head to what the song led her to believe was true.

"That doesn't concern you. We're going right now." Jack yanked her away and proceeded to make his way to his limo.

Alyssa shook her head at the memory. The kid Will was talking to. It was the kid with the drum! The tear on her cheek dried up as the anger catapulted out of her eyes. "Where are we going you twisted bastard?"

"We have a meeting at the sanitarium." Jack flipped open his cell phone again. "I don't care if their ready, it's time right now. Old Town won't know what hit them. I want the fat fuck drugged right now and I want all of them dead! I fed them and kept them alive in the way they wanted to live, and this is how they repay me? Fuck them, they all die! Do you understand me? I am on my over there right now to make sure that Santa is silenced for good so for your sake he better be."

Alyssa had a jolt of fear and dread attacking her stomach as they disappeared in the back hallways of the casino, heading for death and mass destruction that was surely somewhere in her future. She was numb knowing that she signed Will's death warrant herself. She would have thrown up if Jack wasn't dragging her so quickly.

# Thirty Eight

Ollie was waiting on the ridge with Uncle Frank and Eve, staring into the canyon that housed the casino strip a few miles away. They had no idea when the magician was arriving. Mort and Stan should be here soon with Frosty. Eve stared out into the night as she spotted four figures slowly coming towards them. A dull pounding could be heard echoing in the distance, a muffled thump, thump, thump.

As they approached, the three Wise men were walking in front of Eddie. They slowly scaled the hill and were up on the ridge within a few minutes, moving more quickly than their old bodies seemed to allow.

"I'm here to help." Eddie said. "That human guy was nice." He opened his drum and handed Ollie the duffle bag.

"Thank you very much." Ollie said, unzipping the bag, pulling out the mason jar. "It's so nice to have an old friend back. Where's the magician?"

"Who?" Eddie wasn't told of any of this.

As if the heavens heard the question, or if Eve sent in an employee request to her Boss herself, Blitzen flew overhead, Mort and Stan enthusiastically riding on his back. They had Johnny Turtledoves between then, a black hood placed over his head, his arms tied tightly behind his back.

"Here he is!" Mort yelled. "Sorry we're late. It's hard to catch a magician, but luckily he's not that good."

A muffled expletive jumped from beneath the hood.

"Is the hood necessary?" Uncle Frank asked.

"Sorry about that. Bad habit, you know?" Mort shrugged and hopped off of Blitzen, Stan following as he pulled the magician off the side and removed Johnny's hood.

"Hello, Johnny Turtledoves." Ollie said.

"You heard of me?" Johnny said like he just found out he was famous. "Have you seen my show?"

Eddie opened his drum and handed Ollie the items that he stashed in it earlier with Mindy. Ollie popped the old black hat into its normal position and handed it to the ego-centric magician.

"I know everyone. The reason you are here is that I need you to make this old black hat magic again." Ollie said.

"I am a magician, not a damned sorcerer! Do you have any idea about the concept of magic, elf? We are illusionists. We create the illusion that we have magical powers, but we are no different than you, other than the size. How am I supposed to do that? My show was cancelled for this? I have a huge television deal coming!"

"You're show sucked." Mort said. "I've seen it. I had free tickets and wanted a refund. Stan liked it though but that was mainly for the girl you had assisting. She could have just stood there and drooled and he would have given her a standing ovation."

"Shut up." Johnny said to Mort. To Ollie: "Give me the damn hat; I'll see what I can do as long as I'm back for the show. Man, Jack is going to be so pissed."

Johnny Turtledoves took the hat and twisted the lid off of the Mason jar, spilling the liquefied snowman into the snow slowly and carefully, keeping him in a contained pool as best he could. Johnny held the hat in his left hand and began circling it with his right. The crowd fell silent around him as they eagerly waited for some otherworldly force to come through Johnny's fingertips.

Johnny closed his eyes and drew upon the power of generations of illusionists that preceded him. He thought of Houdini, Copperfield, Henning, Siegfried and Roy, Penn and Teller and even David Blaine. The images of them passed through him quickly, knowing how they did most everything in their repertoire but not performing them nearly as well as his predecessors.

He thought of Criss Angel, the MindFreak himself, whose illusions were difficult to interpret as anything but otherworldly, taking hours to be frustrated by the brilliance of his effects and the inability to figure them out. He wasn't thinking of the make-a-coin-disappear, he was thinking of the grandiose illusions: sawing himself in half for public inspection, pulling a woman apart in a park, all of those types of illusions defied any normal explanation, other than being touched by a higher power, no matter how much you scrutinized it to be rational. It was this type of illusion that he was thinking of, to summon the gods that touched Criss to maybe help him through this dilemma. Hell, it justified the name of the show so there must be something to it.

As Johnny circled his finger around the top of the hat his mind fell into an abyss of self comfort. The world around him was crystal clear and completely silent. He saw nothing but the hat before him in a blue sky over a pure white ground. He was caught in a trance in a parallel universe that he hoped that not many people shared. Either way he was happy he was starting to find this sacred corner of the otherworld.

The hat started to jump in Johnny's left hand. It wasn't going more than an inch, but that movement alone showed everyone that it was working. Small glitters of gold started to come out of Johnny's fingertips, circling the hat slowly at first, lifting it in a glittery sphere that was its new home. The old black hat hovered from him, flying like a Frisbee in slow motion to the puddle at his feet. His fingers were still moving and his left hand was still in position, as if the hat never left. The stars flew around in a grand, beautiful fury, as if the stars themselves actually knew the purpose for which they were called upon.

As the hat glided down and hit the puddle, the gold glitter made its way through the cold water, pooling it up and slowly turning it white. The lump in the middle got higher and higher until it was once again the size of a two-armed biped made of snow. The hat was on his head and he quickly began to dance around. He had no eyes, no nose or a mouth to think of so he danced around in a frantic circle, like he was trying to get out of a paper bag. Ollie gave Frank the coal and the button and gave Eve the corncob pipe.

"I can't reach up there. And he's jumping around like a drunk." Ollie started to laugh a little bit. "Maybe we can keep him like this for a little while? Maybe take a picture of him for later?"

"That's just not right, Ollie." Frank said.

Frank circled with Frosty, keeping himself in what he perceived as the front of the snowman. He quickly popped the coals in his white sockets. He ran around with him again and tried to place the button in proportion to what would be his nose. Eve blindly stuck the corncob pipe in where his mouth would be and he suddenly stopped in place.

"Well, this is better." Frosty said in full Jimmy Durante mode. "That jar was giving me a horrible cramp."

Frank looked at the magician who was coming out of his trance. "Can you do this with a lot of other hats?"

"You can probably use the magic from that one." Johnny said, exhausted. "I never thought that was possible. I've never done that before."

"You've never had anything to believe in before but the ticket price." Ollie said to him. "I'll get everyone's hat. Frosty, please come with me."

Ollie and Frosty walked away down Wonderland Road, leaving everyone else in complete and total shock that they actually witnessed what was once just a myth. By the time the elves met Frosty in the first place, Frosty only had the story of how he was made. Nearly everyone chalked it up to just being extremely creative. They had no idea it was true until now.

"We need to get everyone out here." Eve said. "It's almost time. I hope Tig got everything ready."

"I'm sure he did fine. He's nuts but he's definitely thorough." Frank said. "I don't know if it's enough though. Jack is going to run right through us."

"Not if they can help." Blitzen said. "Look behind you."

Frank and Eve looked to the hill situated behind the town. It was hard to see this late at night with a lack of light, but as they stood there, they saw something unbelievable as their eyes acclimated. Five thousand elves standing at the ready and about a hundred reindeer scattered between them. The fog was encircling the army as they stood there. They all had their hats on backwards and all looked pissed off at the world as they stared through the dusk and onto Wonderland Road.

"Who the hell are *they*?" Frank asked.

"The Southies." Blitzen responded. "When they came in to challenge us at the races I called in a favor and they all came. I think that evens things out between us."

"Blitzen I have no idea what to say. This is incredible." Frank said as he stared at the army behind them.

Frank got goose bumps knowing that a lot of people were standing up for this. Even the South Pole elves were sticking up for this cause. They were notorious for being constantly irritated that they only got the production overflow and were considered the elf sweatshop of the holidays.

"Don't thank me. If this little plan of ours doesn't work out, Vixen has a lot of paying off to do, and we definitely don't want or need to see that in the stables. She's a screamer and gets very loud." Blitzen snorted. "Does anyone have a cigar? It may be my last, you know? I have to go out with some style."

"I'll find you one." Eve said, smiling. "Just for the record, angels don't do this sort of thing often. Quit smoking, huh?"

Blitzen nodded to Eve, knowing that either way he had a feeling that this would be his last stogie.

"I'll get the troops together." Frank said. "It's do-or-die time. Blitzen, you know what to do next, right?"

"I'm on it, man." Blitzen said as he oozed with pride. "There are good times ahead, human Frank. Good times. Tell the angel I'll be back for my stogie."

Blitzen silently lifted off and flew away, out of sight in seconds. Hopefully Frank would see him again. The one thing he couldn't stand was the uncertainty of it all. Either way someone you knew wasn't going to be the same ever again, for good or bad. It was the strangest feeling in the world, a feeling that Frank thought no one should have to endure.

# Thirty Nine

Frank always knew in the back of his head what had to be done to make this successful. He knew the layout of the grounds between Old Town and the city like the back of his hands from all of the runs that he's made throughout three years.

Eve did a preliminary sweep of the vast field of snow which would most likely be tinted with red tonight. He figured that Jack's army would be coming towards Old Town at full throttle with guns blazing. He also knew most of the elves first hand and had a pretty good idea that they were in no position to formulate a strategic battle plan for a battle no one thought they'd be having. Time and urgency were working in their favor. They were lucky enough to be able to be trained to fire a weapon in the first place, let alone mount a strategic offense.

Not to forget that the elves were kind of heart naturally. All the tinting in the world can't make someone learn to kill when your whole life's purpose was devoted to the theory of loving and giving. On top of that it wasn't Jack Frost's way to be smart about it. If he sees a problem he eliminates it. Frank was hoping that haste would be Jack's problem tonight and eventually be his downfall.

Ollie just stood there and stared into the moonlit horizon with his chin held high.

"There will be a lot of lives lost tonight, my friend." Ollie said. "I don't think it will ever be the same regardless of what happens out there."

"Times do change Ollie." Frank said. "We have to accept that. What we can't let happen is going to the extremes as a result of it. Change is good if you incorporate it into what's already there, not completely rearranging tradition. Some lives will be lost, but they will be lost with honor, trying to bring back what needs to be found again."

"And what is that, Frank Foster?" Ollie broke his gaze to look at Frank, a tear frozen to his left cheek.

"Faith, Ollie. We need faith in each other. We just need to find where and when faith vanished in the first place and get it back. However that needs to be done remains to be seen. We can only get the faith back in the people up here, I have no idea what kind of effect tonight's events will have on the rest of the world."

Ollie just continued to stare into the horizon, the quiet calm overwhelming him. Sadly war was a necessary evil. He hated being in this position but knew no other way.

"We need to get these men into position." Ollie said, not wanting to do it in the least bit.

# Forty

"We're ready, sir." Tig said, flipping his shield up. "The Southies are a mile out on each side of the perimeter of the valley. When the lines meet, the Southies will bring up the rear and we'll have them surrounded." He nodded his head hard, flipping the welding shield down with a loud, echoing crack.

"Weapons?" Frank asked.

Tig and Eve stood next to Frank and Ollie on the ridge.

"We're not using any." Tig said through his shield. "It was Ollie's call, not mine."

"We are not compromising who we are, Frank, no matter what the outcome." Ollie's stare was stern, Frank's equally so. "We are fighting for what we are. If we change that the war would already be lost before it started. There would be no hope."

"So what are we using?" Frank stared at Ollie like he was about to strangle him.

"Bring them out boys!" Tig yelled towards the main part of Wonderland Road.

An organized thud grew louder as the footsteps approached down Wonderland Road. They were heavy, like giants, all walking in unison to hide the numbers. Frank stared down the strip as twenty small-skyscraper-sized nutcrackers marched down the street. Their painted stares ominously looking towards the city as they marched, their eyes opened wide with war painted on their wood. Their arms were stiff and their legs were now jointed to accommodate the movement that they've longed to have since their creation.

They were all in their traditional clothing, the furry black hats and blue jackets were painted on with precision. As they marched behind the red painted nutcracker Generals their mouths opened and shut in accordance with the giant levers on their backs. The wood in their mouths was reinforced with steel, making it sound like a giant machine press going off to war.

"The magician blessed them." Tig said. "He was on a roll and it saved a lot of time not putting together remote units that big. Each one is equipped with a high-powered ice ball thrower. They have water cooling units in them to retain their solidity. They won't kill but it'll hurt a hell of a lot." Tig smiled at the creations as he told them to stop about three feet away. "Their arms are fortified with flamethrowers and are equipped with fireball disbursement systems. We are all linked up so we can communicate with each other in the process."

Frank just stood in awe as he stared at the giant army of wooden men who were obviously ready to unleash some holy hell into the night.

As they all stood there assessing the army an elf ran around them, quickly and haphazardly placing hats in a circle around them one by one. There were hundreds of hats, all different styles of elf design, all laid out on the snow. Frank had no idea what the little elf was doing.

They just stood there and let the elf proceed, all hoping that he did indeed have a purpose. As they looked, the hat bearing elf held his finger up to his lips to tell them not to even bother with the question. As the elf made the motion, the ground beneath them started to shake and rumble. Instinctively, they all held each other to spare someone accidentally being thrown off the cliff.

As they watched, all of their mouths opened as the hats started materializing snow underneath them. They swirled into snowballs and grew bigger and bigger until each snowball was supported by a larger one, which was supported by two stumpy legs. Two fat arms sprouted out on each one of them, the snow crunching against itself into a choir of beautiful creation.

"This is your front line." Tig said, flipping his shield up again. "They can patch any bullet holes put into them as they walk. They're surrounded by body parts. And I have one more thing to show you." He motioned for the decoy squad to come down. "You can't have a battle without toy soldiers, now can you?"

The toy soldiers were all repainted for the situation. Their uniforms were gleaming red, the pink spots on their cheeks refreshed and refurbished into a tribal war paint design. They were all modified and twenty feet tall. They were all created by Tig to act as the first line out of the gate, followed by the snow men and women, the two lines of nutcrackers and finally the elves themselves. Ollie definitely knew what he was doing in the process of protecting lives and general military tactics. It was damned impressive for a conspiracy-theory nut job.

"This is unbelievable." Frank said. "You did all this in an hour?"

Ollie nodded. "I told you before. The world is pretty big. We have to do a lot to make sure it all goes okay."

Eddie Drummer ran up from wherever he was hiding and started playing his dad's beat on the drum. "I'm ready." He said.

"You're ready for what?" Eve asked. "You're staying right here with me. It is against who I am to let you go out there."

Eddie was starting to cry. "I don't have a family. You guys all at least have each other. If I never find my family, I at least want them to be proud of me for doing *something* to help."

The adults all looked at each other, knowing that none of them possessed any right to tell anyone not to get involved, no matter what the age. Everyone here had their own reasons for doing this and no one was going to tell Eddie that his reason wasn't good enough. Hell, his reason was the basis for what they were doing in the first place, family.

Without a word they all silently agreed that everyone was involved so it was everybody's right to fight for it how ever they saw fit. It was all of their legends that the world remembered and honored. They needed to be remembered around the world again and live up to their names to retain them.

"Eddie, you lead us out, but I want you in the back as soon as we see the opposing line coming, understand?" Uncle Frank looked sternly into him.

"But, I can fight!" Eddie yelled.

"We are not fighting! We're defending, Eddie. Plus, what if your family is looking for you later and you're not there? Is that fair to them?"

"No, I guess not." Eddie put his head down.

"You lead us in with your march and get out, Revolutionary War style. I am not letting you get killed. Stay up at Ollie's house until you see it's clear, in the library. Got it?"

"I got it!" Eddie yelled back.

"I'll bring him back to Ollie's house as soon as he stops playing." Eve said. "No one will touch him, I promise."

Eddie smiled and started banging his drum. Pah-rum-pum-pum-pum rang through the night sky as he descended the hill. In perfect unison to his beat the army fell into place, battalion by battalion.

Nutcracker mouth chomped to the Drummer boy's beat, all of the feet falling into cadence.

Frank and Ollie mounted two Southie reindeer and acted as the generals of the evening, leading the army down the hill and into battle. Snowmen, toy soldiers, nutcrackers and elves marched down the hill in that order, ready to take on anything.

"After I get Eddie out of there I've got you covered up high." Eve said. "My sisters are on their way. Good luck to all of you out there. May God be with us."

"Amen." Frank said.

Frank nodded to Ollie as they slowly descended into the sunken valley's battlefield.

Step.

Step.

Pah-rum-pum-pum-pum.

# Forty One

I finally reached the sanitarium around ten o'clock. All of the diversions worked well, only delaying me about a half an hour. I still have two hours to grab Santa, find Alyssa and unravel this nasty knot of a world that I have been running in for the last couple of days.

I reached the huge metal door and pulled it open, almost separating my shoulder in the process. As luck would have it the cold out here made it impossible for the door to behave silently. The echo of the deep shriek echoed for what would probably be miles behind me. I just stood there and listened to the mayhem starting to unfold miles behind me.

I took a deep breath and entered the main hallway of the Sanitarium. It was a long hallway that was so dimly lit that anything could be hiding in a corner somewhere just waiting to kill me for my meds. I have not been known to be scared of much, but that awkward feeling of relieving myself in my Armani suit were becoming too frequent. The lump in my throat wasn't helping either.

Some lights hummed above me like bug zappers and some just blinked out of control as I started humming *Goodbye, Yellow Brick Road* to myself. If this sanitarium was ever low on residents, just walk through the halls and you'd be crazy enough when you finally got to the reception desk. When I got up there I noticed that the lady elf behind the desk was old and mean, angry at something she didn't want to share. She looked at me like I was not on the same level as her as far as the world goes, and couldn't care less who I was, but rules are rules. The huge blister on the tip of her nose looked like it was going to pop at any moment.

"Name, please." The angry elf asked in a voice that sounded like it just polished off a pack of cigarettes.

"Dr. Steven Chow. I have an appointment. I am here to assess the condition of Mr. Kringle. He also needs his last shots."

I tried to sound as convincing as I could, pulling up whatever useless television knowledge I have accumulated over the years. The one name Candy Cane could have gotten and I have to pull off being Asian in the process. This was going to be a hoot and I really wanted to pop that thing on her face.

"I don't see you in the appointment book." She said, flipping through the appointment book in front of her. She was looking up at me, probably thinking to herself that I looked as much like an Asian person as peanut better looked like moo goo gai pan. This was going to be difficult.

"Jesus Christ! I made this appointment last week!" I yelled as Dr. Chow. "I have to have my report on Frost's desk by tomorrow! Kringle is up for shots and I have to re-evaluate his mental condition before I administer them." Shit, I was convincing myself I was a doctor and I had a sudden craving for steamed dumplings.

"Well, I can't let you in, young man." She said, standing on her chair to be eye level with me.

Again I pulled out the cell phone that was given to me as a prop for my charade. It worked for Jack Frost; this insane little lady should be no problem.

It had no signal or no plan, but it did have power so in case she wanted to use it I should be okay. I dialed a few numbers and hit the non-functional send button like I did when I was the breast doctor-gambler at the casino.

"Hi, this is Dr. Chow." I said to the dead air in my ear. "I am here at the institution and there's a…" I focused on the name tag, "Wilma Whipple that won't let me in. She says I am not on the log. This is a Goddamn nuisance! I am leaving here if I don't get access to do my job! I have a family that I could be with!"

I paused and nodded a few times to answer the imaginary boss on the dead phone. The gnome was nodding with me. Good, it was working.

"Yes." I yelled. "You want to see Wilma after she lets me in? I'll send her right up." I hit the cancel button and flipped the phone closed.

"Who wants to see me?" She asked.

"Oh, you have an appointment with Mr. Frost as soon as you buzz me in." I said, cocky as all hell.

"I can't go up there! He'll kill me!" She was visibly panicking as she hit the button to buzz me in. "He's been in a bad mood all week."

"Maybe because you give everyone shit for being here." I smiled at the little bitch with the huge zit. "Good luck with that meeting. Merry Christmas."

I held up the phone in front of me and pretended to snap a picture of her.

"Yeah, that zero tolerance crap sucks." I said. "You should learn to be a little more trusting. I'll have this picture on a milk carton later tonight."

This was well beyond my sarcastic cockiness, but the lady was a damned troll. I smiled at her, knowing she'd be fine but confused, maybe even a little mad. But at least she'd be alive and not near me ever again with that growth on her face.

"Tenth floor. You can ask a nurse up there to let you in." Wilma was white with horror as her head turned with my every movement.

I walked through as she buzzed the door and was met with every traditional horror movie hallway I have ever seen. It was all of those cheap horror movies that rip themselves off all into one big cliché. The greenish walls had the stereotype wet look from a drip that came from nowhere plausible. Pipes that were overgrown for the ceiling made clinking noises for no apparent reason. I even noticed the puddles on the floor, again more products of that pesky mystery drip. It always made me wonder where all the orderlies that were mopping the floor vanished to. Certainly someone should be living up to legal codes of sanitation. Not just here but in the movies too. I'll have to agree that it certainly is hard to find good help these days.

There was no one on the floor to help me find anything. Where the hell is the elevator? There was nothing on this floor at all, not even any rooms, just the ominous pipes dripping doom all over the place. I had no idea what I was doing and got a strange feeling in my gut telling me that I was going to fail miserably. Down the hall, I heard the noise of people cheering for something. Maybe my gut was telling me that I was actually going to find *Fight Club*. I did, however, have the urge to say the word hello into the emptiness of the hallway, just to make the movie cliché complete. I didn't though. There were more important things on the plate this evening.

I followed the noise down the hall until it ended at the only door that was in here. It was a rusty old door with a window so dirty that the orderlies inside all had a brown, watery haze. From the look of it, they were all human. I opened the door with yet another creak, silencing the cheering with a group stare in my direction. They all looked at me like I farted in an elevator and denied it.

"I don't mean to interrupt you, but can you lead me to the tenth floor? I have an appointment." I was scared shitless. These places freaked me out in the movies and the orderlies were generally all nuts.

One of the overgrown men looked right at me. He looked to be Mexican, his hair in a ponytail and goatee. He was huge and apparently pissed off that I was there. "Are you a doctor or something?" He said with a thick accent.

"Yes I am." I said, worried that my voice was trembling.

"Good, we'll get you to the tenth floor, but first we need your advice." He said, leading me into the crowd.

There were eight orderlies standing around in a half-circle, a dirty mattress standing against the wall about ten feet beyond them. The Mexican guy pulled up three elves from behind another huge orderly, pulling them up by the collars of their terry-cloth patient robes. He had two in one hand and one in the other. "Which one do you think is more, how do you say, aerodynamic?"

"What are you talking about?" I had no intention of finding out why they needed to know this. Dr. Steven Chow has no time for this.

The Mexican orderly continued without explaining. "Andrew over there thinks this pudgy one is. But I am leaning towards this skinny lil' fella." He was alternating his arms and lifting them up for my approval.

"I think the little one. The pudgy one will get more momentum though." What the hell was I saying? This was some twisted carnival bullshit. I wanted to vomit at my participation in damning this elf to whatever fate was in store for him.

"I'll put a hundred on the fat one!" The one that looked like a Viking said. "Are there any takers on that action?"

"I'll take that spread!" Another one yelled. "The skinny one is going to make it!"

The Mexican guy looked at me and smiled. He was missing a prominent tooth. "Thanks, Doc. As soon as we do this round, I'll take you up there."

I nodded and had absolutely no idea why. This was crazy but since I was in a house of crazy, I just rolled with it. What was I expecting? All of the orderlies having a picnic lunch and talking about marriage?

As I stood there the Viking guy grabbed the pudgy little elf and waved him back and forth. As he got momentum he tossed the pudgy little elf across the room. As the elf hurled towards the mattress he fell short by about a foot, hitting the cold floor under him. The orderlies that bet on the skinny one cheered as the pudgy elf whimpered across the room in the medicated state he was in.

A large black orderly came over, picking up the skinny little elf. He quickly threw him towards the mattress. They all waited as he was flying through the air. A moment later he hit the mattress with a dull thud and he slumped to the floor, landing on top of the pudgy one who was trying to walk away.

Money eventually changed hands and everyone cheered. Down here, it seems, losing was okay but throwing elves was the essential passion of these animals.

"Come on and follow me even though you gave me some bad information and that fat one. You should be paying me" The Mexican guy said. "I will take you up there. Just be prepared."

"Thanks." I said, baffled at the fact that *Fight Club* was actually a monetary elf-tossing event. I was wondering how serious the man was about me owing him money. The borrowed suit I was in didn't come with a wallet full of cash.

"Who are you going to see?" He asked as we left the room and entered the creepy horror movie hallway again.

"Kringle." I said, not wanting to explain.

"Oh, here to see that crazy old bastard? He thinks he is still all magical and shit. Promised me a bike when I was six, shit got stolen and he never replaced it. Some nerve, huh?"

The orderly talked over his shoulder to me as we walked.

"This is what it's all about now." The orderly said. "Money is what we're all about up here, doc. Frost won't let us play in the casinos, so he sanctions these elf games down here."

"He sounds like a real hero." I said.

"He has brought the world to us, doc. We were nothing before he came to run things. He gave us women, money and gambling and as you can see by our appearance, those things don't come by too often. Hell, Frost has sports books betting on us. We broadcast this shit for the casino on Fridays, for God sakes! All the things you can ever want, he gives you." He stopped and stared at me. "And we all would kill to protect this way of life. So make sure that your exam goes well, doctor."

A man that tosses elves just threatened me. I am at the highest point on Earth and oddly enough just reached a new low. I just decided to keep my head just as low and follow him.

We reached the elevator that seemed to be hidden in the wall and eventually made our way to the tenth floor. Great, the elevator smells like urine. Hopefully it wasn't from Dr. Chow.

# Forty Two

The orderly and I reached Santa's cell door within thirty seconds of getting off the urine box. The orderly fumbled with an old fashioned key ring that was straight out of a spaghetti western's jail cell and within seconds the large lock snapped open. As he waved me inside he stared at me hard enough to make sure that I knew that he would kill me if I messed with the way things were. I smiled, and for the first time since I could remember, I felt okay dying if it was for the right reason. Hopefully it wouldn't be by the hands of this guy.

As I walked in the door slammed shut behind me, making me jump. The light bulb above me was broken so the only light in the room was provided by the huge moon outside.

As I slowly walked to the chair that was sitting in the middle of the room I was frightened when I actually saw Santa's thinning gray hair streaming down and becoming translucent in front of the moon. I rounded the front of the chair and stood just there frozen in shock. I was humbled like anyone should be humbled when they see an idol in front of them, especially in the condition that he was in.

It *was* Santa from what I concocted long ago in my head. There was no mistaking it. His rosy cheeks were sunken into his face like his graying leather skin was shrink-wrapped to his skull. His eyes were all blood-shot as he tried to look up at me, the crust in the tear ducts crackling with the sudden movement. By the bulb in his nose, I didn't have to be an actual doctor to see that his nose was broken on the bridge. He had matted blood in his crusty beard and his clothes were draped on him like he shrunk while wearing them. He must have been ninety-eight pounds. I couldn't help but to let some tears out.

"It's no use in crying, young Foster. They can't kill me." Santa said in an incredibly low voice. "I am in idea, and you can't kill that."

"You're alive, though. I don't understand." I said, not wanting to look at him. It was sad seeing him so different than what everyone was used to.

"I always will be, Will. As long as we succeed, that is. They can beat the idea, Will. Soon the idea will be no more. Greed will win eventually. It always does. We have had a good run of it though, in my personal opinion."

"Well, we're leaving tonight, Santa." I said, sounding like the cliché heroic jackass that I laugh at in movies.

"What we need right now is right in this room, Mr. Foster. What you need is right here in the room." He slowly nodded to a dark corner where the moon light was absent.

I followed his look and walked over. I immediately fell to my knees and cried in anger at what was laying in front of me. Alyssa was laying there in an evening gown, her hands hog-tied in front of her tightly, which were tied to her hog-tied feet. She had some sort of a gag in her mouth.

I reached over and quickly took the gag out of her mouth and placed me ear next to her lips. My heart jumped when I heard and felt her breathing. I untied her hands and gently shook her shoulders until she was awake.

"Alyssa, I am so sorry." I said. "I never meant for this to happen." I kissed her on the forehead.

I don't remember ever feeling so guilty. Since I have known her, I promised myself if I ever got to know her that I would never let anything happen to her. I couldn't hurt her. Even after all the hurt that was given to me and all the emotional hurt that I have unknowingly given to a lot of people I just couldn't bear to see this.

"Santa, we're leaving now." I said, the anger boiling up in me as I stood up. "When we get to Peary's Point, if this thing is reversed I need you to promise me that you will take her home tonight."

"Will, I want to go home *now*." Alyssa said, standing up and getting her balance after being out for so long. She was bleeding from somewhere on the top of her head.

"You are going home tonight, Alyssa. No questions." I looked at her for a long moment.

Jack Frost was officially pissing me off to a level that I didn't know existed.

"I will take her home, Will. You have my word." Santa said. "Now, how do we get out of here?"

Alyssa had so many emotions running through her and some of them had the look that they involved how she felt about me. You can't mistake that look. I shrugged it off so my heart didn't change its mind and let her stay for my own selfish reasons. I opened my jacket and pulled out an envelope with her name on it.

"Read this when the time is right." I said, handing her the envelope. She took it and folded it, squeezing it into the front of her dress.

I walked over to the window which went from ceiling to floor. I checked the material in the jacket over my elbow and decided that it was enough to cushion the blow. Without thinking I smashed my right elbow into the glass, shattering it into a hundred pieces all over the floor. I felt the blood running down my arm as I realized how seriously I misjudged my jacket's durability.

"Will, there are bars on the windows! You do realize that, right?" Alyssa was looking a little nervous.

I pushed on the bars easily, making them dislodge and fall ten stories down into the snow below. "The Welder was out here about two hours ago." I said, smiling.

As I was reveling in what I had done, the door slammed open and Jack Frost stepped inside. Mort and Stan were with him, both holding ice-shooting crossbows which were instinctively aimed at me.

"Well, it seems like you want to fuck up my holiday." Frost said smiling. "You know with all the money I make, the best investment to make is always going to be investing in information. My people would kill their own families to make a buck."

"You are seriously demented, you know that?" I said, getting more irritated with this guy with every moment our paths crossed. "You are absolutely sick in the fucking head." I looked at Mort and Stan. Mort winked at me as he held his aim.

"Not demented, Dr. Chow. Or should I say Will Foster? You had me fooled for a while. You have played a good game, but this old man is over. Come on now. You look as much Asian as I look like I'm a black man."

He had a point. I'll give the asshole that one.

"You raped what Christmas was all about!" I yelled, baffled that I was talking to a crazy blue man in an institution on the North Pole, standing next to an emaciated Santa Claus.

"Rape." Jack smiled. "I was never into rape. Hookers yes. I mean you can turn any honest girl into a hooker if the money's right. There's no use in rape, words will drop panties quicker than forcing them off. People just lack the confidence to lie; rapists take the easy way out. Women have no problem doing what they do for free if there's a hefty paycheck attached to it. People like eating humbugs, tripping out and screwing a tart in the ass on a Friday night. Then they give me all of their money on the chance that they will hit the jackpot and get to straighten their pathetic lives out when it's all said and done. They've created their own vicious cycles, I just exploit them."

"Why not try to fix them?" Alyssa asked. "Haven't you ever thought that maybe they just need some help?"

"Listen, I am no guidance counselor." Jack said. "I'm sure Will here can attest to the fact that they are so full of shit anyway. People around the world have the attention span of a shock treatment laboratory rat. It's all porn, drugs, fucking and stealing. There's never enough stimulation for anyone. They always want more, Will."

Jack was staring straight into me.

"Everyone in the world has some sort of attention deficit disorder." Jack continued. "That's what killed your version of Christmas, you sanctimonious shit head."

Jack walked over and smacked Santa in the back of his head.

"Do you think anyone cares about being surprised?" Jack continued. "No, people like immediate results. They like to get what they want and they like to get it now to be better than the asshole neighbors on the block. Hell, even your baseball is tainted. Steroids are breaking records built by honest men and its okay. Hell, the actual league condones it! People are complacent as long as they benefit from the immediate results. It's all about the destination, not the fucking journey."

Jack rolled his eyes and absently looked around the room.

"Do me a favor, Will." Jack said through an evil smile.

"Ask your hottie companion over there what she wants for Christmas. And then go and get it for her, pay top dollar and I guarantee that dress drops to the floor, shortly followed by the best sex in your pathetic, self indulged life."

"She's not like that." I said loudly through my gritted teeth.

Its one thing to mess with me but to disrespect Alyssa makes me want to kill the bastard on the spot.

"Not like you'd know, you rag-toothed prick, we're not even together." I said. "I respect her way too much to put her through that. She has a family to go home to. Now, why don't you let her go? It's me that you want."

Jack just started talking again. "Not that you two are going to live long enough to play this out but do you have any idea why I found you here so easily?"

Honestly the thought had crossed my mind.

"She gave you up." Jack told me. "I threatened her and she sang like a little songbird, giving you up to save her own ass."

I looked at Alyssa and felt like I was just kicked in the stomach. She looked to the floor, obviously upset that Jack actually called her out on it. I was pissed but really couldn't blame her. She never fully let me into her life anyway. I chalked it up to natural progression.

Jack nodded his head to the elves behind him. I didn't even see it coming but knew it was about to happen.

An ice bolt ripped through the air and speared into my right shoulder, spraying blood spatter behind me. Mort was very agile with his weapon so I trusted him to not hit me in the heart, but Jesus this hurt. Jack laughed as he pulled out his handgun. I fell on the floor, trying to bite the pain as the white heat took my vision away. Alyssa's screaming didn't help matters much.

I landed on the edge of the window, looking down at least one hundred feet straight to a cold death. I saw a red light in the distance coming towards me. Right on time, I thought through the pain spells. I can't give up now, this was almost over. I rolled back, righting myself and getting up again. I motioned for Alyssa to move behind me.

"Any last requests before I kill all of you?" Jack asked us like the Good Samaritan he would never be.

I looked over at Alyssa and back to Jack.

"I would like to say something to Alyssa." I said to Jack. "I promised her for Christmas that I would do something that didn't involve money." This was going to turn into a damned madhouse in about thirty seconds.

"How touching." Jack said. "I would say no because I really want you dead. But, in the spirit of things how can I refuse? One last traditional thing before the world is mine, go for it!"

Jack told Mort and Stan to stand down. They stood down, waiting for their cue from me as they aimed their weapons at my face. My shoulder was bleeding and it hurt like crazy. I was almost ready to fall over.

Santa looked up at me like I was totally fucking crazy. He winked at me, knowing what I was about to do but had no idea if I had the balls to do it. I was guessing he saw the red light too.

I turned around and stared into Alyssa's eyes. As always, it gave me goose bumps and butterflies, even five years later. Again I felt like passing out but this time it wasn't from the pain.

"Pay attention to the song." I said as I moved her towards the open window. "I know you ratted me out but it's okay. This is the one time you're going to have to trust me."

I looked directly into her sad eyes. The comfort of knowing that we were connected in this crazy universe warmed me and made my shoulder feel a little better for the time being.

I cleared my throat. Even under these circumstances I wanted to impress her. I will always want to, no matter where we are.

"Think of your favorite *Creed* song." I whispered.

"Will, no I can't." She looked at me as she was placing the song in her head, pulling out of the jukebox in her memory banks.

"*One Last Breath*, right?" I whispered again, the irony of the title hitting me like a guillotine blade that's been sitting in the sun too long.

Alyssa nodded.

"Sing the chorus." I told her. "Sing it to yourself look me in the eyes. Don't stop looking at me, do you understand?"

A tear rolled down her cheek as it came across and made sense to her. She loved this song but it finally sunk in that this might be the last time that she ever sees me. Or it was also a look of denial? Maybe she was happy that she converted me into a *Creed* fan. For whatever reason she hesitated. I never thought we'd part like this either...but she had to be safe. I winked at her and looked towards the window.

"Will, I can't!" She whispered to me. "I won't do this. I can't leave you here to go through this and I'm sorry for telling Jack. You have to believe me."

Mort pulled out a laser light and blinked it twice out the window. Jack's back was to him so he didn't notice a thing.

"Trust me. I would never hurt you." I whispered back. "Enjoy your family and your life; I know they all love you. I hope everything works out for you, Alyssa. Just so I know that you know, I have been in love with you for a long time and always will be." I let that sink in and kind of got lost in the moment. *"Six feet ain't so far down."*

I sang the chorus lowly again as I slowly backed away from her. The tears were coming out of me now too. She was the most influential woman in my life, the only one I would marry at a moment's notice. I was holding onto telling her that I loved her for a long time, fearing that it would ruin what we had. I know it will but I have a feeling that I will never see her again.

Alyssa was completely different than any woman I have known, a woman that would straighten out the way I saw people and give me new life in what I was looking for in a woman. She was my world but it hit me that she really never wanted me to be in any part of hers. I never fit into the world she had constructed for herself and in this instant, as she backed into the window, I understood that. She was a world of secure, impenetrable walls that she was safe in with the people she knew. There was no more room for me no matter how many signals were sent out.

I moved in and kissed her, one final thing before she leaves me forever. It was selfish but I thought it could be overlooked by her. I'm sure it would be. It was warm and beautiful and much better than I imagined it would be. Alyssa was sobbing while the song ran through her head again.

I stared at her for a moment with tears coming from my eyes and with a gentle shove I pushed her out the window.

Alyssa screamed for a half second and then it immediately stopped. The wind below was the only thing that disrupted the awkward silence now, howling around the insane walls I was standing in. In an instant the woman I would marry was gone, sinking into a winter oblivion on the back of a reindeer.

I ran and skidded over to the edge and I saw she landed on the back of Rudolph who was waiting about six feet below the window, just like we planned. He saw her and jolted up to catch her as she fell. From what I could see she was looking up at me as she clutched Rudolph with both arms tight around his thick neck.

I whispered goodbye and cleared the tear from my eye as the second ice bolt slammed into my back. I screamed like a broken madman and fell to the floor again, more blood spatter slapping the walls. Jack walked over to me and kicked me hard in the ribs. I heard one snap and lost my breath.

"You may have saved her for now, but you two are dead, you have my word on it.. She meant nothing to any of this and more importantly you meant absolutely nothing to her."

Jack started kicking me again, snapping another rib.

"You're something else." He said. "Take all of this punishment for a chick that sold you down the river. And you told her you loved her! How much pain do you really need to confirm that you're a schmuck?"

"She meant everything to me and chivalry will never die." I said through a broken chest, trying not to laugh the least bit. "My job is done, so finish me off asshole. My life is complete. She knows how I feel and I'm okay with that."

Blood started pouring out of my mouth. I knew in my heart that tonight was going to be the last night on this earth. I'm just glad I finally told Alyssa the truth.

Jack had Mort and Stan come up and try to get me to my knees. Jack always wanted an execution-style killing under his belt and what better time than now?

As the elves righted me I grabbed them and with each hand spread my arms wide. The pain was unimaginable as I threw the two elf militant-allies out the window. I screamed at the white pain ripping through my chest, another rib cracking in the process. It felt like it was piercing a lung.

"Nice move, Mr. Foster." Jack said. "That must have hurt."

Jack smiled and hit me in the face with the butt of his gun, breaking my nose the same way Santa's was broken. More blood shot out of my face and it felt like my whole face was cracked beyond repair. My eyes were producing tears fast and furiously.

Jack laughed again, pulling his gun in front of me and moving the barrel from my face towards the middle of my body. He pulled the hammer and quickly shot me in the stomach. I didn't think it was enough to kill me; it didn't seem to be his style.

I tried to scream but the cracked ribs muffled my breath and the blood started to pool in my throat. I just thanked God that Alyssa wasn't here to see this. I laughed to myself knowing that I always said I would take a bullet for her and I was a full shooting and multiple beatings into it. Now that's dedication for ya. Now if I could just get her to care. All of the sound I tried to make became a muffled cry into the dirty floor.

"Is that all you got, Snaggletooth?" I said through the blood rushing down my face, into my mouth, mixing with the blood from my throat.

"Nah, we're just starting. You're still breathing right?" Jack clearly was enjoying this.

I heard a whistle outside the window as the wind picked up. I somehow got back to my knees again and waited for Jack to right his gun into the bleeding skin of my forehead. He finally did, like clockwork, and when the barrel touched my skin Santa leapt up and bit him hard in the wrist. Jack loosened his grip, thankfully before it went off.

"Nip at this, asshole!" Santa yelled as Jack's wrist was spewing dark blue blood.

As Jack stumbled backwards I leaned over and grabbed Santa. With one painfully numb move I slid both of us to the edge of the window and out. We fell for a few seconds and something snapped near my collarbone as I landed on a huge furry body.

"Glad to see you two." Blitzen said, making me grab on. "We have to get to Peary's Point, so hold on!"

I just watched through red eyes as my blood saturated into the fur on Blitzen's back.

"Please let me die." I said, not wanting to continue breathing. It just hurt too damned bad.

Santa landed on Donder and was trying to grab on as best he could with whatever strength was left in his body.

Mort and Stan were on Dasher, holding on for dear life as tears were running down their faces. Mort has shot at me before, but not with as much accuracy nor with me requesting it. He was a changed elf, and two pulls of the trigger slapped him in the face with exactly how backwards he was. With the other five remaining reindeer in tow, we sped off to Peary's Point to finish the mission, the team flying faster than they ever have before. I half hoped I wouldn't make it there. I had no idea how much more I could handle.

"You are one crazy son-of-a-bitch, Foster!" Blitzen screamed over his shoulder. "I'm starting to like you."

Blitzen laughed as he picked up the pace with his running feet. I screamed into the howling air, just wanting the pain to be over, just wanting my life to be over. My breathing was limited to tiny inhales through a broken face, trying not to breathe so hard that my lungs actually collapse. It was bad enough that two ribs were puncturing them, but making them bigger with every breath was the worst thing to imagine in the cold of The Pole. Not to mention that every breath meant an extra coat of red on Blitzen's fur. My stomach was fucked up beyond any reasonable repair.

It was eleven o'clock. We only had fifty-nine minutes to fix the world, broken or not. Fifty-nine minutes that would seem like an eternity in a cold, cold Hell.

# Forty Three

On the battlefield bullets were flying from Frost's front line so fast that that made one constant sound, the rapid fire sputtering turning into a solid tune of mechanical mayhem. They were about fifty yards away from the front line of snow men, blowing holes in the snow soldiers as they walked.

Frosty was leading them and reaching down, filling holes as he walked briskly into the oncoming soldiers. The other members of his sudden warrior family were all doing the same: patching arms and legs, replacing coal so they could see. They were all an average human's height, so the line of Frost's elves could not see over them as they got closer to each other.

Behind the snowman line the toy soldiers were being fired up. They raised their clunky wooden guns from their straight arms and started unloading ice balls into the line of militants. All that was heard in the night air were hollow thuds of the firing units followed by the yelps of fallen elves all over the snow in front of them.

Bullets were being deflected off of the steel-lined surface of the toy soldiers and nutcrackers behind them. With each step the nutcrackers opened their mouths, the wooden lever on their backs operating on their own, up and down at a frenzied speed. With each time the jaws separated, huge ice balls the size of small boulders fired out into the oncoming brigade, followed by a lot more screaming. They began walking faster, bringing the frequency of the ice balls to about fifteen in five seconds.

"This is the coolest thing I have ever done!" Stan yelled from the cockpit of the main nutcracker which was coming up in the middle of the line. Mort and Stan had theirs on reserve and just got back so they had some catching up to do.

"Me too!" Mort yelled. "Don't get cocky!"

"Where have I heard that before?" Stan asked through his head set as he fired off another small burst of ice.

"No idea but it sounds cool!" Mort said.

As he was screaming, an RPG slammed into a toy soldier in front of them, blowing it apart as millions of wood chips flew off into the field around them. Wood was flying everywhere, deflecting off the front of the nutcracker line like a hailstorm. The snowmen had splinters poking out from every angle.

The smoke in the air made it near impossible to navigate through as Mort increased his ice ball output. He was shooting blindly but had to do something.

The snow men made a sudden reassessment of their situation and all simultaneously decided to roll themselves into the opposition, wooden splinters in all.

"Men!" Frosty yelled. "It was an honor and a pleasure serving with you!" The gunfire was whizzing around him as he yelled. "Commence Operation Porcupine!"

Frosty got down and submerged his legs in the snow, quickly turning himself until he was a snow ball with enough snow to keep the wooden points exposed. The others in his unit followed until all of them were rolling into the nasty elves, taking down hundreds in a storm of impaling fury.

The snow was beginning to turn red as they materialized themselves back into snow-human form. Whoever was still standing after the attack was now successfully trapped between the snowmen and the frontline of toy soldiers that were still marching forward. Frosty looked in front of him, ordering his platoon to keep moving forward to immobilize the second line of Frost's armed elves.

Tig was in the third largest nutcracker on the line and was in the middle of Mort and Stan. His nutcracker stared at the enemy with blue war paint painted on one side of his face.

"We just need to hold them while the Southies get into position! Increase firepower! More balls!" Tig was in full attack mode as he screamed his orders over the intercom.

"They blew apart a soldier!" Mort yelled into his head set, hoping Tig would hear it. They were fighting with snow and ice so the loud factor never came to be. "Who was in it?"

"Hester Heppity!" Tig yelled back. "She was a good woman! She knew what she was getting into! Don't lose concentration! We can feel sorry for the losses later, soldiers!"

A tear flowed down Mort's cheek. He'd known Hester for a long time and couldn't bear never seeing her again. Quality time lost, if only he knew how close the end was going to be.

"What do we want?!" Tig yelled into his own cockpit. "FREEDOM!"

Tig looked out the back window of his warrior nutcracker and looked out upon the foot soldiers of Old-Towners, all gearing up for war with nothing but the tools of their trade and their bare hands. They were ready to bleed for this. They would not kill, only in self defense, but the scent of blood in the air made it almost impossible not to want it.

"On my mark, I want everyone to rush the line!" Tig yelled. "We can take them by sheer force! Cover me with fire and ice!"

Tig suddenly flipped a wooden switch that he had installed in his nutcracker. A few loud clicks were echoing through the night as the top of the nutcracker's head flipped open.

Tig silently counted to three as the seat he was in thrust itself out of the nutcracker's head, catapulting Tig into the sky with a sudden jet burst of flame under him. His ejector seat shot him straight up in the air and directly into the battle zone. As he cleared the nutcracker's head, an RPG slammed into it, blowing it to bits as he soared above it.

The heat from the RPG's was starting to melt the line of remaining snow people. They were trudging along the line, packing more and more snow into their sweating frames as bullets shot pierced them. With every step they were getting an inch shorter. If this was going to end it has to end soon or Old Town would soon be decimated out there.

Tig landed in the middle of Jack Frost's army, suddenly surrounded by a hundred elves, all armed with MP5's. They had all of them pointed at him but didn't shoot. The shock that a kamikaze elf just jumped into the lion's den was enough to halt them momentarily.

"Now, let's see who's standing after this!" Tig yelled.

Tig flipped his welding shield down and turned on his torch, adjusting the unit on his back. With a flip of his left hand, he opened up the flame to flamethrower level and started circling around, shooting like mad. The elves got closer to him as he circled.

"Can't shoot me, huh?" Tig yelled. "It's not in your blood to kill anyone, you limey bastards! You can't change that!"

The circle was within an inch of the circling flame, which was about fifty times longer than a normal torch, thanks to some back-end modifications made in his shop.

"But one more thing you can't do?" Tig made sure the torch to gun level, hitting every one as he circled. "Hold on to a really hot gun!"

Each MP5 started to glow red as he spun around, burning the hands that held them. Red hot submachine guns were being dropped in the snow, one after another, followed by the yelps and screams of the mildly burned elves.

The Old-Towners were approaching, all of the arms of the wooden soldiers firing fire and ice, slowly making weapons drop all over the place.

One by one, as Frost's elves dropped their weapons, they began to pummel Tig as he was facing someone on the other side of the circle. They rotated and took kidney shots, head shots and systematically got him to the ground where they continued to bash him until he was a bloody pulp. The flamethrower extinguished as they all cheered within the confines of their little mosh pit.

Blitzen flew in at what seemd like two hundred miles per hour, clipping Frost's army one by one, sending them flying backwards until they unconsciously skidded in the snow about a hundred yards away. The smoke was making its way over to where everything was going down, making it to where Blitzen would hit anything that moved, regardless of what side they were on.

"SOUTHIES!" A South Pole elf by the name of Houlihan screamed from behind the melee. "SOUTHIES formation, ten hut! Give up or we'll give you a fight! This is your final warning! If you don't go along with it, we will kick your fucking asses into Kingdom Come! Jack Frost ain't here to back you up, you little piss ants!"

The army of Southies emerged from behind Jack Frost's line of madmen, surrounding them to the point that they had absolutely nowhere to go. They pulled in closer and closer, bringing everyone into within a foot of each other. The Southies all started yelling in unison, stomping up and down on the ground, pounding their feet and fists into the snow in a tribal rhythm.

Within a moment their stomping got unimaginably louder. The noise wasn't coming from them anymore as they pounded the snow beneath them. As everyone stopped in the frozen shock of what was coming, the remainder of Jack's army dropped their weapons.

From behind the line of Southies a fifty foot piece of white fur stomped into the battlefield. It was the Abominable Snowman, coming to rid the field of the remaining elves in Frost's army. He had a werewolf's snout and was drooling in anticipation of finally eating someone. It's been a long time since he had a good dinner.

The monster stomped in and picked up elves one by one, throwing each one dozens of yards at a time into whatever direction that he wished. There were shouts accompanying the abominable roar that echoed across the vast white battlefield. You could almost hear the saliva dripping into the snow.

Jack's soldiers ran to each of them, refusing to give up as the Abominable Snowman screamed again, igniting the air with anger. He picked some elves up, looked at them like appetizers and just continued throwing. It wasn't just Frost's army, there were old-timers being thrown just the same. Within minutes the beast had made a clearing in the carnage, enough for the Southies to move in.

Frost didn't send the order to retreat so his men reassembled as best they could. The Southies met them with angry fists, causing a riot of fist-fueled mayhem in the snow banks of the valley. The Southies were second fiddle to everyone for a long time, so this was a long time coming, their anger and resentment coming out in the form of pain. This was the first time that the South Pole was going to get its fair shake in the equality of elf-kind so they took it personally. Each punch landed had the power of ten angry human men, breaking noses and teeth as they pounded their point home. One by one, Jack's men were falling into the snow, blood spraying everywhere. The others were fodder for the big white beast.

Houlihan whistled for a reindeer so he could assess the damage from above. As he mounted one of his favorite Southie reindeer, Bloodbath, he surveyed the bloodshed. Jack's army was down to about a strong two within minutes from the time that they were surrounded. They held up a white handkerchief in a dignified showing of surrender.

"Gentlemen!" Houlihan yelled. "It is finished. They are holding up the flag of surrender! Frost's army is no more!"

Houlihan looked down from Bloodbath and saw the lifeless body of Tig, an elf he has known for years. He hovered over it for a long, sad minute.

"Will someone please get Tig up so we can bury him in honor and get that hairy beast under control before he actually eats someone?"

Houlihan shook his head as he continued looking down at the carnage below. He couldn't believe that such a peaceful place would be turned into the horror that he was hovering above. As he looked for more damage he sighed when he saw that most of the population of Old-Town was either severely wounded or dead. There were pointy shoes pointed up to the sky and bloodied knit hats strewn all over.

"Get the rest of these men and women too! All of them! This was a bloody battle, but we shall honor all of its warriors! Are there any misunderstandings?" Houlihan started to cry, an emotion he didn't remember ever feeling.

Ollie and Uncle Frank flew up on the other two reindeer, paralyzed by the sight below them and below them.

"This is the saddest day in the history of the North Pole and it's even sadder for the history of the world." Ollie said, sobbing at the view of his dead friends down in the field below.

"They did what they needed to do." Houlihan added. "We all did, Ollie and I think that's pretty damn heroic. They died like warriors."

"Heroism shouldn't end only in bloodshed." Ollie replied.

"When you're willing to die for what you believe in, you're a hero no matter what the situation. The most effective heroes, Ollie, are the unsung. Their greatness lies in the fact that you would never know they exist, but you feel the positive effect of their lives."

"You're a smart man, Houlihan." Frank said. "Thank you for all the help. Is that huge snowman okay or is he going to go ballistic?"

"He will be fine. He's a Southie so he understands. He will not harm anything even though he has every right to." Houlihan said.

"Well, let's hope we can finish this so we can fix it." Ollie said.

"And don't thank me for participating in a revolt, human. War never deserves thanks. Now let's get to clearing this out and getting medical attention to whoever needs it. It's a mess down there. You have to be strong to see what's down there, I tell ya."

Houlihan shook his head and started his descent into the war zone below.

"I'll make the arrangements to take care of the deceased." Ollie stated. "But I take no pride in it."

Houlihan and Uncle Frank just nodded, not wanting to proceed but knowing it needed to be done. Uncle Frank looked out into the dark horizon and hoped to hell that Will was somehow still breathing.

# Forty Four

Santa and I were not so gracefully dropped right under the North Star. Hitting the snow from five feet in the air was enough to break the remainder of my ribs and reassure my collar bone that it was indeed fucked up.

This was Peary's Point, there was no doubt about it even though my eyes were extremely blurry and watering. There were more stars than sky up there, the North Pole beaming down like a plane flying at a low altitude over our heads.

"Will, I would like to thank you." Santa said through his restricted air pipes. "Not many people would risk their lives for someone and you've done it twice in about two hours. Not bad for a writer from Florida."

I was just on my back just staring at the stars and just plain trying to ignore the pool of blood under me, staining the snow crimson red. "No problem, Santa." I said, trying to sound cool. It made me laugh a little, causing daggers to stab at every part of me.

"What is it that you want for Christmas, Will?" Santa just stared up into the sky.

"With all due respect, sir, I don't thing that is ever going to be answered and I really am not thinking about it. I'll be lucky to make it through midnight." My body instinctively revolted against conversation by catapulting blood from my lungs. "So let's just wait for this miracle to happen so I can go on to Heaven or Hell, which ever."

"You'll make it, Mr. Foster. You have found something you lost a long time ago and it will help you if you let it."

"What's that?" I coughed, not finding anything but pain and misery at the moment. The North Pole wasn't exactly what I'd imagined. I just wanted to see the North Star beam its light down and take me to whatever home that would take me. Hell, maybe it was a ride on a comet like that crazy cult a while back, right now I'm up for anything.

"It was faith." Santa sounded almost like he was never hurt. "You found faith in other people again. You fell in love with the way someone was, Will, even though you knew that love would never be returned to you." He coughed again. "That's what the world is missing. Faith and love without expecting something in return for it. And what's more important is that you have found some faith in yourself. Everyone in the world should think like a child. All of the thoughts are unfiltered and undiluted. That's what you did. You gave your heart to that girl and made her fuller, even if it doesn't look that way."

I was fading in and out with a much quicker turnaround time. I heard everything he said but couldn't move to comment on it. I tried closing my eyes but couldn't figure out if they were bleeding or just frozen open. I just wanted to have this all over; the pain was way too unbearable.

"So what is it, Will? What would you like for Christmas?" The more and more he asked the question, the more it sounded like he was just trying to pass the time and irritate me. Maybe he learned his little bag of cruel tricks from God.

The inside of my head is feeling like a fog machine set on high and the rest of my body is numb.

"I would like to die knowing that I asked this. So if it's possible I want to wake up next to Jennifer Love Hewitt tomorrow morning. It would be really nice waking up next to her smile every day. It would be like Heaven."

I tried to smile, my face and muscles were so frozen that they hurt. Hell, even in dying I was going to be a wiseass. It was truly a wish but I knew even in the state that I was in that it was inconceivable.

"You know I can't do that, Will." Santa chuckled in his bony little frame.

"It was worth a shot. I've never had luck with the women that were ever actually attainable so I figured I'd go all out and just go for it. And as far as she goes it don't get any better." I said, telling my mind that I shrugged.

I just stared at the North Star through blurry eyes when it came to me. Call it a realization, call it an epiphany, I could care less, all I know is that it's clear as day.

"There's one person that I want to make sure has a nice Christmas." I said, more blood spilling from my mouth.

It never came to me before but there was one person that helped me and has no idea how or that she did at all. It was the first time I felt a commitment and it wasn't in the traditional way.

"There's a girl I know named Kelly. She's one of the prettiest people you can ever meet, the kind of girl that stops you in your tracks when she looks at you. She works at the coffee shop I used to stop at all the time."

Thinking about this is strange but it all made sense.

"Wednesdays and Thursdays were the only days that I looked forward to and no matter what happened during that week, I always knew that she would be there." I told him. "She was the most reliable person without even knowing it. We got to know a little bit about each other, she has a fiancé and that was fine. I was just relieved to have someone interested in what I was doing and where I was going in life. And on the other side, I was equally interested in where she was and where she was going, all of it through a drive-through, sometimes inside. It went beyond customer service and we always kidded about getting married. I know it was only kidding around, but in a strange way, it made me feel great. I would never do anything to jeopardize her relationship, it's none of my business, but I just want her and her boyfriend to have the best Christmas they've had. She deserves it and he deserves it for being the other half of her. She was the proof that a smile can change someone's world. Hell, her smile alone made me commit to something and made me a happier person, even though it didn't show."

"Even after I was laid off," I continued, "I drove way out of my way to make sure I was there most of the time. I know this is dumb but that's my wish. Give her the world, Santa. She was a major part in me trying to be a part of the world again. Hell, it made me realize that Alyssa wasn't the only woman in the world. Alyssa was the only one I wanted and still want but Kelly taught me that there's mistletoe hanging everywhere, you just have to pay attention enough to notice it. Not literally but you know what I mean."

I coughed hysterically and spit more blood into the snow. "And tell Alyssa that when I said I loved her, it wasn't in a stalker way, I just liked the person she was and I hope her life turns out beautifully. And I hope that she at least remembers me."

"Will, I will definitely relay that and I'm sure she will. It's an honor to be here with you tonight. No matter what happens, you have my eternal respect, even though I smell like reindeer pee." Santa was smiling hard enough for me to feel it.

"Well, isn't this romantic?" Jack said, popping up silently right over me. He pointed his gun right at my face. Jesus I didn't even hear the snow crunching.

"Hi, Jack." I said, not caring if he pulled the trigger. In a way, I was hoping that he would. "I'm glad you're here. I need to thank you."

Jack looked at me like I just hit him on the head with a cartoon hammer. "Thank me for what, you silly shit head?"

"It was you." I smiled through my broken face. "I had to come up here to stop you from whatever *Pinky and the Brain* world domination scheme you were hatching, but I found out what I was made of in the process."

I tried my best to roll over and get to my feet.

"Don't worry." I said. "I'm in no condition to lunge at you."

I have no idea how the hell I was doing it, but within a second I was standing directly in front of Jack, his gun still pointed at me. Silently, I thanked the heavens and all of the gods through the history of time for making snow cold enough to numb my body.

"Thank you, Jack." I told him. "You did the biggest thing in the world. You helped someone overcome their past and actually live actively in the present. And there are no two bigger things in the world than love and faith. You tried to strip it away from the world but gave it all to me, and I can't thank you enough for it."

I looked him straight in the eye, feeling a little bit sorry for him for what he has become.

"Oh, that's precious." Jack smiled with his razor teeth. "What kind of romance novel did you pick that up from? You've been watching some women's programming maybe?" He laughed like a maniac into the calm air. "I didn't give you anything you human fuck! Now if you'll excuse me, you have a date with a bullet."

"It's because you refuse to see it Jack." I said.

I actually had confidence for once in my third decade on this crazy little planet. Normally I'd be shitting my pants at someone holding a gun to my face but I didn't care right now. Whether it was that I was in such pain that a bullet would be a welcomed friend right now or the fact that I was so numb from the cold that I thought I was invincible, I didn't know but for once I was standing my ground. Not for myself but for all the people who have lost track of what's important in life.

"You were an only child, right, Jack?" I asked, noticing that my body felt a lot better than it looked.

"I don't need to explain myself to you, asshole." Jack yelled. "Right now all of your little new-found friends are being decimated at the hands of my army."

"You can't kill them, Jack." I said, knowing that they would fight to the death to regain what has been taken.

"Maybe I should keep you alive and drag you through the bloodshed. That's what's wrong with you people. You used to have such faith in everything. You based your governments on the concept of a higher authority and then told everyone that they have the freedom to believe in what they wanted. Oh, but then you people chastise them for what they believe because it's not what the governments were founded on. See, Mr. Foster, it all starts with faith. You believe in something but it gets all out of whack and what you believe in turns into a rebellion. Your beliefs suddenly aren't good enough so you rebel and believe in them so hard, not even your family counts if they don't live by their standards. You lose the faith just by believing. Ahhh, it's the great oxymoron."

Jack just stared at me and smiled like a mental patient from the Sanitarium.

"Do you realize that almost all of the death and all of the wars in the world were in the name of whatever god that the people involved believed in?" Jack adjusted his hair. "You wear your gods on your lapel and have pissing matches to show that yours is better. What the fuck is that? Thou shalt not kill is turned into killing in the name of the best god in the sky. One Nation Under God? Which God are you picking today?! The one they tell you to believe in or one that you choose?"

"What does that have to do with anything?" I had no idea where he was going with this. Part of my mind thought that he was actually going mad, not like it was much of a leap from where he was before.

"It has everything to do with it." Jack said, and I could have sworn I saw a tear. "You all sing your little songs about being with people you love on Christmas and all that other bullshit and what does it get you?" He didn't wait for an answer. "It gets you long lines in malls, fulfilling an obligation to get someone something, something bigger and better than the other ones. It's all narcissistic, Will. It's about making yourself feel good by exploitation, which feeds into the fame-obsessed culture that you people live in. You're all forced to be the person with the biggest gift so you can find a place in your family as the one to top. It's seeking fame and acceptance on a smaller scale and everyone's guilty. Except me, of course, because I got wise to it and helped it grow. Hell, it was going there anyway. Am I really that criminal? We all exploit things. I just make money doing it."

"You're insane. There are still good people out there." I said.

"Where are they? The world is like my army, Will. Greed and anger turned magic into obligation and money. There's no way to stop it. Everything is corrupt. Hell, you can have your kids turn on the sports channel and have them learn poker. It's a great game for them to get good at, lying to win other people's money. Is this starting to make sense to you, Foster child?"

He knocked my head with the gun.

He just kept rambling. "It's the world that's breeding liars and killers and not caring about it because the ratings are good. Turn the other cheek, so to speak. The cheaters will always win because it's good fucking money all the way around. It's all about the money, about recognition. It's about driving around in a hundred-thousand dollar car and laughing at the people who live in the shit boxes. My god is better than your god. It's all a pissing match Will and God takes a back seat to all of it. If anything, God created it, right? Hell, you should applaud me for giving people a haven to do it in that is away from everything." He looked at me with determined eyes, his gun pointed again at my face. "You can have a cashier telling a woman "Merry Christmas" as she's five people back with a cart load of shit that she waited until the last minute to buy, and I'd be willing to bet the cashier would get a big 'Fuck You' in return for her efforts. No one cares about other people if they're not in their little circle of the world. No one cares about you, not even that hot little woman you came here with. Where is she, by the way? Ahh, the going gets tough and hottie gets going, is that it? Face it, faith is dead already and hope is not very far behind."

"She's safe and on her way back to her family, where she belongs." I said, getting irritated to the point of shooting myself with his damned gun.

"Oh, and about that fat sack of shit lying over there? Well, he's not what he used to be, but…" A tear rolled down Jack's face, looking at Santa bleeding in the snow. "He was a dying breed, giving gifts to people for no reason. His way of thinking is so archaic. It's about time this thing was over and done."

"Then why are you crying?" I said, staring directly into him.

Jack smacked me with the butt of his gun, opening another gash on my head. I tried not to, but I fell in the snow again anyway, making more snow turn red. He walked over to Santa and squatted over his beaten, near-dead body.

"I hope you found what you were looking for, Jack." Santa said through his broken lips. "I underestimated you."

"I found everything that I was looking for, Kris. I have everyone in the world now thinking I am the guy providing happiness every year even though its only contrived and well-covered misery. There's no more wanting and waiting. There's only asking and getting." Jack pushed Santa's hair off of his forehead. "It's quick, simple and to the point. Who needs faith and mystery?"

"Please kill me." Santa said. "End this now and you can have everything. Just let Will go. He tried but he can do nothing more for me. I know why you are doing this."

"NO!" I yelled, feeling like I was being cut open by a drunk surgeon. I tried to make my way over to Santa. The world needed him, not me. In the grand scheme of things, I was a little speck on the globe compared to him. I couldn't even get through to a woman that was close enough to be my wife. She even left without a thought.

Jack aimed his gun and fired, a bullet slamming into my right lung. At least I thought it was my right lung, I had no way of knowing. That is, except for the breath that seemed to leave me with the bullet. I refused to fall back, crawling more slowly towards Jack and Santa.

"You are one tough little mother fucker, you know that?" Jack said, firing his gun again, the bullet grazing my skin past my left temple. "You're stupid and crazy, but tough. Now why don't you be a good boy and just fucking die, already!"

"No!" I yelled. "I took a beating for a woman that couldn't care less if I ever took another breath, so I damn sure will make sure that Santa is okay. Call me crazy, shoot me all you want, I refuse to die before you're gone."

I got back to my feet and blood literally was flowing out of me like an IV bag was just stabbed by a pissed off patient with a cafeteria spork. Jack got up and walked towards me.

"Okay, I've played enough with you." Jack sprinted to meet me and held me close with his left arm around me. With his right hand, he squeezed the trigger about twelve times. I lost count after the shot to my head. His gun tip was resting on my stomach as the bullets ripped through it quickly.

I saw nothing but white and was sure that the time was finally here. I was finally going to the other side and was ready to take it on with open arms. Tough as I seemed to be, everybody had a limit and I was long overdue. I didn't cry. I didn't scream. I think I actually just smiled at the irony of it all. I found a way to let things out and be a better person and I am taken immediately from the world by a blue sociopath. That seemed balanced.

I didn't know what to do so I just reached out and hugged Jack, pulling the ring out of my pocket in the process.

"Thank you, Jack." I said. I can die knowing that you helped me find out who I really was." I looked at my watch. It was five seconds until midnight. This was the only shot I had. It was the last and only shot to fix things and breathe my last living breath. Either way, I am going to end tonight. I might as well go down fighting like a banshee.

Jack just stared at me, wondering why in hell I was still able to talk, no less hug him.

"I was brought here to make you do a good deed and you've done it, Jack." I said through a bloody smile.

That white light I was looking at wasn't heaven at all, it was the North Star. The light from it came down to my chest, penetrating the ring that I put between. It started to vibrate violently between myself and Jack with enough intensity to drop us where we stood. A stiff wind could drop me where I stood. Jack was the only reason I was still standing at all. I stared at my hands and because of the lack of blood I was matching Jack in skin color.

"What the hell is that?" Jack screamed.

"It's the North Star!" I yelled back. "Your world is going to end right now along with me! You've done a good deed Jack. That's what Christmas spirit is all about! It's the one flaw in your twisted little plan that you never saw coming."

Jack squirmed while trying to break free from my grip. The light was blinding and it started to hum loudly like electricity. By a minute after twelve, the power was enough that it blew us apart, skidding us into the snow around ten feet away from each other. Puffs of snow blew up around us like we just crash landed from Mars.

Jack was laying there staring over to Santa, who was still bleeding to death. I just stared at the sky, hoping to hell that I would feel better someday or just make my way up to heaven. Either way, I just hope it happens quickly.

"What have I done?" Jack asked himself, staring at the crippled old man in the snow.

Jack just started sobbing out of nowhere. He crawled over and kneeled next to Santa, putting a hand on his bleeding head. He was careful not to touch the bridge of his nose. Looking at it, Jack could see it was still broken in three places.

"You were the only one who watched out for me, Kris." Jack said through some long hidden tears. "You were the only one to bring me gifts when there was no one else there to do it." He sobbed onto the wounds, leaning down to kiss Santa's forehead. "Since my parents left I had no one. I had no idea why they left, Kris. I had to hustle to make anything work, that's all I knew how to do. You were the only person in the world that saw past the hideous smile that made my parents leave, Kris. And how do I repay you? I made you a bleeding mess in the snow. I just wanted to say that I'm sorry but I don't think it would come close to being enough, considering what I've done."

"Jack, its okay, there's still time to fix this." I didn't know if this was a show or that he had actual feelings. I turned and started crawling towards Jack and Santa.

"No one cared, Will." Jack said to me. "No one. I was left alone because of what I looked like. I only got mentioned in one song and it was about my teeth, how am I supposed to feel? I was associated with killing living things. How do you think that affects a kid?"

"Jack, it's okay. We all make mistakes. That's what we do."

I froze staring at them, realizing something horrible about myself and all of this.

"Jack, we're the same." I told him. "We let what life brought us dictate how we live now. It's all rebellion, Jack, just like you said. But you know what? Despite all of it, I had a great childhood. All of us kids had a great childhood and have great lives and I just had to learn that it was all connected to a bigger plan. The good and the bad are all connected. I like who I am and all of the people I have ever known had something to do with that, even the evil people who did those things to me. People ask me all the time if I would change anything in the past and I tell them no. If I did, it would tell them that I am not happy with the way I am. You are the one that helped me realize that by making me come here. I wasn't brought here for that. I think I was asked to come here to save *you*, Jack Frost. My problems ended with about two people. Yours affected the whole world."

Jack put the muzzle of the gun up to his temple. "This is the only way to turn things around." He was crying hysterically into the night. He pulled the trigger, firing only a small tuft of snow into his blue temple. The snow fell silently to the ground.

"You don't want to do that." I said, unable to move. I tried moving my limbs, each one giving an inch in their own sweet time. "Violence no longer has any power up here, Jack. It just won't work."

"How else am I going to live after this? I have nowhere to go and no one to go there with? What the heck is left?" Jack was confused that he was no longer able to use foul language.

I had no idea if I was on a trip to Heaven or Hell or if I was still here. I couldn't open my eyes. It felt like there were about a hundred pounds on my lids. My ears were popped, the air muffling my ears like I was listening to a seashell. In the distance, I heard Eddie Drummer playing his tune. The sound was drawing closer and closer by the second. I just heard my cue and passed out face down in the snow.

"It's all back to normal, Jack." Santa said, the pounds slowly and methodically filling out as he stood up, making me slide into the snow. His cheeks began to get rosy and the jelly in his belly started to jiggle. "And it's all because of you. I have to give credit to Will Foster for doing it, but you've finally found your way, my son."

Jack turned around and saw all of the elves, some from his army, encircling them. They were all dressed in their traditional uniforms: hats, shoes and ears all pointing north, towards the North Star. The snowmen were all there, some filling the holes as they walked, followed by the toy soldiers and the nutcrackers all walking in unison.

Uncle Frank and Eve walked with the three Wise men and Eddie Drummer. Eddie wasn't banging his drum at the moment, just looking down at me trying to find a visible breath. He stood over me, waiting for some sign of life. My wounds were all closing but there was nothing happening in the field of mobility. I couldn't get my eyes to open. The seconds ticked by and slowly I felt the blood rush back through my veins. As I slowly rolled over, Jack and Santa joined Eddie and were standing over me. They looked like three football players huddled over me as I got conked on a fall into the end zone, from my point of view.

"I knew you'd be okay, Mr. Foster." Santa said, jiggling and rosy as ever. "You are welcomed officially to the North Pole." He laughed so hard it was infectious. The group forming around us started clapping.

Eddie's eyes widened as the cast of the casino's stage show walked up the embankment. There were eleven drummers walking up to Eddie, playing the famous song. He knew them from somewhere but couldn't place from where. It's been a long time.

The elder Drummer kneeled down in front of him. "I wrote that for you son." He said, a tear popping from his eyes. "I'm glad you remembered how to play it."

"Daddy?" Eddie asked through nervous tears.

"Yes son. From now on, we will always be the Twelve Drummers drumming. I promise. No matter what life brings us, we will stay together until the end." He gave Eddie a hug that was years in the waiting.

"Alyssa's back with the Welder." Uncle Frank said. "He's getting the sled ready for tonight and she wanted to wait there. I guess she's worried that she'll be stuck here again."

Uncle Frank had sorrow in his eyes. I smiled, silently telling him she *should* go. It was better this way.

"I think in this case she's better off with me being a distant memory of hers." I said.

I smiled, knowing in my heart that this was true. She would never see me as more than the guy to talk with to pass the time, albeit a fucked-up one.

"I would never be as important to her as the people she knows and I can accept that. Hell, I will never matter as much to her as she did to me but it isn't my place to ensure a spot in her existence. That's okay with me, I enjoyed every minute that I've known her and would change none of it." I smiled to myself, knowing in my heart that I would really never see her again. And I was oddly okay with it.

"You'll see her again, Will." Uncle Frank wouldn't give it a rest.

"No, I don't think so." I smiled. "And that's okay, *really*. I have some work to do on myself first. If you see her, let her know I wish her nothing but the best, huh?"

Uncle Frank nodded.

The Herald Angels, Dawn and Eve, flew in and grabbed Santa by each arm. "Hark!" They sang into the air, making sure we all cleared the way. "We need to get him back to his sled! He has a world to tend to."

"Thank you, Will Foster! You are forever on the Good List! But lay off of the pornography, okay?" Santa yelled as he was being whisked away by the angels.

Santa called to all of his reindeer, one by one, each forming a single file line behind him. As they did, they all looked at me and smiled. Rudolph blinked his nose twice and mouthed the words 'Thank You, friend'.

"And what about me?" Jack asked. "I didn't have anything before all of this and I'll have nothing after it. What am I supposed to do?"

I rolled my eyes. "Have you ever tried talking to people? Get to know them? Who knows, maybe you can even help them spread some cheer. Maybe you had everything in front of you but chose to focus on the negative side."

"No, I haven't." Jack quickly rolled his eyes back to me, knowing I was right.

"Well, I think it's a good idea to start. I'm sure Santa will help you out. If you ever need it Mort and Stan know where they can find us. You're part of my family now, Jack, no matter what."

Jack smiled, his teeth somehow looking less threatening.

I put my hand on his shoulder. "This place is cold enough, but being alone is probably the coldest place you'll ever be." I patted him on the shoulder again and turned around to walk away. "Uncle Frank, let's go home. We have some presents to open tomorrow morning."

"Oh, and guess what?" Uncle Frank asked.

"What?" I asked, not knowing what the hell he was even thinking of saying. I never wanted news from him again.

"Our entire family is there. I just wanted to let you know so you weren't too surprised when we got back." He said with an idiot's grin.

"I'm relieved." I said.

"Relieved? Why?" Uncle Frank started laughing.

"As dysfunctional and not into our feeling as we are, I have the greatest family in the world and I wouldn't change it for anything."

"And you want to hear the weirdest part?" He asked. "They just showed up unannounced! I went back to get some things and they were all just there, decorating the tree. That's weird, huh?" Uncle Frank was absolutely puzzled.

"Not at all, Uncle Frank. Christmas is all about the spontaneity and the surprises right? Oh, and thanks again for signing me up for this. It was the strangest thing I've ever been through but the best. I can't thank you enough for it. If there's anything you need from me, please let me know."

"Can I borrow twenty bucks? Gus is being a real asshole." Uncle Frank laughed into the night like a madman as we started walking back toward Wonderland Road.

# Forty Five

I stood silently in the middle of Wonderland Road. The businesses that were dark for so long now finally had light in them. It as only about two in the morning but it seemed like yesterday that everything took place, when it was only a couple of hours in reality. Hell, I have no real perception of reality anymore. I never in my life anticipated going to war and facing off with Jack Frost to save Santa Claus. It was just a ridiculous thought that happened to be true.

Regardless, Wonderland Road was a solemn place tonight. Santa was on his way to make sure that Alyssa got home and that all of the children in the world were taken care of. When the world woke up in the morning, hopefully there would again be smiles on the faces of the children as they were surprised at what they secretly wished for. Every single one of the mall Santas got their orders in early like normal. So if it all went without a hitch everything should be fine. They would have to wait until morning to find out.

Mort and Stan stood beside me. Jack Frost was behind me next to Eve, Dawn and Uncle Frank. The remaining portion of the population was behind us, patiently waiting for the procession. Ollie was up front, staring up the street to the back end of Wonderland Road. He motioned for all of us to remain silent which was no hard task as no one uttered a word in over an hour.

The South Pole elves systematically and slowly brought the fallen elves down to the middle of the street, pallbearers to the masses of elves that were slain. They were humming *Silent Night* as they worked to honor the fallen. The coffins were all handcrafted by the remaining elves after Santa left. As the last of what seemed to be hundredth casket came down, Tig was placed in the front next to Harriet. Ollie turned to face the crowd.

"Ladies and gentlemen, this is not the event I had planned for Christmas." Ollie was getting choked up. "I just wanted to say that these elves before you deserve all of your respect for laying down their lives so that we may live in peace and harmony and ruled by nothing but unadulterated love for life. There is nothing more to say, only that I have nothing but gratitude towards them. They need to be remembered for who they were in life, not what they turned into or what they lost. We are all one again and that deserves our prayer and eternal gratitude. Let's all bow our heads."

Ollie had a speech prepared but couldn't muster up the strength to speak it. I couldn't blame him.

"May I say something?" Jack walked to the front of the grieving crowd. Ollie stepped out of the way reluctantly, not fully trusting the new Jack Frost on his sudden turn to the Good List.

"I think that would be a good idea for all of us to hear." Eve said from behind me. "I think we all need to be assured that this is finally all over, once and for all."

Jack stood in front of all of the people that he has basically destroyed in the past few years. No matter what he has ever done, it took an insane amount of courage to confront all of these people in this setting. The caskets behind him might as well have Jack Frost imprinted on them. He looked at everyone with absolute remorse in his eyes. There was so much regret that was pouring out; it almost didn't need to be stated. Yesterday I would have never felt this way, but today I felt incredibly sorry for this man.

Jack cleared his throat. "I don't know how to say this so I'm just going to start." He cleared his throat again. "I don't know where in my life I got so turned around. I have no idea what wiring inside of me went terribly wrong that I actually executed genocide in a city of peace. I was so caught up in making a name for myself that I put everyone in harm's way and I cannot express enough the grief I feel due to the grief that I caused. And I see around me all of the looks on whether I should be trusted and I understand fully that I will not be for a long time to come. But what I also see is a group of people that have let me attend this as part of your town. As part of *our* town. I think that all of the fallen behind me are not the only heroes here. You all are role models and I have a great respect for all of you."

"That doesn't bring our family back!" An elf screamed out.

"No, it doesn't bring them back." Jack said. "But I think there is a way that I can make this right. Dawn, Eve...can you come up here?"

Dawn and Eve walked up to stand next to Jack Frost, one on each side.

"Sugarplum, I need a favor from you and Dawn." Jack asked Eve, who was blushing a little at the mention of her receptionist name that she dropped at the moment she fled up to the roof. "I need you to perform the transference."

"Transference hasn't been attempted for a hundred years, Jack and when it was it nearly killed him. I have no idea if I remember how to do it." Eve seemed very uncomfortable with the last minute request.

"Angels never forget." Jack said, smiling. "I need you to try it on me. The remainder of the Christmas Spirit that was used to fix me should be enough to perform it."

"Jack, this is crazy! It can kill you if you aren't prepared for it!" Dawn was being defiant by angel's standards.

"These boxes behind me didn't deserve to be filled by anyone other than me." Jack said. "This isn't a request, Eve. It's my one Christmas wish and as being on the temporary Good List, I expect that wish to be granted. You take the lead in Santa's absence, correct? So it's your call. These people didn't deserve all of the loss."

Dawn and Eve looked at each other and decided silently that they would try this archaic ritual for Jack. They didn't want to pass up an opportunity for a nice gesture from a man so used to having evil ones.

"Close your eyes, Jack." Eve said. She grabbed Dawn's hands, creating a circle around Jack Frost. "This may hurt a little bit, Jack."

"Again, look behind me." Jack said.

Dawn and eve shut their eyes and started to hum one note. It was a low note that went on forever without a break in the tone. They walked around Jack with their hands still clasped together. As they walked faster, a funnel of wind started to spin into the sound of the hum, encasing Jack in a beautiful vortex of blue and white. Snow whirled around him as he tilted his head towards the sky.

The angels moved faster around him until they were barely visible in the wind that they were creating. All that I saw was Jack in a moving tunnel of snow. As I stared at him I started to notice a white ectoplasmic thread protruding from his heart. It wasn't a substantial substance but looked like pure light. It grew thicker and longer as it spindled its way from his skin. It stretched upwards to the sky as it reached, by the looks of it, fifty feet long and about ten feet wide.

The end of it finally slithered out, joining the rest of the cloud of light above him. He was screaming in pain as the last bit flew upward into the night's sky.

Dawn and Eve stopped suddenly in the same places they were standing in before the ritual began. The tone coming from them did not change, if anything it got deeper.

The angels finally broke their grasp and reached towards the light. Their hair was flying away from it in the same direction of their robes. The feathers on their wings were fluttering in the wind. They kept humming and in an instant, clasped their hands together again in a thunderous clap.

As the sound echoed through the valley, the light divided and shot itself into all of the caskets on display on Wonderland Road. Within seconds, the spectacle was all gone and Jack slumped to the snow, completely drained and near lifelss.

We all stood motionless, staring at the *Raiders of the Lost Ark* thing that just happened in front of us. Nothing was happening, not that any of us knew what to expect as far as results. Dawn and Eve were the only ones that knew anything and they were just as silent about it.

To break the silence of the night Tig slowly opened the lid to his casket, climbing out and into the snow. He felt his uncovered face and shrieked into the night sky.

"Where's my shield? I'll get a flash burn!" Tig said as he if just woke up from a nap, not getting his breath back from the dead.

As he hit the snow all of the other caskets were opening one by one. It was creepy and beautiful all at once, the elves finding their lives again and getting more breath in their lungs. Jack was still slumped down in the snow, sitting on his knees, completely void of breath.

"They're back!" Ollie exclaimed. "I can't believe it but they're back with us!"

Ollie was jumping up and down like he just won the power ball. I couldn't help but cry. It was too bad that Alyssa was missing this. She would have liked to see the result of everything we've been through, she would at least think it was pretty cool to look at. She would have been happy with a happy ending, to know that we succeeded. Hopefully, living in the world now she would know anyway. I just hope she knows I'm still alive.

Dawn and Eve squatted down next to Jack and gave him a gentle blow of air to his face. A slow second later, Jack regained consciousness and was met with a thunderous applause from all around him.

"I'll bet you've never gotten a kiss from an angel." Eve said.

"No, I haven't. That was the most painfully peaceful thing I've ever felt." Jack said, standing up and straightening out his pant legs. "Why couldn't you do that when I was lacking in morals?"

"That's the story of our lives, Jack. It's painful and peaceful." Dawn said, smiling. "You did it. And maybe if you asked nicely on the kiss things could have been different. You just never know."

Off the cliff in front of Old Town, noting was heard but the crumbling of building off in the distance. As each one came close to the ground it disappeared without a trace. Within ten minutes, Frost's city was nothing but a blank canvas of winter and snow.

As we stood there watching the city go away, Santa flew above us on his hemisphere switch, his bells ringing happily in the night air. Frosty surfed down the hill, singing on the top of his Jimmy Durante lungs until he was heard by all.

"*Sleigh bells ring, are you listening?*" Frosty sang. "*In the lane, snow is glistening. A beautiful sight, we're happy tonight…*" He stopped right next to Jack Frost, placing a fat, snowy arm around his shoulder.

"…*walking in a winter wonderland.*" Jack finished the lyric.

Jack led the group into the rest of the song, the Christmas Spirit lighting up the North Pole brighter than it has been in years. Jack Frost has finally come home.

# Forty Six

So here I am sitting on the porch of Uncle Frank's cabin. Behind me my whole family is sitting there talking around the living room which, by the way, was completely refurbished from the attempted elf attack a few days earlier. 'Troy' even looks okay again. I don't know who fixed it but I wasn't about to ask. It's Christmas Day and it was the first year that it was actually calm and peaceful, even though Uncle Frank was telling the story at the top of his lungs to the rest of the family.

I placed my feet on the railing of the deck, staring out into the lake about a hundred yards in front of me. The water was completely still, the occasional fish jumping out for some fresh air and a subtle splash to keep me interested. The wind was down, as well as the temperature, which was a little below zero. I didn't feel cold even though my nose was completely numb.

I was sitting there wondering why on earth I was even here. I contemplated different theories on the situation, from "destiny having a wonderful way of working in the world" to "people are meant to do things" and "there's a reason for everything". All of these theories were fine but they didn't exactly give me the sense of closure that I thought they would. What I thought about was something incomprehensible.

I was meant to meet Alyssa. It was fate that brought us to know each other so well and it was fate that will dictate if we will ever see each other again. I know that we will probably never speak again, we've been through a cold hell together but in the end it strengthened the feelings she has for her family and it strengthened the way I feel about her. She realized what was important to her. I am sure in some way that I am important to her, as well as our time together was, but it isn't the right time for her to think about it and I have to respect that. I can't make anyone admit to something they don't feel like admitting to.

I am grateful that I had the opportunity to know her for the length of time that I have. She has shown me things emotionally that I haven't felt in a long time. She brought out the school-boy nervousness of a crush that you can't muster up the courage to ask out. It was the eternal butterflies that never seemed to go away when you were in the same room together. She made me realize that you can connect with a person in the world in a way that was so different from the way I connect with people normally.

I found that I had the capability of creating laughter in her that would light up the world if only for a few minutes, making a bad day just a little bit brighter. No matter what has happened in the past, all the drugs I've done and all of the horrible ways I have treated people over the years, Alyssa's relationship to me was one of newness. It never felt old talking to her. It was a relationship in the most primal state. I got to know her and nothing physical ever happened between us.

That's why I made the dreadful mistake of letting her know that I was in love with her. She was the one person I looked forward to talking to every day. I looked forward to her cackle and her never-ending nervousness. I missed doing the mundane tasks for her personally just because she would put them off for whatever reason. Yeah, friends have told me I'm nuts and she using me but I insist to this day that this was not the case. I just enjoyed making her happy for the short time that I had with her during the old days.

I've been told on the way back here that she did, indeed, sell me out to Frost. The old me would have been pissed off about it. The great thing about today was that the information made me smile. This was a new me. She made her decision out of love for others, not from a hatred for me.

Is she safer away from me? No, she was never in danger in the first place. I would take a bullet to this day to make sure she was never hurt. The only thing I hope she knows is that I hope she's happy with the rest of her life. I hope she realizes one day that she was responsible for a different way that I looked at things. Just by being a wonderful person, she taught me that you don't need to have the destination, but it is truly the journey that helps you. I am still truly a difficult person to love, but at least I have something to work on.

"I'm glad to see that you finally see it, Will." Eve walked up to the side of the porch, scaring me enough to almost jump in with the flying fish. Her wings were standing calm behind her back.

"Are you into mind-reading too?" I laughed.

"Trick of the trade, I'm afraid. I am not particularly comfortable with it, to be honest with you."

"What brings you here?"

"I have something for you." She said.

I had no idea what was going on here, but I got butterflies. I was hoping that maybe it was Alyssa or Kelly or maybe Jennifer Love Hewitt. I knew it wasn't but my stomach refused to deny the possibility of it.

"What is it?" I asked, raising an eyebrow.

Eve motioned her first finger for me to follow her. Not realizing my legs were numb I stumbled up to follow her to the side of the cabin. As I got there, I saw Ruthie standing with Johnny and Bianca.

"Thank you, Will." Bianca said, Johnny nodding accordingly.

"What are you thanking me for?" I asked, completely confused.

She slid aside and behind them stood two snowmobiles, two bikes and all of the toys they could have dreamed of.

"I saw these this morning because of you." Bianca said, running up and hugging me around my waist.

"But, I don't understand." I said. I was flattered that it happened, but didn't know how it all came to be.

"Let me show you." Eve said. She started singing *Silent Night* softly into the calm air, the forest rustling in response. As she continued, I saw people coming out from behind the trees.

"It can't be!" I yelled, happy to see all of the tree people coming up in front of me. Ollie was in the front followed by Tig and all of the reindeer. Behind them the entire population of the North Pole came out, all singing along with Eve. There were seven Herald angels hovering and singing above the trees. It was all I could do to keep from losing my composure.

Mort and Stan were standing there also, smiling at me. Manny and Mort seemed to have found their friendship again and Stan seemed to have made quite the impression on Candy Cane Mindy. They were attached at the hip. Or more accurately, Stan was on her hip, bringing his face closer to her chest. It definitely seemed that everyone's wish had come true this morning. Did I really miss Jennifer Love Hewitt upstairs? Did Uncle Frank sneak her in for me?

"Mr. Foster?" A deep voice asked.

I turned around and saw Santa and Mrs. Claus standing in front of me, looking like they should..

"You helped me and I don't think I can ever thank you enough for that." Santa said, pulling me into a bear hug.

"You and Alyssa brought my husband back to me." Mrs. Claus joined in the hug as the caroling echoed softly through the trees and bounced off of the motionless lake. The fish at least had a beat to try and jump to.

"And the one thing I have been missing for a long time is back, Will. You have no idea what that means to me." A familiar voice said.

Santa moved out of the way. Jack Frost was standing behind him. I almost instinctively jumped, knowing that all of my memories of him were relatively sadistic and cruel.

"Will Foster." Jack said, smiling normally, completely at peace. "Santa raised me when I was little and I spit it right back in his face. What I put you through will always remind me of how much I needed him. I apologize to you and I am forever in your debt. Whatever you need, you let me know and I will get it for you legally."

"You owe me nothing, Jack." I said. "We all go down some wrong roads. Some of them are paved for us. Sometimes we just need to swallow the pride and ask for directions. You're a good man Jack. We helped each other, okay? Is that fair enough? We'll just put it behind us and start out as friends."

Jack Nodded and smiled.

"Oh and here's a gift for you, Will." Santa pulled out a little box wrapped in a red bow.

I opened it slowly and stood motionless for a few seconds, caught up in what was in the little box. I smiled and let out a tear into the cold air. I reached in and grabbed the coolest gift that anyone could have given me.

It was a container of rice pudding and a spoon. There was no note with it but I got the message. It *was* from Alyssa. I remembered her making me try it because my personal menu consisted of peanut butter and cereal. Every Friday she made me try something new, rice pudding was the only one that made it.

"You will always be part of our family, Will. Alyssa is too if she needs it. You are both welcomed at the North Pole any time you wish."

Santa shook my hand and nodded to me.

"We must be going, Mr. Foster." He said. "It's been a very long week and I think I can use a hot chocolate and a nap. And, thanks to Jack and my wife, I think I'll start a diet. I haven't felt this great in a long time and I was flying into chimneys like a crazy cat burglar! Ho, Ho, Ho! You can't really see it but I lost fifty pounds!"

Within an instant, all of the North Pole residents were waving as they marched back into the trees, the carol fading off into the woods that I was hiking to not long ago.

"Is there any turkey left?" Ruthie asked.

"Of course there is. Go on in, I'll be right there." I said.

Ruthie and the children went into the cabin as I heard various hellos from inside the living room. I just turned around and looked at the lake again.

"Just for the record, the reindeer can still talk." Blitzen said, coming up over my right shoulder. Wedge was standing with him. I jumped again. "We're just not as strange now. Just don't tell anyone."

"Your secret is safe with me." I said. "For the record, people would think I was fucking nuts for mentioning it."

Blitzen laughed. "Oh, and there's this." The reindeer said, motioning for Wedge to hand him a small tube.

I opened it and saw a beautiful Cuban cigar.

"I still smoke them in private but you earned this one, kid." Blitzen snorted as I took the stogie from Wedge.

I tried to thank them but they started walking away almost immediately to catch up with the rest of the group. As I looked over my shoulder Wedge was running back up to me at full speed. Within a second he stopped and kicked me in the shin as he was laughing.

"OW!" I screamed.

Wedge laughed and ran away quickly to catch up to Blitzen. "There's a doozy for the road!" He cackled as he disappeared into the thick woods.

I laughed along with him and realized that saving Christmas was only part of the whole equation. I was roped into that. Alyssa was my journey. I was meant to have her in and out of my life. Love without anything in return. Alyssa will always be Christmas to me from this point on. She's the one gift I can always hope for and the one gift I will always be thankful of ever getting. Well, there's always next year.

The biggest thing that I've learned is to have faith and to have respect for the faith other people have. Don't let faith dictate you, let it guide you and everything will be okay. Is it so much to ask for a little optimism and unconditional love?

I propped my feet up, popped the top of the rice pudding and lit the cigar, puffing the smoke into the air. And with a crazy childlike enthusiasm I buried the spoon into the rice pudding and began to eat the best meal of my entire life.

**The End.**

Note from the author:

Have a Merry Christmas, Happy Chanukah, Happy Kwanzaa and have a Happy Whatever-It-Is that you celebrate. Whatever your version of the Holiday is, enjoy it and celebrate the hell out of it.

**Also available from this author:**

# The MacGuffin Files: Carats and Cold Meat

Greg Jackson was born in upstate New York. He moved to New Jersey when he was not even a year old. Then he terrorized the residents, um, lived in other parts of New Jersey until the age of fourteen. He attended High School in the Tampa Bay area of Florida and resides somewhere in Tampa Bay to this very day.

Please visit my website (or not, it's completely up to you):

**www.lankymania.com**

www.ingramcontent.com/pod-product-compliance
Lightning Source LLC
Chambersburg PA
CBHW050507260626
47157CB00004B/1219